HARD LIMIT

A ST. LOUIS MAVERICKS HOCKEY ROMANCE

BRENDA ROTHERT

KAT MIZERA

CHAPTER ONE

Sheridan

"This was a bad idea," I muttered, staring out the window of the limousine as it inched through St. Louis traffic. "Maybe we should turn around and go home." I turned to my best friend, Vanessa, and she quirked a brow at me.

"We're not going home," she said quietly, folding her arms across her chest. "I did not get all dressed up to sit at your place eating cheesecake. It's going to be fun, Sheridan. You haven't been out in over a year. It's time and we both know it."

"I don't know if I'm ready to be in the spotlight. You know how mean the press can be and I'm not... the same."

"Of course you're the same!" Vanessa snapped.

"I've put on twenty pounds and the camera adds another ten, so—"

"You were in a life-threatening accident. It's a miracle you're not in a wheelchair. You're going to walk in there tonight like the badass you've always been and own it. Besides, the focus tonight is the charity, not the celebrities who are going to the fundraiser."

"I bought the table in your name," I said. "So maybe no one even knows I'll be there."

Vanessa rolled her eyes. "Would you stop? It's going to be a blast. It's a freakin' bachelor auction! Of professional athletes! I've got a thousand dollars put away for Nash Reilly from the Mavericks."

I laughed, relaxing for the first time all night. "I thought you were hot for that new pitcher for the Cardinals?"

"We'll see which one strikes my fancy." She arched her brows and grinned. "Maybe I'll take both."

"I could use a little fancy striking myself." I sighed. "It's been more than two years since I've had sex."

Vanessa shuddered. "Jesus, woman, that's a streak that needs to end right fucking now. You need to talk to your lawyer and—"

"Not tonight." I held up a finger. "This is my first time out since the accident, and I just want to hang out and look at hot guys and have a glass of wine and laugh with my bestie. Can we do that?"

Her eyes met mine. "Absolutely."

"Sheridan, do you want me to escort you right up to the front?" My driver-slash-bodyguard Flynn lowered the partition. Though I didn't own the limo, we'd rented it so he could drive Vanessa and I to this event since he provided my security when I left home these days.

"The bulk of the press will be up front," I protested.

"Dropping you at the front would allow you to walk the shortest distance though," he pointed out.

I loved Flynn ninety-nine percent of the time. Right now, I hated him.

Because he was right.

"Okay. The front it is." I stiffened my spine and sat up straighter.

I could do this.

I'd been through worse and wasn't going to let a broken back derail the rest of my life. Even though it was turning out to be harder than I'd ever imagined.

He pulled into the lane for VIPs and flashed our pass to the security guard who waved him through. When he stopped the limo at the red carpet that led to the front entrance, a few dozen reporters surged forward, anxious to see who was getting out.

"Let's go," I told Vanessa. "But you first, okay?"

"I'm all about the attention!" she laughed, holding out her hand to Flynn, who had come around to the passenger side to help her out of the car. There were some camera flashes, but no one recognized Vanessa Cruz, my best friend since we were fifteen, the Chief Operating Officer of my new plus-size lingerie company, and the smartest woman I knew.

Flynn leaned back down and reached out a hand to me.

"You got this," he said in a tone so low only I could hear.

I took a breath before letting him help me out of the limo. I tested my footing; I was wearing the highest heels I'd worn since the accident—rhine-stone-covered sandals with two-inch wedge heels. I straightened up and smiled as the first flash went off. Then I heard the whispers.

"Holy shit, it's Sheridan Lee!"

"Hey, Sheridan, look over here!"

"Sheridan, you look amazing!"

I smiled and waved, walking slower than I would have thirteen months ago but with an even, steady gait, the way my physical therapist had taught me. Learning to walk again as an adult was hard.

"Are you going to start modeling again?" someone called out.

"Sheridan, how's your back?"

Luckily, we made it inside before I had to answer any questions and I exhaled heavily.

Okay, the first hurdle was a success. Now I could sit in a chair, have a glass of wine, and enjoy the auction, which I was actually looking forward to. I didn't plan to bid on one of the bachelors, but I'd donate a few thousand to the cause. Anything to do with helping pediatric cancer patients was right up my alley.

The room was beautiful. Tables covered in elegant white tablecloths and topped with floral centerpieces surrounded a large T-shaped stage that divided the room in half, and two well-stocked bars and buffet tables were set up on each side of the room. A DJ was playing dance music and my body itched to move. Really move. God, I'd loved to dance BA.

BA and SA.

Before Accident and Since Accident.

That's how everything was classified in my life right now.

"Here we go." Vanessa put a glass of white wine in front of me and sank down beside me. "The party starts now. You hungry?"

"Famished," I admitted.

"I'll go fill a couple plates for us to share and then we can look through the program, see what else is on the menu." She winked as she walked away and I shook my head fondly.

We'd been through a lot together over the last thirteen years, but nothing as traumatic as my accident. And Vanessa had been at my side every step of the way, holding my hand, encouraging me, and kicking my ass when necessary.

I took a sip of wine and looked around, wondering how many familiar faces I'd see.

I did a double take when I saw the owner of the small, local modeling agency, where I'd gotten my start, walk in with her husband and I resisted the urge to wave. Though I loved Delia Hammond, I didn't have it in me to retell the story of the accident, my recovery, physical therapy, or, of course, answer the number one question on everyone's mind: Are you going back to modeling?

I had no idea.

"Yum!" Vanessa set down two plates heaped with what appeared to be every item on the buffet table and sat down again. "And for dessert, they have salted caramel chocolate mousse or white chocolate raspberry cheesecake. Want to share both?"

Vanessa weighed a hundred pounds soaking wet but ate like an NFL linebacker. I hated her sometimes, but I just smiled and shook my head. "I'll have a bite of each, but I need to focus on losing another ten pounds."

She rolled her eyes. "Fine." She popped a bite of prosciutto-wrapped mozzarella in her mouth and then opened the evening's program on the table so we could look at it together.

"There's your boy." I pointed out the Cardinals' new pitcher, Scotty Dominguez, on the first page. He was five-eleven with long-lashed dark eyes and short, dark hair cropped close to his head. But man, he had the world's best lips. Between the lashes and the lips, he could be on magazine covers.

Vanessa cocked her head. "He's sexy. But let's see what else is out there."

We flipped through the pages, checking out each bachelor that would be available tonight and I paused once we got toward the end of the program. "Now that's a guy I could climb like a tree," I murmured.

"Who is he?" Vanessa frowned.

"Defenseman for the Mavericks," I said thoughtfully.

"Hockey?"

I nodded absently, reading the short blurb about him. "Holy shit, he's six foot six, two-fifty."

"And you love that long-haired Viking look," Vanessa said, peering down at his photo. "He looks spectacularly underwhelmed in this picture."

I chuckled. "I'm sure the single guys were forced into this."

"Oooh, he's Swedish. He's younger than you too. Only twenty-six."

I grinned. "I'm only twenty-eight, but I can cougar that boy all night long."

We laughed together and it felt good to enjoy some sort of normalcy after the year I'd had. A big event like this was different than having a movie night at home, and I allowed myself to get into the spirit of the evening's festivities. It was for a good cause, and if we could joke and laugh about hot guys and sex for a couple hours, all the better.

The auction started promptly at nine and though I'd told myself I wasn't going to bid on a date, my glance kept dropping to the picture of Lars Jansson. Physically, he was the man of my dreams, but obviously I didn't know him. He was probably a womanizing jerk—a lot of athletes were—and that wasn't my thing at all. Even before the accident, I'd been careful to stay away from people like that. I had enough drama in my life.

As a plus-sized woman, I was used to comments about my weight. As the most recognized plus-sized supermodel in the world, I was used to people tolerating my body type because I was beautiful, wealthy, and successful. And I would never, ever settle for a man who didn't love all of me. I'd done that already and I was still working on dealing with the humiliation. Going forward, I planned to be in complete control when it came to relationships, dating, and even one-night stands. Not that I'd ever had one of those.

Gazing down at Lars's picture, I wondered if he looked as good in person as he did in the photo.

Vanessa gave me a nudge, bringing me back to the present. "Your boy is up soon."

The last guy had been auctioned off for four hundred dollars, which didn't seem like a lot, but I'd also never heard of the rookie running back for the city's newest football franchise, the St. Louis Sentinels. The high-profile players were being saved for last, and Lars was somewhere in the middle, so I figured he'd be auctioned for a little more.

You know you want to bid, Sheridan.

The devil on my shoulder seemed to be speaking directly to my libido.

"Too young, right?" Vanessa was asking me, motioning to the baseball player who'd just flexed his muscles on the stage. He was laughing, obviously having a good time with this, pulling off his dress shirt and waving it around as a bunch of twentysomethings started bidding.

"He's probably not old enough to drink," I told her, laughing.

"Probably not. And I'm torn between Nash and Scotty anyway."

"Bid on them both," I teased her.

Her eyes gleamed. "Damn, I would if I thought I could get away with it!"

Three more guys were auctioned off and then they announced Lars. I sat up straighter, trying not to look too interested, but holy hell; he was even hotter in person. He was big all over. Not just tall, but muscular and broad shouldered. His thighs flexed as he walked across the stage, muscles bulging beneath his dark gray dress pants, and his shoulders seemed to take up the whole room.

"You're not really going to bid, are you?" she asked, her eyes widening slightly.

"Maybe?" I glanced at her.

"But—"

"He doesn't have to know." Our eyes locked and then I turned to face the stage as the bidding started.

"Two hundred!" One of the twentysomethings

sitting near the stage jumped up, waving her bid paddle. We'd all received one when we arrived, and everyone's information was already on file, so the money transaction would be seamless.

"Two twenty-five!" One of her friends stuck her tongue out at her as they laughed.

"Two fifty!"

"Oh, for fuck's sake," I muttered under my breath.

Lars did *not* look happy to be there and each time someone called out a bid, he jumped a little. Not only did I want to jump his bones, I also had the most irrational need to protect him. Which made no sense for a big professional hockey player like that.

"Three forty!" The first young woman called out again.

Lars was simply standing at the bottom of the stage now, and while the other guys had laughed, flirted, and had fun with it, he was somewhat wooden, the smile on his face obviously forced. But he was beautiful. His long, blond hair fell past his high cheekbones, almost to his shoulders, curling the tiniest bit on the bottom. His eyes were electric blue, even from ten or fifteen feet away, and when we made eye contact, I almost spontaneously combusted. That was the final nail in the coffin of my self-control and I slowly got to my feet.

"Three fifty!" One of the other ladies called out.

That was all it took. I smiled at Lars and held up my paddle. "Ten thousand."

"Excuse me?" The emcee paused. "Number twenty-four—did you say ten...*thousand*?"

I smiled at the three young women who were now shooting daggers at me with their eyes before I turned to the emcee. "I did."

"Now that's what I call donating to charity!" The emcee was pleased as punch. "Lars Jansson goes for ten thousand dollars! Do we have any other bids?"

I sat down with a smug smile.

The emcee grinned as he spoke. "Number twenty-four wins Lars Jansson for a whopping ten thousand dollars—the rest of you boys have some work to do!"

Everyone laughed, but my eyes were on Lars. And then his met mine. For the first time since he'd come out on stage, I saw a glimmer of his personality as he took a moment to study me. Mostly, I saw curiosity, but there was also a hint of annoyance with a dash of...interest?

Before I could figure it out, he was gone, striding backstage.

"This right here is why we're besties." Vanessa dissolved into laughter and I joined her, my eyes never leaving Lars's retreating back.

I'd either done something really liberating or incredibly stupid. Either way, I'd just won myself a date with a professional hockey player who looked like a Nordic god, and for the first time in thirteen months, I was excited about something.

CHAPTER TWO

Lars

Mavericks Group Text

Wes: Boys, this is your captain speaking. I want every member of the team to join me in congratulating Nash and Lars, who are selling their bodies to raise money for charity. Nash brought in 7K for a night with a cougar, and Lars brought in 10K, courtesy of a supermodel. Enjoy those dates, guys—and update all of us here afterward.

Boone: I hated to miss that auction but I had to. How much of a cougar are we talking? Is Nash's date at a nursing home?

Nash: No dude, maybe like 50 and she's hot.

Beau: Dude, cringe. My mom is 50.

Nash: Is she hot? Can I get her number?

Beau: FU

Drew: Lars is going out with an actual supermodel?

Wes: Yep, Sheridan Lee.

Ross: Holy shit! She paid 10K to go out with Lars??

Lars: What is a supermodel?

Nash: It's a generous person who spends an evening with a total dipshit to benefit charity.

Lars: I just googled her. She's more famous than me.

Ross: Dude, she's way way way more famous than you. More famous than any of us. She has a clothing line or something and she's on the Forbes list of wealthiest women in the world.

Lars: She could have paid more than $10,000 then.

Nash: You're lucky she paid anything at all for you. Put some duct tape over your mouth and the date will go great.

Lars: You're just jealous.

Nash: Nah, cuz I know you'll blow it. You'll make some stupid comment and then wonder why she doesn't like you.

Wes: Check in here after the dates, both of you. Let's see who ends up with a second date.

Lars: Okay.

Nash: Deal.

NASH WAS RIGHT. I didn't have the best track record with relationships. But I didn't care, because I wasn't looking for one.

Eat. Sleep. Hockey. Occasionally get laid. That was all I needed.

I'd dated a woman who occasionally spent the night after we slept together when I was in the minors, and she always complained when my alarm went off at five thirty in the morning. She'd wanted to stay in my apartment while I worked out, but there was no way I was agreeing to that. She'd bitched the entire way out the door the last time we'd been together, and I'd decided then and there— no more women staying the night. My morning workouts were nonnegotiable.

It wasn't just that, though. I'd seen what my friends and teammates had to go through with their wives and girlfriends. If they asked where their significant other wanted to go for dinner, it was always, "Oh, I don't know." But if one of my teammates suggested a restaurant, it was, "No, I hate that place."

My teammate Drew got stuck watching stupid shit like *Big Brother* and *The Real Housewives of Beverly Hills*, because that was what his wife Nina wanted to watch. He spent forever at the grocery store trying to find the exact brands of ingredients she put on the grocery list, and he took her to fashion week in New York City and to Broadway shows just to make her happy.

Fuck that. If I went to New York City, I'd be watching baseball and hockey games. My teammates in relationships just didn't seem to get it—you could have all the sex you wanted without the bullshit.

When I walked to my locker after a post-practice shower, Nash was at his locker nearby, getting dressed.

"When's your date with the supermodel?" he asked.

"Saturday night."

"Mine's not until next weekend. I have to figure out what we're going to do. What are you guys doing?"

I shrugged. "Whatever she wants, I guess."

Nash glared at me. "Don't be an asshole. You're supposed to plan the date."

"How? I do not know what she likes."

"Ask her. It's not that hard. She paid a lot of money for this; at least act like you give a shit."

"I do give a shit," I said, narrowing my eyes at him. "She's beautiful. I am wanting to go out with her. I will have her decide what we do so she likes it."

"No. You're supposed to make dinner reservations somewhere nice and then plan at least one other thing."

I scoffed. "Bullshit."

"He's right, dude." Our team captain, Wes,

clapped me on the shoulder. "Hadley would have my ass if I asked her on a date and didn't plan anything."

"You're married. You do not go on dates anymore," I pointed out.

"Just because you're married doesn't mean you don't go on dates anymore."

I exhaled, frustrated. "What I should do then?" I sighed, remembering my last session with my English tutor and immediately corrected myself. "I mean, what should I do?"

"You've got her number, right?" Nash said. "Text her. And don't be an asshole about it."

A flare of aggravation rose in my chest. "I am not an asshole."

"No, but people have to get to know you before they realize that. You're about as charming as that *It* clown."

"Who is that?"

"He's an asshole, trust me."

"You are saying I am clown?"

Nash slipped on his sneakers and grinned at me. "Sometimes, dude. Plan the date. It's not every day you get a shot with a supermodel."

I finished getting dressed and walked out to my Suburban, trying to think of an idea for a date. Dinner was a given, but where? I'd have to google the best St. Louis restaurants and check their ratings. And whatever we did after that, it couldn't take too long, because I had to be in bed by eleven. Ideally, our date would be dinner and sex. I'd have to wait and see if Sheridan liked me enough for that.

My downtown apartment was just a ten-minute drive from the arena. I parked in my spot beneath the building and took the elevator up to my floor. When I walked through the front door, my housekeeper Rosalina called out from the kitchen.

"Mr. Lars, how are you?"

Like me, English wasn't her first language, so we got along great.

"I am good. How are you?" I asked, walking into the kitchen.

"I got stain out of counter," she said, pointing to the kitchen counter near my sink. "You no more let cat walk on counters."

On cue, my cat Loki jumped onto the kitchen island and gave Rosalina a look. Then he walked over to me and I ran a hand down his back.

"That was my fault," I said as I smoothed his gray fur. "I left some V8 juice there."

"Cat is boss around here!" Rosalina said, throwing her hands up. "He shit on floor in laundry room!"

"He was aiming for his litter box," I said, shrugging. "Right, Loki?"

Rosalina shook her head and scowled, going back to her work, cutting the homemade granola bars she'd baked me. She was a five-three, fifty-five-year-old mom of three grown children who'd been working for me since I moved to St. Louis. Over the past four years, we'd gotten pretty comfortable around each other.

My cat, on the other hand, she was *not* comfortable with.

"You go!" she said to Loki, shooing him away with her hand. "You no get hairs in my food!"

I picked Loki up and cradled him in my arms, petting him as I asked, "Rosalina, if someone was taking you on date, where you would want to go?" Catching myself, I spoke again, saying the words in the correct order. "Where *would you* want to go?"

She looked up from the granola bars, peering at me over the dark rim of her glasses. "Mr. Lars, no date for me. Not since many years."

"But where would you want to go?"

Rosalina considered her answer. "Nice restaurant. Eat steak."

"What else? Should we take a walk?" I spoke slowly, wanting to make sure I worked on my English since enlisting the help of a tutor. I'd been in America for years and I planned to stay, so I wanted to speak the language well.

Rosalina shrugged. "Walk is boring. Take boat ride or…flying machine." She gestured in the air with her hand.

"Helicopter?"

She nodded and smiled. "You have date, Mr. Lars?"

"Yeah, Saturday night."

"You need haircut."

I shook my head. "No, I don't look good with short hair."

Rosalina frowned in disagreement, but said nothing more about my hair.

"Dress nice clothes," she said firmly. "No holes. No shoe with toe showing."

"I will."

She gave me a stern look. "No too much perfume."

I smiled. "It's cologne for men, Rosalina."

"No too much," she repeated. "You give her… what is it?" She cringed and held her head.

"A headache?"

She nodded. "No too much."

"Okay."

She squared her shoulders, looking satisfied that she'd given me enough dating advice.

"Granola bars," she said, holding up the container

she was moving to the island. "No leave lid open or demon cat will get."

She was fond of calling Loki a demon. I'd only had him a couple months, and she hadn't gotten used to him yet. My teammate Wes and his wife Hadley were raising our late teammate Ben's children, and their little girl Annalise and I had become good friends. The cat had been her idea, and I'd been unable to refuse her. We went to a shelter one Saturday morning "just to look" and left with the gray bundle of fur she'd named Loki immediately.

He'd grown on me quickly. And I knew Rosalina would warm to him eventually. She cleaned, cooked, ran errands, and took care of all of Loki's needs for me. She didn't live with me, but she spent a lot of time at my apartment, and when I was on the road or at practice, Loki was her only company here.

"Chicken and vegetable," she said, pointing at the refrigerator. "Supper."

"Sounds great, thanks."

She gathered her things and put on her coat, then said, "You pick clothes for date. I see them tomorrow."

I smiled. "You want to help me pick out something?"

She gave me a look I knew well, her lips set in a tight line. "I tell you if clothes look bad."

"Okay, thanks. I'll pick something out and show it to you tomorrow."

Buttoning up her coat, she said, "I go now. Granddaughter has piano show."

"Okay, see you tomorrow."

She walked out without another word, as always. She was no nonsense, which was a perfect fit for me. I didn't have the patience for small talk.

I sat down on my favorite recliner and pushed the footrest out, and Loki jumped into my lap immediately.

"We've got research to do," I told him. "We will find the highest-rated steakhouse in St. Louis and something else to do with Sheridan after."

He purred in agreement. Once my research was done and I made a reservation, I'd pick out some clothes for my date and catch up on the shows I'd recorded. Then dinner, and after that, bowling night with a few of my teammates and I'd be in bed by ten.

The single life was the life for me. I loved women —and sex—but dealing with one every day? Having someone else decide how I was going to spend my time?

Hell no. Other than Loki, I'd never have a life partner.

CHAPTER THREE

Sheridan

I HADN'T BEEN nervous about going out on a date since I was a teenager, but tonight I was. Tonight I was fifteen again, going to the movies with the most popular boy in school, and wondering if he was going to think I was fat. I'd always been on the heavy side, but modeling had changed my outlook on that. Not that I didn't struggle against a world that was still infatuated with the size zero, but my career had taken me places that very few people reached. Up until the accident, I'd stopped worrying about my weight, my sluggish metabolism, and all the things that made me who I was. Tonight, however, I was anxious about all of them, and it made no sense.

Yes, I'd put on weight since the accident. Yes, I had a date with one of the hottest professional athletes I'd ever laid eyes on. And yes, it had been far too long since I'd had sex. But I'd stopped caring what people thought of me a long time ago. I'd made enough money over the years that I didn't ever have to work another day in my life if I didn't want to, but that wasn't the point.

I just wasn't completely sure what the point was.

The point was that I was nervous *as fuck*.

The point was that I wanted to have fun tonight.

The point, and what it really boiled down to, was that I'd paid ten thousand dollars to go out on a date with this guy and I wasn't sure why. This was probably a terrible idea. I'd almost called and cancelled half a dozen times.

My phone buzzed, indicating I had a text, and I glanced down, knowing this was it.

Lars: I'm here. Black Suburban.

Sheridan: I'll be right down.

I'd told him I'd meet him downstairs because there was nowhere to park on my street, so I nervously wiped my hands on my thighs, grabbed my purse, and slid my feet into my shoes. I'd opted for tight black jeans, a leopard print top that made my waist look tiny and showed a little cleavage, and black flats. My hair was down, makeup subdued but on point, and I'd gotten pretty much every hair on my body below the neck waxed.

The elevator let me out on the ground floor and I saw him before he saw me. He was standing on the sidewalk, leaning against a black SUV, arms folded across his chest as if daring my doorman to tell him to move. I took a moment to take in his tall, muscular body and bright blue eyes. He really was a beautiful man.

One night, Sheridan, I reminded myself.

That was all this could be and I couldn't lose sight of that.

"Going out, Ms. Lee?" Barney, the weeknight doorman, asked. "You look wonderful."

"Yes. First date," I told him, wrinkling my nose.

Technically, also the last date, but I didn't tell Barney that. I wanted to pretend tonight could be the start of something new, even though I knew in my heart it couldn't.

He glanced out the door. "Is that…?" He squinted, trying to get a better look.

"From the Mavericks," I said, nodding.

"You tell him I said to take care of you!" he called after me.

I laughed. "I will. See you later."

Lars looked up as I walked through the doors,

immediately taking a step toward me, his eyes on mine.

"Sheridan. Hello." He seemed as nervous as I felt, reaching out to give me an awkward one-arm hug. God, he wasn't just hot, but he smelled nice too.

"Hi." I smiled up at him. I was tall for a woman at five foot eleven, but he still had seven inches on me since I was wearing flats. "Thank you for picking me up."

"Of course." He opened the door of his SUV and held out a hand to help me climb in. The seats were soft leather, reminding me of my Mercedes Maybach, which I hadn't driven in a year. I really missed driving. I got the green light from my doctors, but hadn't had a reason to yet.

Lars got behind the wheel and I tried not to stare. He had a great profile, with high cheekbones leading to a pronounced chin, and a straight nose. The bit of scruff on his face only increased his sex appeal, and I turned to stare straight ahead before I started drooling.

"So you've never been to the Gateway Arch before?" I asked, opting to keep conversation simple. Earlier in the week, we'd decided we would check it out after dinner.

He shook his head. "No. I keep busy with hockey."

"I've lived here my whole life and haven't been to the top either. I mean, my mom worked two jobs when I was growing up, so there wasn't any money for that kind of touristy stuff, and then once I started modeling, I was always traveling."

"You have been modeling a long time?" he asked.

"Since I was fourteen." I paused. "When did you start playing hockey?"

"I cannot remember. Maybe four or five? I have played my whole life."

His accent was strong, though I understood his words clearly. "Did you grow up in Sweden?"

"Yes. In Sundsvall, which is in the north and east of my country. Close to the sea."

"I'll have to look it up," I told him. "I like learning about new places. Everyone always recognizes the capital cities, like Stockholm, but you don't hear much about the smaller towns."

He nodded, pulling up in front of Carmine's Steak House. A valet opened my door, and I carefully stepped down, always cognizant of how I positioned my body. One bad step or twist could send the muscles in my back into spasm overdrive, and I didn't need that tonight.

We were shown to a table in the back and Lars pulled the chair out for me. He was a little quiet and reserved, but that was okay since I could talk enough for five people.

"Tell me something about yourself," I said once we'd ordered. "Do you have siblings?"

"I have a sister, Ingrid. She is married with three children."

"Are your parents still in Sweden?"

He nodded. "My mother, yes. My father died when I was three."

"Oh, I'm sorry. Your mother never remarried?"

"No." He paused. "And you? Brothers or sisters?"

I shook my head. "No, it's just me. My father left when I was a baby and Mom didn't want to have any more kids. She didn't remarry either. She lives about ten minutes from here."

"You are close?" His blue eyes met mine.

"Very. You?"

"No. Not so much. My mother, she is more excited about the grandchildren than hockey."

I widened my eyes in surprise. "Really? That's a shame because hockey is awesome and you're amazing on the ice."

He looked shocked. "You watch the Mavericks?"

"Of course! I go to as many games as I can every season, depending on my travel schedule."

"You travel often for modeling?"

I nodded. "I had to take some time off because of

an injury, but in general, yes. I'm usually in Europe a few times a year and I used to go to New York once a month."

We chatted about random topics all through dinner, with me doing most of the talking and him giving short answers whenever I asked him questions. I liked men who didn't spend the whole evening talking about themselves, but in this case, it meant I spent most of the meal talking about myself, which I also didn't like.

"We go to Arch now?" he asked as we walked outside, one of his hands at the small of my back.

"Do you still want to go?" I looked up at him curiously, wondering if he wasn't that into me, if I'd talked too much, or if he was just shy.

"Yes, of course."

It was a short walk from Carmine's to the Arch and he hesitated as he stared up at the top. "This is very high," he murmured.

"Are you afraid of heights?" I asked.

"No." He frowned, but we continued inside the building.

At the ticket counter, he bought two passes and looked around. "Is there elevator?"

I shook my head. "It's a tram."

"Tram? What is tram?"

"Like a gondola or a little car. A cable pulls it to the top."

"A cable?" He looked wary. "I am a very big man. This is safe?"

"Of course." I smiled and held out my hand. "I'll hold your hand if you're scared."

It seemed like it took him a second to realize I was joking but then he smiled back. "Perhaps this is good idea."

I slid my fingers through his and found his hand warm and dry. And big. Like the rest of him. I honestly couldn't get a read on him. I kept wondering if he was having fun or if he liked me. I'd never met anyone as guarded as he was, but holding his hand was nice—it was one of my favorite couple-ish things. I enjoyed physical intimacy like sex, but there was something about holding hands that just got to me. To me, it expressed an emotional type of intimacy, a sense of affection and comfort. Maybe I was weird, but the way a guy held my hand told me a lot about him as a man and that, combined with my gut, told me Lars was a good one.

Too bad this couldn't be anything more than one date.

"This will hold us?" he asked, staring at the car that would carry us up one side of the Arch and then down the other after we reached the top.

"Millions of people ride it every year. Don't worry—I've got you." I playfully squeezed his hand and we moved toward the small, rectangular opening when it was our turn.

To be fair, the tram was small and Lars was practically a giant, so he had to duck really low to get in. He didn't look comfortable as he sat down, so I sank onto the seat next to him and slid my fingers between his once again.

"Don't worry," I whispered against his ear. "It's going to be beautiful when we get to the top."

He nodded just as the tram started to move and the pressure of his hand on mine increased in direct proportion to our ascent. The movement reminded me of a Ferris wheel, slow and somewhat rickety, so by the time we got to the top, his hand was sweaty and mine had gone numb from how hard he'd been squeezing it.

"It's okay," I said, sliding out of the car and looking around. "See?"

We entered the observation room at the top. It was smaller than I'd expected, but had a row of windows you could look out to see the view. So worth it.

"Oh, it's beautiful," I breathed, looking out at the Mississippi River and the western part of Illinois.

Lars didn't say much, more interested in

watching me than the view, but I thought it was breathtaking. Maybe not as magnificent as the view from the Empire State Building or the Eiffel Tower, but impressive nonetheless.

"I spend so much time on the go," I mused, moving to the other side where I could see the St. Louis skyline. "I rarely take the time to appreciate the majesty of my hometown."

"I think this is true for all of us," he agreed quietly. "I never look for tourist places in Sweden."

Our eyes met and something sparked between us, briefly, like a flash of lightning. Damn, he was so hard to read, but he also wasn't like anyone I'd ever met before. Maybe that was why I liked him.

"You ready to go?" I asked when I'd finally gotten my fill of the view. I would have loved to stay up here for hours, but I sensed his discomfort and didn't want to force him to stay any longer than necessary.

———

WHEN WE GOT BACK to the ground floor, I spotted the gift shop and had an idea, hoping to get a feel for the man behind the mask.

"Let's go in the shop real quick," I suggested, feeling giddy when he reached for my hand and nodded. He was much more relaxed now that we were on the ground and followed me amiably.

"Would you like a souvenir?" he asked politely, cocking his head.

"Yes, but I want you to pick it." I grinned at him. "You go buy me something to remember our first date, and I'm going to go buy you something. But you can't see it until we're both done. How about we meet out front?"

He hesitated. "Yes. Okay." He turned abruptly and went in the other direction, leaving me staring after him curiously.

I knew what I was buying him the minute I saw it —a replica of the Arch made from one of the cables used for the trams. It was kind of silly, but maybe it would remind him of me.

I paid for it and waited for him outside.

He joined me a minute later and immediately held out a bag. "For you."

"Thank you." I opened it and pulled out a mug with a picture of the St. Louis skyline on it. Well, I couldn't give him points for originality, but at least it was one of the nicest mugs in the store. "Oh, this is pretty. Thank you. I'll have my tea in it every morning."

"You are welcome."

"Well, this is for you." I said, handing him my purchase and watching as he slowly opened it.

"This is…" His voice trailed off.

"Made from the same cables that carry the tram up and down. So you'll remember your first, and probably only, trip to the Arch."

Surprise flickered in his eyes as he stared at it. Then he put it back in the bag, wrapping it up carefully before turning to me. "This will be nice memory. Thank you."

"Thank you for indulging me tonight. I know you didn't really enjoy it, but I loved it. It was *so* beautiful up there."

He reached out and put one of his big hands on the side of my face, his eyes softening as he looked at me. "Not as beautiful as you."

Oh. Wow. It was his turn to catch me by surprise because I hadn't thought he'd even noticed me. "Thank you," I whispered, suddenly unable to find my voice.

"Sheridan." His eyes were a deep, rich sapphire color as he stared down at me.

"Y-yes?"

"I can kiss you?"

"Oh. Yes. Definitely."

He leaned in, sliding one hand around my waist and

drawing me closer. He slanted his head and touched my lips with a soft, gentle caress. His mouth was tender for such a big guy, and my heart thudded with inexplicable excitement. When he nudged my lips apart with his tongue, I leaned into him and closed my eyes. I hadn't thought we'd stand right outside the building making out, but here we were, and holy shit, could he kiss. His tongue was both teasing and dominating, working me up without him doing anything else.

I could have stood there kissing him all night. He was that good. And it had been too damn long for me. I wanted him so badly I could taste it, but I hadn't been able to figure him out tonight, and didn't dare make any assumptions.

Luckily, I didn't have to.

"My place?" he asked in a gruff voice.

"Where do you live?" I asked.

He named a neighborhood about twenty minutes away and I shook my head.

"My place is closer."

CHAPTER FOUR

Lars

Wes: Am I the only one still up at 1:06 a.m.? Benny is teething and he only sleeps for two minutes at a time. I just offered him five grand to sleep for four hours.

Wes: Hello…? Anyone. I'm bored as hell here, guys.

Wes: Lars, wasn't your date with the supermodel tonight? How'd it go?

Wes: Or is it still going…?

"Wow," I said as Sheridan led the way into her apartment.

It spanned the entire twenty-third floor of a

renovated downtown St. Louis warehouse building and had an industrial feel, with high ceilings, exposed ductwork, and red brick walls.

She secured two dead bolt locks on the black steel door that she slid closed behind us as I admired the bold artwork on her walls.

Her apartment wasn't what I expected. I thought it would look like an interior design magazine, with high-end antiques on display. Didn't all super rich people like antiques?

Sheridan didn't seem to. Her furniture was leather and looked very comfortable. There were blankets and pillows all over the place, bookcases filled with books, candles, and framed photos.

"I just need to text my head of security real quick and tell him I made it home okay," she said, typing on her phone.

"Wow," I said, picking up a framed photo from a shelf so I could see it better.

It was Sheridan, looking fresh faced, a little younger and absolutely stunning in a red two-piece swimsuit, her dark hair wet and slicked back. She was standing in knee-deep, bright turquoise water, the setting sun painting the sky shades of orange, pink, and purple behind her.

"That was in the Maldives," she said, walking over to me. "It was taken five years ago by Harry

LeCompte. He was a legendary photographer—my absolute favorite to work with. That was our last shoot together before he died of a heart attack."

"Oh." I turned to look at her, momentarily stunned by the color of her eyes—a mix of caramel, gold, and dark green—which were framed by thick, dark lashes. "I am sorry."

"Thanks." She gave me a soft smile and I returned the frame to its place on the shelf.

"And this one?" I asked as I pointed to another framed photo.

It looked like she was in a jungle, but she was dressed in a white sleeveless pantsuit and red patent heels, looking off to the side with a pissed-off expression on her face.

"Oh, yeah." She groaned. "That was a high fashion shoot at Tongass National Forest in Alaska. It was absolutely freezing, and the photographer took forever to get what she wanted."

"Is that why you were so angry?"

She laughed. "No, that's just how high fashion poses are. We're supposed to look borderline angry or distracted. Kind of like how you never see the Kardashians grinning."

I considered this for a moment. "I thought they were always angry."

Sheridan moved a few inches closer to me, her

eyes bright as she tipped her chin up so we were eye to eye. "You're kind of a serious sort, Lars Jansson."

"I have been told that before."

"But you also happen to be sexy as hell."

My blood pumped hard as she licked her lips. I'd never met a woman who was so confident, but also not full of herself. I'd seen how beautiful she was the first time I looked at her that night at the auction, but tonight, seeing her smile as she filled in the gaps in our conversation, I got to see the part of her that had nothing to do with her looks.

Conversation wasn't my strong suit. But making a woman feel good—that I was damned great at, and I knew it.

"You are also sexy as hell," I said, brushing her hair back from one shoulder and laying my hand against her neck. I stroked her cheekbone with my thumb.

She gasped softly. "That feels good."

"What do you want tonight?" I murmured.

"You." She put a palm on my chest, her eyes widening. "Holy shit, it's so hard. It's like..." She moved her hand to the side, and then down to my abs. "Like rocks. You know I don't have abs, right?"

Her tone was teasing, but still, I had learned from experience that anytime I was with a woman and she asked me a question, I should compliment her, just to be safe.

"I like that you're soft," I said, putting my free hand on her back and leaning closer. "And you are also…curved. It's very good."

She smiled, her eyes dancing happily. "I *am* curved."

"You tell me what you want tonight," I said, easing my hand beneath the back of her shirt.

"Because I paid for it?" Her expression became uncertain. "Do you feel like you have to have sex with me because I paid for this date?"

"Not at all. I want to, very much. But only if you want me, too."

"I do."

I leaned down and captured her lips in a kiss, my body tight and tense with arousal. I had the occasional one-night stand, but it had been a long time. And I usually found those women on Tinder. I didn't go out on dates like Sheridan and I had tonight. I'd spent the whole evening admiring her, my desire for her building to the point I could hardly stand it.

And now, finally, I didn't have to hold back.

She moaned and pressed her body against mine, the kiss becoming more intense. I ran a hand over her round, voluptuous ass and groaned. God, was it sexy. I wanted so much more. When I put both hands on her ass and squeezed, she moaned into my mouth and grabbed a handful of my long hair, tugging roughly.

Fuck. It was on.

I bent slightly and picked her up, eliciting a stunned gasp.

"Lars, no, I'm too—"

"Wrap your legs around me," I told her, and she complied.

She felt so fucking sweet molded against me, her legs locked just beneath my waist. I had to take the occasional break from kissing her to make sure I wasn't about to trip over something and fall.

"Where's your bedroom?" I asked her as I pulled away from a long, hungry kiss.

"Keep walking this way," she said breathlessly. "First door on the right."

Her apartment was the size of a fucking IKEA store. Once I finally reached the hallway and I had a clear path, I broke into a run. She squealed, squeezing her legs around me tighter, and laughed.

The lights were off in her bedroom, but there was enough of a glow coming in through the large windows that I was able to find her bed. I set her down and eased up the bottom of her shirt, kissing her stomach. She squirmed and laughed again.

"Oh, God. Sorry." She laughed. "I like it, but it tickles. No one's ever kissed me there before."

I pushed her shirt up farther, and she grabbed it and pulled it off over the top of her head.

Holy fuck. I knew her breasts were big, but the sight of them in the lacy bra she was wearing was absolute perfection. Her large pink nipples showed through the delicate fabric. I ran my tongue over one and she moaned.

That was all the encouragement I needed. I spent the next ten minutes lavishing attention on her breasts —licking, sucking, and nipping them before finally taking her bra off. The entire time, her hands were in my hair, tugging hard when I did something she loved. She still had her legs wrapped around me, too.

It was heaven. She smelled lightly of coconut and her skin was so soft. Every moan made my erection strain against my pants.

She pulled my shirt off and ran her hands over my sculpted chest and shoulders, making an "mmm" sound as she did. When I unfastened her pants and moved down to her ankles to pull them off, she gasped again.

"I just need to close the blinds real quick," she said, scrambling to the side of the bed and grabbing a remote.

"Why, can people see in?"

There was no building across from hers, only the view of the night sky.

"No, but—"

"Leave them open," I told her. "I want to see you."

"Yeah, but—"

"You're the sexiest woman I've ever seen. Let me look."

She sighed softly and set the remote down. "Okay."

I couldn't keep my gaze from her as she came back over to the bed. Her dark hair was spread out over one shoulder and another section fell just to the top of her breasts. Her panties were lacy, like her bra.

We were both on the bed on our knees when I kissed her again, holding her body tightly to mine. I cupped her ass again, groaning. I'd never get enough of her ass.

"You feel so good," she whispered against my lips.

"So do you."

"I'm kind of…" She pulled back and met my eyes in the moonlight. "I don't know how to say it. It's been a while since I've, you know, and I've only been with one man before."

I dropped my hands from her ass.

"Oh. It's okay, Sheridan. We don't have to do this."

"No! I want to do this. We're doing this. I'm just…awkward, I guess."

I smiled. "There's not one thing about you that is awkward. You are perfect."

"God, I want you so bad."

"Lie down," I told her.

She did, and I eased her panties down, then kissed my way up her thighs. She fidgeted a little as I got higher.

"Sorry," she murmured.

"It's okay. It tickles?"

"No, it's just…no one's ever done that to me before."

She was waxed and trimmed neatly, and I kissed the spot right above her pubic bone. "Done what?"

"Um…you know, had their mouth below my waistline."

I got to my knees and looked up at her, confused. "But you are one of the most beautiful women in the world. Do you not like that?"

"I don't know, because no one's ever…"

"Can I?"

Her sigh was ragged. "I mean…you don't have to."

"I want to."

I didn't just want to. I was dying to. I put two

fingers in my mouth and then used them to tease her slowly, trying to relax her. She moaned and opened her legs wider as I coaxed her clit. I didn't need to ask her if she liked it—she did. When I slid my fingers inside her and flicked my tongue over her clit, she groaned loudly.

"Oh my God, that feels good."

I made it last, bringing her close and then slowing down several times. Her body was so damn responsive, her pussy soaked and her hips bucking by the time I let her come. And when she did, it was with a long, deep cry of satisfaction.

Her hips dropped back to the bed and she laughed softly. "Lars?"

"Hmm?"

"I've never felt anything that amazing in my life."

"I am glad."

"I hope you have condoms."

"Yes, I have a twelve pack."

She sat up on her elbows and gave me a sexy grin. "Get one on."

I quickly got off the bed and took a roll of condoms out of my pocket, then unfastened my jeans and pushed them to the floor with my boxers.

"Whoa," Sheridan said from the bed. "That's…wow."

Glancing down and then back up at her, I tore

open a condom packet and rolled it on. "It is larger than average, but I will not hurt you, I promise."

With a single note of laughter, she said, "I'm not worried about it. I was just…surprised. Pleasantly surprised."

Lowering my brows, I said, "You thought I would have a small penis?"

"No! I just didn't expect it to be the size of my forearm, that's all."

"It is not that big."

"Lars."

"Yes?"

"Stop talking and fuck me."

CHAPTER FIVE

Sheridan

I knew the moment I woke up that I was alone in my king-size bed and I sighed as I rolled over. Having his huge, warm body draped all over mine as we'd slept had been…wonderful. In fact, everything about last night had been wonderful. I'd never come so hard, so many times in a row. No one had ever touched me the way Lars had. It was almost scary how good in bed he was.

Not that I had much to compare him to, but I knew instinctively that the physical connection we'd had wasn't the norm. I'd lost track of all the ways he'd pleasured me, and my body tingled from both the memory of his lovemaking and the faint soreness between my legs. We'd had intercourse four times, in between bouts of kissing and oral, and I'd never been with anyone as big as Lars. Sure, I had a selection of toys I used to pleasure myself, but Lars was better—and bigger—than all of them put together.

It was ironic that he'd left without saying good-bye. I'd been worried about how to kindly get him out of my apartment in the morning. I didn't have room in my life for a guarded professional athlete who'd spent most of the evening giving me mixed signals. Hell, I barely had room in my life for anyone. Between my lingerie company, physical therapy, a bazillion different doctor appointments, and trying to figure out what I wanted to do next, I had a lot on my plate.

Today was Sunday though, the only day of the week I allowed myself the luxury of doing nothing. I didn't think too hard, work, or even usually talk to anyone, though Vanessa always checked in. I washed up and pulled on yoga pants, an old, oversized T-shirt, socks, and sneakers. I'd have coffee, stretch, and then head up to my studio, which was a separate loft in this building. No one knew about it, not even Vanessa. It was the one place I could go when I needed to escape everything—even myself. I could paint, draw, listen to music, watch shows on the

DVR, and daydream. I tried to relax there, lose myself in art and solitude, though it didn't always work out that way.

Despite my best efforts to put Lars out of my mind, it was impossible to stop thinking about him. My body ached in the best possible way as I walked into my studio, a cup of tea in my hand. I'd put it in the mug Lars had bought me last night and I thought back to me telling him I'd hold his hand if he was scared. That had been my first taste of those big, beautiful hands of his. The same hands that brought me so much damn pleasure. I inadvertently moaned as I pictured the way he'd looked as he'd slid inside of me. The expression on his face had been one of pure rapture, as if he'd loved the way I felt just as much as I'd loved the way he made me feel. As if our bodies were made for each other.

I was tall and full-figured, so I'd never been with a man that much larger than me. And it was fucking amazing. I felt small and feminine in Lars's arms, a feeling I rarely got to experience. Watching him get off was the type of thing women fantasized about. Well, I did anyway. It was raw and guttural but also sexy and intimate. He'd laced his fingers through mine that first time, pressing them into the mattress on either side of my head and crashing his lips to mine. Watching the pleasure on his handsome face had been breathtaking.

It was the type of thing a woman could get addicted to, so it was probably better that he'd left without a word. It was also kind of funny that he'd felt the need to sneak out, like I was the type of woman who might beg him to stay. I wanted to fall in love again someday, but not now. Not when my life was still so chaotic and filled with uncertainty. And certainly not with quirky, man-of-few-words Lars.

No thinking, Sheridan, I reminded myself.

Sitting in front of one of my easels, my fingers worked of their own volition, sketching out an outline of his face. I closed my eyes, letting the memory of his expressions as we'd made love shutter through my mind's eye. I tried to capture the essence of what we'd shared on my canvas, wishing I could have him sit for me sometime. I'd probably never see him again, but I didn't want to forget what we'd experienced together either.

My phone buzzed and I glanced down, seeing a text pop up from Vanessa.

Vanessa: You were supposed to call me when you got home. You okay? Did you have fun? Where the hell are you?

I figured she'd panic if I didn't respond, so I texted her back.

Sheridan: Had a great time! I'm working on some sketches for the summer catalog, so I'll call you tonight after I get some work done, okay?

Vanessa: You'd better!

I put my phone down and went back to my drawing. I wanted to get this done before the memories started to fade.

————

My week started with a staff meeting discussing the summer catalog, which I hadn't worked on at all yesterday, despite what I'd told Vanessa. I knew what I wanted, though, and I'd bang out some designs tonight. My lingerie company, Sheri Lee, had grown in leaps and bounds over the last year. After my accident, I hadn't been able to do much of anything related to modeling, so I'd started designing lingerie for women who looked like me. Women who had big breasts, big behinds, and thicker waists. My goal had been to create lingerie that made larger women feel sexy while simultaneously masking some of those problem areas that inevitably took us out of an intimate moment.

My best seller was a teddy that featured a

gorgeous push-up bra with lacy material that flowed below it, all the way to your hips, so it covered a round belly, stretch marks, and other areas women often liked to de-emphasize. The material was soft but sturdy, the bra giving maximum lift while the rest of the material was sheer enough to still be sexy. It was available in ten colors and three different fabrics, and I'd made a million dollars on that product alone. The winter catalog that had just come out featured a wedding night version and preorders were through the roof.

So business was good, and I had a million more ideas, but Vanessa was urging me to slow down and not overwhelm my market. We had a great business model, and she thought expanding too fast would be a mistake, but I wanted to release a swimwear line for the summer. So my focus was to talk her—and the rest of my team—into it.

It took me most of the week, but by Friday I could breathe again. We'd come to a compromise on the swimwear line and since I was going to model a few of my favorites, we were planning a photo shoot in the Caribbean for February. It had been a long, productive few days, and I'd just sunk into my massive tub with a glass of wine when my phone rang. I always kept it with me since the accident, in case my back spasmed and I couldn't get up, so I reached for it lazily, expecting it to be Vanessa.

Instead, Lars's name flashed on the screen and I stared at it for a second.

Why was he calling me?

It rang four times before I finally hit the button to accept the call. "Hello?"

"Sheridan. It's Lars."

"Uh, hi."

"How are you?"

"I'm okay." I wasn't sure what to say to him because I honestly hadn't thought I'd ever hear from him again. "But I'm kind of confused. Why are you calling?"

He paused. "Because I want to see you again."

I couldn't help but laugh. "Seriously? You snuck out of here like a thief in the night, I don't hear from you all week, and now you want to see me again? I'm not interested in being your hometown booty call, if that's what this is about."

"Booty call…" His voice trailed off. "This is not that."

"Then why did you leave without saying goodbye?"

"I left because I did not want to wake you and I had to go to the gym. Then we left for road trip. We return to St. Louis tomorrow. Are you angry?"

I sighed. "No, I'm not angry. I'm just…surprised. Usually, after you spend a wonderful night with someone, you call or text or give some signal that you're interested. You ghosted me so I assumed… well, obviously I thought I'd never hear from you again."

"I am sorry. I thought it polite to let you sleep, but I want to see you again." He paused. "Do you want to see me again?"

My brain almost short-circuited from a combination of confusion, excitement, and concern.

It was supposed to be a one-night stand.

He'd disappeared for almost a week and I'd been okay with that.

But now he wanted to see me again.

And I wanted to see him.

Shit.

This was a mistake.

It *was*.

Right?

Going on a date with Lars had been risky. Even 'though I wanted to spend another night with him— badly—I knew better. I couldn't afford to have the news get out that I was seeing someone, because trouble would literally come to my doorstep if it did.

"I want to, but I can't," I said, wishing things were different.

"Why not?"

Huh, I hadn't been expecting that question.

"Well, there are a lot of reasons." Lie. There was only one reason. "I'm just getting back to work after being gone for a long time after my accident, and that takes most of my time and energy. I'll be traveling again soon, and then I'll be even busier. I also like to keep a low profile, and you're anything but low profile."

"What is low profile?"

I smiled. "It means you attract attention."

There was a pause on the other end of the line, and then Lars said, "You enjoyed the sex."

It wasn't a question, but a statement. My smile widened.

"I did, yes. And you did, too. But adult responsibilities call. Maybe when things settle down for me, we can get together again."

Another pause. "Okay."

"Bye, Lars."

"Goodbye."

CHAPTER SIX

Lars

I'D NEVER GET USED to ice baths. Sinking into the freezing cold tub of water shocked my system every time.

That was the point, though. It woke my entire

body up after my pregame nap and had been part of my routine since before I went pro—ice bath for ten minutes followed by my pregame meal.

"Lars!"

I opened my eyes to see a red ball flying toward my face. I reached up to catch it just in time and then turned to see who'd thrown it.

It was Ross Camden, a second line forward. He was grinning and I was scowling.

"Good reflexes," he said.

"I will hurt you if you throw anything at my face again."

"What should I throw it at then?" he asked, grinning.

"I will shove this ball up your ass until it comes out of your mouth," I said, dunking it in the ice bath. "I am rubbing it all over my balls right now."

"Dude." He furrowed his brow. "Disgusting."

"Do not talk to me on game days. Or look at me."

He put his hands up in the air. "Fine. You don't need to be a dick about it."

I held the ball up and asked, "Do you want it back?"

He cringed, grabbed a towel from a stack nearby, and held it out. "Just put it in the towel. I'll disinfect it later."

"What's that for?" Nash asked as he passed by after taking a shower.

A long, hot shower was part of his pregame routine. I didn't know why he did that—it would relax me, and that was not how I wanted to be when it was game time.

"It was just for fun, but then Lars rubbed it all over his balls because he's an asshole," Ross said.

I sank back down into the chilly water, ignoring him.

"I haven't forgotten about your date with the supermodel," Nash said. "I'm going to keep asking you how it went until you tell me."

I sighed heavily. He'd been nagging me to tell him about the date since the morning after, and I was getting sick of him asking.

"I do not want to talk about it," I said, not looking at him.

He cackled. "You were yourself, weren't you? You barely smiled, looked indifferent the whole time, and then wondered why she didn't want to jump into bed with you."

A flare of aggravation started to rise within me. My teammates knew damn well that I wanted to be left alone on game days. My first season with the Mavericks, I'd put a sign on my locker telling people not to talk to me on game days, but some teammates ignored it. Nash was my best friend on the team, but he still enjoyed messing with me.

"Go away," I said.

He didn't.

"When's the second date? I'm guessing never?"

"Who says I want to go out with her again?"

Nash scoffed. "I'd bet my earnings from this game that you do. Between one and ten, you're usually around a level-five asshole on game days, but today you're more like an eight. You either went out with her and it didn't go well, or it did go well and you asked her out again and she said no."

"Go fuck yourself."

"I'll tell you how my date goes."

"Don't care. Fuck off."

"Okay, but seriously," he said. "Did you order me some spaghetti Bolognese?"

"Yes, but I will eat it myself if you don't leave me the fuck alone."

He chuckled. "No, you won't. You eat one order of that chicken spinach pasta from Giovanna's before every home game and that's it."

The timer on my phone sounded and I reached for the towel next to the tub and dried my hand off before turning off the timer.

"Go see if the delivery guy came yet," I said, standing up.

"Okay. Did you tip him yet?"

"Yes. I paid for everything."

"Thanks, dude."

"You are welcome. Now leave me alone."

I dried off and dressed, then went to the weight room so I could eat my pregame meal in peace. After I finished, I drank the sixteen ounces of water I'd brought into the weight room with me, and then sat down on a mat and closed my eyes.

Before every home game, I did things the exact same way. I tried to mimic my routine during road games, but it wasn't as easy. Even on the road, though, I always did this part.

This was my time for a mental run-through of my opponents. First thing this morning, I'd watched game film of Nashville. I knew every offensive player's stats from last season, but I still liked to watch film before every game.

As a team, their record was 45–28–9 last year. Their team captain, Jack Cavanaugh, was the one I had to keep the closest eye on. He had a face-off win percentage of 57.43 last season, as well as 67 take-aways and 21 giveaways. As someone who didn't turn the puck over much but was good at stealing it, he was the kind of player who won games.

I had teammates who played with their hearts. Wes Kirby was one of those. He had keen instincts and I admired that about him. My instincts had never gotten me far—I relied on statistics to guide many of my decisions on the ice.

The timer on my phone sounded once again, indicating it was time for me to eat two Reese's Peanut Butter Cups. I went back to the locker room and took out the package, eating each one the same way. First I ate the crinkled edges around the cup, and then I ate the center.

"Yo," Drew said, sitting down next to me. "I know you don't want to talk, but I just wanted to say, if you need someone to confide in about your date, I'm always here, man."

I shrugged. "It was good. I enjoyed it."

"Good. You guys going out again?"

I eyed him suspiciously. "Did Nash tell you to ask me?"

"No."

Drew was our goalie, and he was the oldest member of the team. He had a wife and kids and wasn't one to mess with people just for fun. Still, I knew Nash well enough to know how persistent he could be, and he was dying to know about my date with Sheridan.

"She does not want to go out with me again," I said, my tone so low it was almost a whisper.

"How come?"

I shrugged. "She said she is very busy with going back to work, and that maybe when things settle down she will have time."

Drew furrowed his brow. "Huh. So give me a quick rundown. How long was the first date?"

I calculated. "Nine and a half hours."

His brows shot up. "Oh. So it was good."

"It was great."

He nodded. "And you guys…spent the night together?"

"Yes. Most of it. I had to leave at three thirty so I could sleep for a little before my workout."

"And she was cool with that?"

I shrugged. "I did not ask; I just left. She was sleeping."

His expression changed, but I wasn't sure why. "And then you called or texted her later that day?"

I shook my head. "No. We had our road trip. I called her the day before we came back."

I didn't understand his single note of laughter.

"Was she happy to hear from you?" he asked.

"I do not think so. She said I…ghosted her? What docs that mean?"

He nodded. "It means you waited too long to call her, dude. If you really like a woman, you need to pay more attention to her. For example, send a text after a date saying you had a great time and want to see her again."

I scrunched my forehead in confusion. "But I called her when I had time to go out. Why would I ask her out when I am in another state?"

"You just do, man. So she knows you're into her."

"I am into her. But Nash is right. I blew it."

"Nah." Drew stood up. "If she answered the phone and talked to you, there's hope. Try again. Send flowers. If she knows you really like her, she'll give you another chance."

"Do you really think that?"

He grinned. "Bro, Nina turned me down the first four times I asked her out. And look at us now, married for like…a hundred and fifty years. Just kidding, she's my ride or die. Don't give up."

I nodded. "Thank you."

"Anytime. Hey, I have to go dress."

"So do I."

I had taped my stick after watching film, so now I just had to put my gear on. I thought about Sheridan as I did, wondering if Drew was right.

Should I try again? It had been a long time since I'd wanted to go on a date with a woman. Usually I preferred drinks, sex, and a middle-of-the-night departure that ensured I didn't have to deal with an awkward morning-after conversation when the woman asked me when I wanted to get together again.

I couldn't stop thinking about Sheridan, though. Even though the sex had been great, it was other things about her I found myself daydreaming about.

Like her smile, which made me understand what it meant when Americans said someone had a smile that lit up a room. Sheridan's smile did that. And her laugh, which made me want to laugh as well.

Drew was right—I had to keep trying. I liked Sheridan too much to give up so easily.

CHAPTER SEVEN

Sheridan

AFTER THE ACCIDENT and my initial recovery from surgery, I'd needed something to get my mind off my troubles, so I'd created Sheri Lee. I'd thrown myself into it thinking I might not ever walk again and I'd need a source of income. Vanessa had been my best friend, sister, cheerleader, and drill sergeant—sometimes all at the same time—and together we'd created a multimillion-dollar company. Today, however, I wanted to strangle her. She was my right arm, but this was still my company, and I didn't know why she was fighting me so hard on everything.

"Okay, let's pause for lunch," I said at Wednesday's senior staff meeting. "I think we all need a break, so let's meet back here at two o'clock." I gazed at Vanessa as she started to get up. "Will you stay, Vanessa?"

She hesitated but dropped back down into her chair.

Everyone filed out, closing the door to the conference room behind them, and I leaned back in my chair, stretching out my back a little.

"You want to tell me what's going on with you?" I asked her.

She arched her brows. "Me? There's nothing going on with *me*."

"Then why are you fighting me on every damn thing I want to do?"

She sighed.

"Nessa?" I never used her nickname at work, but she was my best friend and I didn't like when we were at odds.

"Look, I'm worried about you."

"More now than, say, thirteen months ago?"

"In a different way. You're drowning yourself in work so you don't have to think about anything else, and you can't keep doing it."

"I don't have a choice. This is my future and—"

"There is no reason whatsoever you can't go back to modeling!"

"You know damn well why I haven't gone back."

We glared at each other.

"Then fix it," she said after a moment.

"It's not up to me at this point. This is a legal battle."

"The more successful we make this company, the worse it's going to be."

"That's why you don't want to do the summer swimwear line?"

"My gut tells me the swimwear line will be a huge success and the more money you make, the more this case is going to drag on."

"What's the alternative? I sit home and mope?" I hated when she was right, but I was between a rock and a hard place, and she knew it.

"I don't know, but I'm worried. This has gone on too long. It has to stop. It's destroying you, Sheridan, and it's killing me to watch it."

"I'm okay. I'm strong and resilient. I'll come out the other side, one way or another."

"Excuse me—you guys want to order from Pino's Pizza?" My assistant, Nellie, stuck her head in the door.

I nodded. "That's fine with me. Greek salad."

"Two," Vanessa called out. "And a white pesto flatbread." She looked at me. "We'll share it."

I smiled. That was my favorite and she knew it.

I'd been trying to lose these last ten pounds, but it was so hard. Weight had always been difficult for me to lose but never more so than after the accident. These days, I did a lot of yoga, but hadn't worked up to cardio yet. My physical therapist was forcing me to get back to normal one tiny step at a time. It made me crazy, but I trusted her; she was the whole reason I was walking again. And I wouldn't do anything that might slow or completely halt my progress.

"Let's focus on the Black Friday specials today," Vanessa said once Nellie was gone. "And this weekend you and I can talk some more about the summer catalog. Deal?"

I gave her a small smile. "Fine. Deal."

"We're also going to talk about Lars."

I groaned. "I don't want to talk about him."

"You like him."

"I do, but a guy who sneaks out without a word isn't the kind of man I want in my life. I've already had a relationship with the world's biggest asshole. I want a guy who's devoted to me. Who loves me more than money or the fact that I'm a supermodel."

"You can't possibly know that Lars isn't that guy after one date."

"Aren't you the one who told me going out with him was a bad idea?"

"Yeah, but maybe I was wrong. Maybe he's

exactly what you need to get out of this funk you're in."

"I'm not in a funk," I protested. Even though I kind of was. I just didn't know what to do about it.

"You are *so* in a funk."

We stared each other down until we burst out laughing.

"Fine, this weekend we'll talk about all the things. But right now, let's figure out Black Friday and eat."

We ate in relative silence with her on her laptop and me checking messages on my phone. Just as the others filed back in around two, my phone buzzed and I was surprised to see a text from Lars.

Lars: Hi. This is Lars. How are you?

Sheridan: Busy today but doing well. How about you? You had a great game last night.

Lars: You were there?

Sheridan: No, I watched on my phone while I worked.

Lars: You work so many hours in the evening?

Sheridan: Sometimes, and right now we're getting ready for the holidays, which will be extremely busy.

Lars: When do you relax?

Sheridan: On Sundays, unless something comes up.

Lars: We will be on the road this Sunday.

Sheridan: Like I said last time we talked, we're both very busy.

Lars: Yes, but a good orgasm will relax you like nothing else.

I chuckled to myself since he had a point.

Sheridan: Is that so? You think you'll give me a good orgasm?

Lars: Didn't I? I thought you had many good orgasms.

Sheridan: I did—great orgasms, as a matter of fact. But I'm still crazy busy.

Lars: I'll do that thing you like with my tongue.

My insides clenched with excitement. He'd tongue fucked me until I'd been both begging for more and begging him to stop. It had been insanely sexy. And despite initially choosing not to go out with him again, the thought of him going down on me was enough to change my mind.

Sheridan: How many times?

Lars: As many as you can stand.

Sheridan: What else?

Lars: What else will I do to you?

Sheridan: Yes. And I want details.

Lars: Anything you want. Do you like ass play?

Holy hell, my panties were about to be soaked. Thinking about Lars touching me there was enough to make me flushed with excitement.

Sheridan: I never have. Will I like it?

Lars: You will if I do it. You've never had an orgasm

as strong as the one you will have with my finger in your ass.

Oh, yeah, my panties were soaked.

Sheridan: My favorite was when you used your mouth.

Lars: My favorite is your ass. I can touch and kiss it all day. And your breasts. They are perfect for my hands.

Sheridan: You realize I'm in a meeting and now I'm all hot and bothered?!

Lars: Then let's find a time to get together to do these things in person. What about Friday?

Sheridan: I can't. I have vendors in from LA and I'm taking them out.

Lars: I'm gone from Saturday until next Friday and then a game next Saturday afternoon here at home. Do you want to go out after the game?

Sheridan: That's my mother's birthday so I've got plans with her.

Lars didn't respond for a few minutes and I tried to figure out what I'd missed in the meeting. Vanessa was talking about the online sale for Black Friday, and whether we wanted to discount the whole site twenty-five percent off or create a coupon code that customers had to type in.

"Let's make it easy," I said. "Just discount the whole site."

"Even the new stuff?" My vice president of sales, Bernie Fisk, asked. "Like the wedding stuff?"

I sighed. I didn't care about this kind of thing. I just wanted to create pretty underwear and bathing suits and go around the country visiting stores that carried our products.

"Sure, let's discount everything. That's the point of Black Friday, right? To kick off the holiday season?"

"I'm thinking a coupon code." The vice president of marketing, Marnie Swail, made a face. "And it's only good on certain items."

"Why?" I cocked my head. "People expect to get good bargains on Black Friday. Let's do twenty-five percent for all online orders. If people want to purchase items in person, then it's up to each individual store to charge whatever they want."

Marnie didn't look happy, but she nodded and made some notes on her pad.

My phone buzzed again and I looked down.

Lars: There is a team party next Sunday at Wes Kirby's house. Would you like to go?

Sheridan: I'd like to see you again, but are you sure you want me to go to a...team event?

Lars: Of course. Why not?

I couldn't think of a response even though there were probably a million reasons this was a bad idea, but I had a feeling Lars marched to the beat of his own drum. Even in hockey.

Sheridan: I don't know. I figure the whole team must know I paid ten thousand dollars to go out on a date with you.

Lars: You paid this money for CHARITY. The date was not the point.

That was true.

The whole idea of dating still made me nervous.

But I kept thinking about the things he would do with his tongue. And his fingers. And my ass.

Holy shit, there had to be something wrong with me.

Sheridan: All right. I'll see you then.

Lars: I will pick you up at noon next Sunday.

CHAPTER EIGHT

Lars

Mavericks Group Text

Nash: Wes! What time are we supposed to be at your house?

Wes: Whenever. Just come after noon. We're eating around 1:30.

Nash: What should I bring?

Wes: You do realize it's 11:45, right?

Nash: Yeah, so?

Wes: We could use a homemade potato salad. Can you bring that?

Nash: Fuck no. I'll bring chips.

Boone: Hey Nash, how was your date with the older

woman? Did she get you guys the senior discount at dinner?

Nash: The only word I can think of for that date is harrowing.

Drew: WTF dude. Do you know what that word even means?

Nash: Yes I do. All I'm saying over text is that she made me call her Mistress Sandra and my ass hurts so bad that I can hardly sit down.

Wes: Forget the chips. Get your ass over to my house ASAP and tell me about this date.

SHERIDAN'S DOORMAN tipped his hat at me as I waited for her to come down for our date.

"Made it to a second date, I see," he said.

"Yes, sir."

His facial expression became a little more serious as he continued. "I haven't seen any men come over to her apartment except her bodyguard since she moved in. She's a nice woman. You treat her right."

Before I could respond, he saw Sheridan approaching the front door, a covered container in hand, and opened it for her.

"Afternoon, Miss Lee."

"Hi Barney. How are you?"

"The sun's shining and I'm talking to a beautiful lady, so I can't complain."

Sheridan gave him a radiant smile and my heart kicked up a notch. I hadn't been able to stop thinking about our phone call the other night, or our date. She was confident, and I found it incredibly sexy.

"Have a good one," she said, giving Barney a little wave.

I nodded to him, and Sheridan hooked her arm through mine and said, "Hey. How are you?"

"I'm good. How are you?"

"Good. It's been ages since I've been to a cookout. I'm looking forward to this."

I walked her to my car and then leaned down to give her a quick kiss before opening her door.

"My teammates can be…much," I said as she got into the car.

She laughed. "I'm sure. Don't worry; I can handle it."

There would be kids at the cookout, so hopefully the rowdy energy and raunchy comments would be minimal. But anytime we were all together and alcohol was involved, things definitely got out of hand.

Wes and his wife Hadley had just bought a new suburban home, and moving day had been bittersweet. Most of the team had been there to help them say goodbye to the home that had belonged to Ben and Lauren, our former team captain and his wife. Wes and Hadley had lived there for a while after Ben and Lauren passed away, giving themselves and Ben and Lauren's children, Benny and Annalise, time to settle into their new normal.

I'd helped Annalise set up her new room. It had wood floors, large windows, and a small nook area we'd filled with pillows. And bookshelves. Every time I went over there she asked me to read her the same book. It was about the Avengers and I had it memorized by now.

Annalise and Sheridan were going to love each other. Annalise had become very special to me since Ben's death. I hadn't thought I was good with kids before, but she made me feel like maybe I was okay with them after all.

"So it's Wes and Hadley, right?" Sheridan asked as I drove. "And Annalise and Benny?"

"Yes." I glanced, once again, at the container in her lap. "What's in there?"

"Broccoli salad. You know, the one with the bacon and sunflower seeds? It's one of my favorites."

"That sounds good. Did you make it?"

She grinned. "I did. It's my mom's recipe."

"I brought pasta salad."

Sheridan arched her brows, looking impressed. "Did you make it?"

I smiled. "No. I am not good with that. My housekeeper Rosalina made it. I hope it is good. She wouldn't let me have a taste."

"I'm sure it's fantastic. You can't go wrong with anything pasta."

"If you are nervous, just stay with me," I told Sheridan as we pulled up to Wes and Hadley's sprawling home.

She gave me another megawatt grin. "Don't worry about me, Lars. I'll be just fine."

We walked around to the back, where a group of around twenty people had already gathered.

"Thor! Thor! Thor!" Annalise cried as she raced toward me, her arms open.

I bent down as she jumped. She wrapped her arms around my neck and I picked her up.

"My playhouse is done!" she cried. "It's over there! Come see!"

"Hey, man," Wes said, approaching us. "Glad you guys could make it. You must be Sheridan."

"I am." She held out a hand and Wes shook it.

"Hi, I'm Wes Kirby." He gave Annalise an admonishing look. "And what did we say about today, peanut? There are lots of kids here to play with. I want you to let Lars talk to the grown-ups. He brought a friend today."

I took his cue and said, "Annalise, this is Sheridan. Sheridan, my good friend Annalise."

"*Best* friend," Annalise said, tightening her hold on my neck.

Sheridan smiled at her. "Wow, it's a real pleasure to meet Lars's best friend."

"Why are you here?" Annalise asked her in an accusatory tone.

"Annalise," Wes said sharply. "That's rude."

Sheridan waved a hand and said, "It's okay, really."

Wes gave her a grateful look and said, "It's not, but we'll address it later in private."

He looked over his shoulder as Hadley approached. "And this is my wife Hadley. I can sense her presence now. It's a little creepy."

"*You're* creepy," Hadley said, grinning and rolling her eyes. "Hi, Sheridan. We're so glad you could join us today. And hey to you, too, Lars."

"Hello."

"Where should I put these?" Sheridan asked, holding the containers of food we'd brought.

She'd grabbed mine when she saw Annalise running toward me. Hadley gestured toward a large table set up on a nearby paved patio.

"Over here. I'll go with you and then we can get a drink."

"Oh, hey!" Nash called as he walked over to Sheridan and Hadley as they left. "You must be Sheridan. Are you wondering how to get a refund on that money you paid for a date with Lars?"

I rolled my eyes, aggravated, but Sheridan just laughed.

"Hey," Wes said to me. "We need to have a little chat with Annalise."

"No, I want to play," she said, wiggling in my arms in an effort to get down.

Wes crossed his arms and shook his head. "You were rude to Sheridan, and I expect you to apologize. That's not how we treat guests in our home."

Annalise looked at me. "Do I have to apologize to her?"

My lips parted with surprise. I still couldn't believe Annalise had said what she did to Sheridan. It wasn't like her. Usually she was a bubbly, happy girl who got along with everyone.

Wes sighed heavily. "It's not up to him, Annalise. And you have to apologize unless you want to watch the other kids play from the time-out corner."

"How long of a time-out?" Annalise asked.

I forced myself not to smile. Wes wouldn't like it if I undercut his parenting strategy.

"Really long," he said. "And you'd still have to apologize at the end of the time-out."

"Don't you want to play with me?" Annalise asked me.

"Yes, I'll still play with you. Sheridan probably will, too. But we also want to spend some time with the grown-ups."

"I don't want to play with her." Annalise scowled. "She's ugly."

Wes gasped and I set Annalise down.

"I'm disappointed," I told her. "That was mean."

Her expression was crushed as she looked up at me and said, "I'm sorry."

"I will see your new playhouse when you are ready to show it to me *and* Sheridan," I said.

"Okay."

"But first, you'll be telling Aunt Hadley about the mean things you said," Wes said, reaching for her hand.

"No!" Annalise protested.

"Yes."

Nash and Boone approached me as Wes and Annalise walked off, and Nash handed me a bottle of Heineken.

"Is someone jealous of Sheridan?" he asked.

"That must be it."

"Poor kid. It's hard to blame her with everything she's been through."

I nodded and took a sip of my beer. I still couldn't believe Annalise was acting this way. I'd been sure she and Sheridan would click immediately. She'd latched on to Hadley hard and recently started calling her 'Mommy', which was bittersweet for those of us who'd known Lauren, but we also understood Annalise feeling like Hadley was her mom now.

"Dude, I broke several traffic laws getting over here as fast as possible," our goalie Drew said as he walked up to us. "I have to hear about your date."

Nash scoffed. "I'm glad my misery is so amusing to you fuckwads." He shook his head.

"It really is," Boone said. "Don't leave us hanging."

Nash looked over both shoulders to make sure no one could overhear.

"So she said she wanted to cook me dinner at her apartment, right? I was expecting a home-cooked meal and sex."

Konstantin and Wes came to join our huddle, both with eager expressions.

"Is this about the date?" Wes asked. "What'd we miss?"

Nash rolled his eyes. "She said she wanted to cook me dinner at her apartment. So I got there, brought a nice bottle of wine too, and when she opened the door, she was dressed in black leather from head to toe."

Boone cackled, putting a fist to his mouth to stifle his laugh.

"She told me I had to address her as Mistress Sandra for the entire evening," Nash continued. "I wanted to pass her the wine and bolt, but she paid seven grand for this date, you know? I felt like I had to give her…something."

"So you gave her your virgin ass," Drew said, shrugging. "Makes total sense, dude."

Nash glared as the rest of us laughed. He looked over both shoulders again before whispering, "I didn't let her do that. She whipped me."

Boone was doubled over with laughter.

"Okay, go back to the beginning," Wes said. "I don't want to miss a single detail. You walk inside, and then what?"

Nash heaved out a sigh. "She wanted me to take off all my clothes and put on a collar. I told her I'd take my shirt off, but that was it."

"And then she whipped you?" Boone asked.

"No, she said that was fine. But she made me eat my dinner out of a bowl on the floor, like a fucking dog, while she sat at the table and told me the rules for the evening."

I grinned and cut in, saying, "I would pay good money for a video of this date."

Nash just shook his head. "I told her I wasn't doing all of it."

"But what did you do?" Drew asked.

Nash hesitated. "I tried to compromise. She wanted to put things in my ass but I said no fucking way. So I…licked her boot instead."

Boone let out another guffaw as we all gaped at Nash.

"You…licked her boots?" Drew asked.

"*Boot.*" Nash held up a finger. "Only one. And it was one lick. They looked clean."

"Oh my God, this is the best day of my life," Boone said, grinning.

"It was ridiculous," Nash said. "Not sexy at all. She pinched my nipples really hard and made me sit by her feet."

"Is she your master now?" Wes asked, trying to rein in his laughter.

Nash glared at him in response. "I let her whip my ass a few times, so she…I don't know, got her money's worth, I guess. It hurt like hell. I have welts on my ass."

"Can we move this conversation over to the grill?" Wes asked. "I have to start the burgers and hot dogs, but I don't want to miss any of this."

"That's all there is," Nash grumbled. "New subject. Will we be celebrating Lars's engagement next weekend? Who brings someone to a team cookout for a second date?"

I shrugged. "I like her. She's great. You are just jealous because I don't have to lick my date's boot."

"Plus she's a smoking hot supermodel," Boone said.

I gave him a warning look. "Don't talk about her."

"What?" He put his hands up in mock surrender. "I say good for you, bro. I'd kill to go out with someone like her."

I scanned the growing crowd for Sheridan. Wes and Hadley had invited all the team trainers and coaches and their families, so there were lots of people around. I finally found her, tucking a lock of dark hair behind her ear as she laughed at something Drew's wife, Nina, had said. Sheridan was surrounded by a group of team wives and girl-friends, looking as if she was chatting with old friends.

Was she faking it? Surely she felt awkward, or at least nervous. I still felt that way at these things sometimes, and I'd known most of the guys on my team for years.

When she looked my way, I gave her a little wave

and an expectant look. She smiled and gave me a thumbs-up.

Huh. Apparently she didn't need me. I went back to my conversation with the guys.

By the end of the cookout, I'd only spent a few minutes with Sheridan out of the five hours we'd been there. All the women had wanted to talk to her about everything from fashion advice to the best selfie angles. It was exhausting to listen to.

"I think we should go out for dinner," I told her as we walked to the car after saying our goodbyes. "It was not a date if I hardly got to see you."

She laughed and said, "I had a wonderful time today, and dinner sounds great."

I had a feeling this was going to be the longest date I'd ever been on. And I was more than okay with it.

CHAPTER NINE

Sheridan

Since we were dressed casually, we found a quaint little restaurant not too far from where I lived and ordered a bottle of wine. I was already looking forward to the naked portion of our evening, and based on the way Lars had been looking at me the last half hour, he was too. I wanted to lean over and kiss him, hard, and taste the wine on his lips, but a public display of affection like that probably wouldn't be the most prudent move at this point. I had a love-hate relationship with the press these days, but it came with the territory. I was a public figure and they had a job to do. Even when it annoyed the hell out of me. I'd gotten used to it, but sometimes I just wanted to enjoy dinner or a night out in peace.

Here in St. Louis, they mostly left me alone unless I was somewhere high profile, like the bachelor auction, but you never knew when someone was going to pop up with a camera and I wanted to keep this thing with Lars as low key as possible. It was just easier that way.

"I'm very sorry about Annalise," Lars said, apologizing for the second time since we'd left the cookout.

"Really, it's okay. Hadley told me about what happened to her parents and how important you've become to her. She's just a baby, you know? She doesn't understand loss and grief and all that stuff. She probably looks at me as someone who could potentially take you from her, even though that's not true, so I can see why she reacted that way."

A faint smile played on his lips as he reached across the table for my hand. He brought it slowly to his mouth, his eyes never leaving mine, and gently kissed the inside of my wrist. "You are a good heart," he said softly.

"Thank you." I smiled back, even as goose bumps broke out on my flesh and my insides yearned for more of his touch.

"You spent a long time talking with Hadley," he said. "Did you get along with everyone?"

"Yeah, they were great," I replied, reluctantly pulling my hand away and lifting my wineglass. "I really enjoyed Hadley. She writes about the fashion industry, so we had a lot to talk about, and Nina's a lot of fun."

He nodded. "I don't know so many of the wives and girlfriends. Only Hadley and Nina. Because I'm single, I don't attend a lot of family events and parties. It was different when Ben was killed. I…" His voice trailed off as he looked away. "I guess I am a loner. But it was important for me to show support after such a tragedy and then Annalise, she became very attached."

"I think you're a little attached to her, too," I teased, smiling over the rim of my wineglass.

"Yes. She is so small. Innocent. I feel very strongly the need to protect her."

"Of course. And that's why my feelings aren't hurt that she doesn't like me. She's jealous. It makes perfect sense."

"She is not usually like this."

"She'll come around. You'll see." I sat back as the waiter delivered our meals and a twinge ripped through my lower back that made me cringe.

Oh, no. Not tonight.

I closed my eyes and took a deep breath, trying to relax.

But it was no use. My back seized up and the pain had me clenching my teeth.

Sonofabitch.

"Sheridan?" Lars asked, watching me carefully.

"I need...to call...my bodyguard."

"Why?" He was instantly on alert, looking around. "What is it?"

"My back...a cramp." I clutched the edge of the table so hard my knuckles turned white. "I won't be able to walk."

"Will you be able to finish dinner?" he asked.

I narrowed my eyes in disbelief. "It hurts to move, Lars."

"What should I do?"

"I just need to get home. I have muscle relaxers. This happens every so often. Since...the accident." Fuck, this hurt. Normally when it happened, I was at home, where I could hobble to bed and take my meds. Now we were in a public place and there was no way I'd make it out to his SUV. This had been my biggest fear about venturing out again.

"I will pay," he said automatically. "Do not worry. I will take you home."

He motioned for the waiter, whispered something to him and handed him his credit card. I closed my eyes and took a deep breath, forcing myself not to let the pain show on my face with so many people around.

The waiter practically jogged back to the table, Lars signed something, and then he got up. My eyes widened as he approached my chair.

"Wait. You're not going to…?"

"I am very strong. Do not worry."

"Lars, don't—"

My heart hammered as I imagined him trying to pick me up and falling over or dropping me in the middle of a crowded downtown restaurant. I'd be a laughingstock.

He scooped me up from the chair and away from the table, his expression as stoic and unconcerned as ever. He wasn't straining and he wasn't going to drop me. No one had carried me since I was a child, but this strong, huge hunk of a hockey player managed to do it.

"Lars Jansson!" a man called from a nearby table. "It's Lars Jansson from the Mavericks."

"Yes, I am Lars."

If I hadn't been in so much pain, his response would have made me smile. Lars was the most unique, straightforward man I'd ever known.

He stopped walking, and I cringed.

"Hey man, can I get a picture with you?" the man asked. "I'm a season ticket holder."

Lars looked at my face and asked, "Do you mind?"

I arched my brows, stupefied, and forced myself to unclench my teeth. "Do I mind? Yes, I do. Will you please get me out of here right now? People are already taking pictures of us with their phones."

He nodded and turned to the man. "I am sorry. I can't do a picture right now."

"Sure, it's okay."

Lars opened the door to the restaurant with his foot, not missing a beat. When we got to his SUV, he gently placed me in the front seat and latched the seat belt so I wouldn't have to twist. Then he jogged around to the driver's side and got in. He pulled into traffic and glanced over at me.

"You are okay?"

"Not yet." I grimaced. "I have medication that will help the muscles relax. A good night's sleep and I should be fine tomorrow. I guess I spent too much time on my feet today."

He looked like he was going to say something but then didn't.

IT ONLY TOOK a few minutes to get home and he double-parked in front of the building. He jumped out and opened my door, waving at Barney.

"What's happened? Does she need a doctor?" Barney came running out.

"No," I gasped, wincing as Lars lifted me out of the SUV. "Just a bad cramp."

"Don't let anyone…take my car," Lars called to him. "What is the word?"

"Tow," I responded automatically.

"Tow!" Lars yelled right next to my ear. "Don't let anyone tow it!"

Ouch. That kind of hurt. But my back hurt worse.

"Don't worry, Mr. Jansson. I'm on it." Barney yelled as the elevator doors closed.

I somehow managed to get out my keys and Lars unlocked the front door without even putting me down, which was something.

"Where is the medicine?" he asked, taking me directly to the bedroom.

"Top drawer of the nightstand." I told him the name of the prescription and he put me down gently before opening my drawer and pulling out the pills. I swallowed two dry, unwilling to wait for water, and rested my head on the pillow. This hurt so damn much, no matter how much progress I made. My physical therapist said it was the muscles trying to protect themselves from strain, which happened often as I became more active. But damn, it had been over a year and I was so tired of this.

"What else can I do?" Lars asked, sitting on the edge of the bed, one hand on my hip.

"Nothing," I whispered. "Thank you for taking care of me. This happens sometimes. Can you bring me a bottle of water from the fridge, please?"

"I'll be back." He disappeared for a minute and came back with a bottle of water and a napkin. He opened the bottle and then set it on the napkin on the nightstand.

"I'm probably going to fall asleep on you," I said. "This stuff is strong."

"It's okay. Just sleep."

He took off my shoes and pulled the blanket over me.

Before I knew it, I was fast asleep.

———

SUNLIGHT WAS STREAMING through the windows when I opened my eyes and I turned over stiffly. The spasms were gone, but I needed to call my physical therapist for a session today. I sat up and, once again, Lars was gone. I didn't remember him leaving, but I didn't remember much of anything when I took the muscle relaxers. They were strong, and I tried to only take them when I absolutely had to because they knocked me out hard.

I sat up groggily and padded to the bathroom. I'd slept in my clothes and a full face of makeup, so I ran a bath while I cleaned up. I made a cup of tea and grabbed my phone before heading back to the bathroom and getting in the tub.

I needed to decompress in a big way. I was pissed at Lars. Going out with him had been a huge risk for me, and once again, he'd just left. What if I'd needed something in the middle of the night? Not that I was his responsibility, but it was the principle of it. What kind of guy just gave the woman he was dating strong medication and then left her without a word?

That's not fair.

The voice in my subconscious reminded me that Lars probably didn't even know what kind of accident I'd had or how badly I'd been hurt. How the doctors had told Vanessa I might never walk again. How hard I'd worked and the tears we'd cried when I'd taken those first steps. The information was out there, but my gut told me Lars wasn't the kind of guy who'd go online to find out things about me.

But I was still disappointed in him.

I liked him so much. I'd never met anyone who

made me feel safe, feminine, and sexy. I was a model, so there were lots of men who thought I was beautiful, but that was different. This was a guy who actually knew me, who'd touched me and made love to me and carried me out of a restaurant. Even now that I was aggravated, the memory of him picking me up like it was nothing made me smile.

I sank into the water, which I'd filled with Epsom salts and a special blend of essential oils, and sighed. I needed to call Lydia, my physical therapist, and see if she could squeeze me in.

The sight that greeted me as I opened my phone made me do a double take. Why did I have dozens of texts, calls, and notifications? My heart skipped a beat as I opened the text app and saw Vanessa's messages first.

Vanessa: Have you seen the news? Are you okay? If I don't hear from you by 10:00 this morning, I'm coming over!

Vanessa: Girlfriend, please respond!

Vanessa: You're starting to scare me!

I quickly called her because Vanessa would call out the Marines if she got worried and that was the last thing I needed.

"What happened?!" she demanded as she answered.

"I had a back spasm and took my muscle relaxers," I said, mystified at her tone. "What's going on?"

"Have you been online?"

"No. I just got up and saw your four hundred texts."

"You might want to steel yourself."

"Why?" My heart started to pound uncomfortably.

"The picture of Lars carrying you through the restaurant is everywhere. Social media is on fire talking about Sheridan Lee and her hunky new hockey-playing boyfriend."

I groaned. "Fuck."

"Has he called?"

"Who, Lars?"

"No, *you know who.*"

I swallowed. "I don't know. I have a million texts and calls. I called you back first."

"He's going to be pissed."

"He doesn't own me! I'm free to do whatever I want, whether he likes it or not."

"Yeah, but—"

"I know!" I hissed. "Okay? I know. Dammit." Tears threatened, and I squeezed my eyes shut to head them off. I wouldn't cry. Not over him. Not ever again.

"You should probably warn Lars."

"He's probably at practice, but I need to look at these messages and see how much damage control I might need to do."

"Look, at the end of the day, a guy carried you out of a restaurant. There's nothing nefarious about it. The whole world knows you broke your back just over a year ago."

"Yeah, but that's not what you-know-who is going to focus on."

"You want me to get the PR department involved?"

"No. Let me just get a handle on things first. Thanks for checking on me."

"Always, girlfriend. I will always check on you."

"Love you."

"Love you too."

I hung up and opened my texts.

Sure enough, there were texts from friends, business associates, even a few journalists I knew, wanting the scoop.

Were Lars and I a couple?

How long had we been dating?

Had I really bid ten thousand dollars to spend the night with him?

This sucked.

There was one message that made me smile, though.

Hadley and I had exchanged numbers and her text wasn't filled with anything but concern.

Hadley: Hey, I saw that Lars carried you out of a restaurant last night. Hope you're okay. Call me when you get a chance.

I found the pictures on Instagram and grimaced. There was no mistaking Lars. There were full frontal photos of his face and though my face was mostly buried in his shoulder, someone had recognized me.

Lars probably wasn't happy about this turn of events, but after the way he'd left me last night, I wasn't going to reach out. If we were going to keep seeing each other—and I had no idea if we were— he'd have to get used to this.

Finally, I opened the thread of text messages I'd been avoiding, and my heart sank.

You fat whore. You think this hockey guy you're fucking actually cares about you? I'm watching, Sheridan —and this isn't going to end well for either of you.

CHAPTER TEN

Lars

Wes: Coach just told me we've traded Keegan and acquired Sawyer Cain. He's legit. Should be a great addition to the team. Starts practicing with us tomorrow.

Beau: WTF! I didn't even know they were looking for another D man...

Wes: Relax, your spot is safe.

Beau: How do you know?

Wes: Guess I don't. Might want to pack your bags just in case.

Beau: Why, have you heard something?

Nash: I've heard Cain's an arrogant asshole.

Beau: I just bought a condo and now I'm going to get traded. FML.

Wes: Quit bitching and play hard. You'll be fine.

Lars: Which line is he playing on?

Wes: No idea. Maybe we'll find out tomorrow.

HOW LONG WOULD it take for Sheridan's back to feel better? I figured at least a few days. Back injuries could be a bitch. I knew that from seeing teammates trying to push through them, usually unsuccessfully. I didn't want to bother Sheridan when she was in pain and have her think I only wanted to sleep with her again.

She'd really impressed me at the cookout. I loved the way she fit in, and the people she engaged with were always smiling or laughing. Hadley had sent me a text after we left the cookout saying how much she liked Sheridan and hoped to see her again.

I was in the locker room changing for practice when Drew came up and held out his fist, grinning. Fist bumps were stupid and I didn't get the point of them, but I liked Drew so I did the perfunctory knuckle-to-knuckle greeting.

"Persistence paid off, I see," he said.

"What do you mean?"

"With Sheridan. You brought her to the cookout."

"Oh." I nodded.

"She seems pretty great. Nina loves her."

"Sheridan is great."

He gave me an expectant look. "So? Did you wake up at her place this morning, or did she wake up at yours?"

"We went out for dinner after the cookout. She had back pain and we had to—"

"Dude!" Nash came over to us, cell phone in hand. "I just have to say that never, in my wildest dreams, did I ever imagine you going viral for carrying a woman out of a restaurant. Lars Jansson? Nope. I would have bet money you'd go viral for punching some guy at Subway because he forgot to put cheese on your footlong, or making somebody piss themselves for chirping at you, but this?"

I gave him an irritated glare. "What are you talking about? Why do you take so long to make a point?"

He cackled and turned his phone so Drew and I could view the screen. There was a video of me carrying Sheridan out of the restaurant last night. She'd said people were taking pictures with their phones, but why was all this stuff posted online?

"What is this?" I asked Nash. "Why?"

"Because she's super famous, bro. She's a celebrity."

I bristled. "I am famous, too."

He rolled his eyes. "Not like her. She's famous everywhere, all over the world. And when someone like her gets carried out of a restaurant by a—" He turned his phone back toward himself and pushed a button on the screen. "—Greek god of a man who could make a nun hot…I mean, that's overly generous. I'm not saying you're *un*attractive, but—"

Drew cut in. "Wait, why were you carrying her?"

"Something with her back," I said. "She couldn't walk."

"Okay, so you took her out of the restaurant, and then what?" Drew asked. "Is she in the hospital?"

"No, she had medicine at home. I took her there and she took her medicine and went to sleep."

"Was she better this morning? Does she need anything?"

I just stared at him silently. After a few seconds, he spoke again.

"Lars. Tell me you didn't fucking leave her like that. Was she alone?"

"I should have stayed."

Drew and Nash gasped at the same time.

"Dude, you are un-fucking-real," Nash said. "You left?"

"She was sleeping," I said, even though I knew he was right.

"Get your phone out," Drew ordered.

I complied, reaching into my locker for- my phone. He pointed at me.

"You text her an apology and tell her you'll be over right after practice. Then order some flowers to be delivered to her house that cost a minimum of two hundred dollars. Make sure it's a big arrangement."

"For flowers?" I balked.

"Just do it, Lars," Nash said.

"And then," Drew continued, "after practice, you go over to her place with some Starbucks and food. Ask her if you could bring her something she needs. If she says nothing, bring stuff anyway."

I sighed heavily. "I am not good at this."

"Just do what he told you," Nash said.

There was some commotion at the door to the locker room, and Drew looked over.

"I think Sawyer Cain is here," he said.

He was right. Wes was leading our new defenseman into the locker room and introducing him to everyone. When he made it to our group, he wasn't even smiling.

"Sawyer, this is Lars, Drew, and Nash. I think you know who they all are. Guys, our new teammate, Sawyer."

Drew held out his hand and Sawyer shook it.

"Great to meet you," Drew said. "Glad to have you here."

"Hey, man," Nash said. "Welcome to the Lou."

When it was my turn to shake his hand, Sawyer and I exchanged a serious look and then I grunted in greeting. I was too wrapped up in how I'd fucked things up with Sheridan—again.

"Don't mind him," Nash said, nodding toward me. "He's an asshole to everyone."

"I am…" I searched for the word, finally remembering it. "Distracted. I am sorry."

"It's okay, man," Sawyer said.

"You want to get lunch after your first practice?" Wes asked Sawyer. "There's a great deli close by, or a hibachi place."

Sawyer shook his head. "Nah, I've got plans already. If you could just show me where my locker is, I want to get ready for practice."

After a beat of silence, Wes said, "Yeah, man. Of course."

He led Sawyer to a locker on the other side of the room. Nash and Drew exchanged a look.

"He seems friendly," Drew said in a low tone.

I looked at Nash, and he knew what I was wondering without me even having to ask.

"Yeah, that was sarcasm," he said.

———

THE WOMAN at the floral shop had helped me decide what kind of flowers to send Sheridan, and she'd texted me back that she'd love something from Starbucks and included her order.

Which, by the way, was absurd. Iced white mocha with sweet cream foam, an extra shot, and extra caramel drizzle? I drank black coffee. I couldn't now and never would understand the lure of sugary coffee. But if it would make Sheridan happy, I'd stand in the longest Starbucks line ever and get her the drink she wanted.

I'd already showered and was about to pick up lunch for the two of us, and her drink, when a Mavericks intern stopped me outside of the locker room.

"Mr. Jansson, Gloria wants to see you," she said.

I frowned. "Gloria?"

"The head of PR for the Mavericks…sir," she said, looking nervous.

"I am in a hurry. Can I talk to her another day?"

The intern was less than half my size, and her eyes widened as she looked up at me. "I don't…um, she said she really needs to see you."

I huffed out a sigh. Sheridan was expecting me, and I didn't want to disappoint her. Again.

"Okay, I will go, but I need to hurry."

The intern had to jog to keep up with me as I quickly walked to the administrative offices located on the other side of the arena. When we arrived in the lobby, she was out of breath as she said, "You can have a seat…anywhere. I'll tell Gloria you're here."

"You said now," I protested. "I am ready now."

"Just…okay," she said, motioning for me to follow her.

Gloria's office was at the end of a hallway. I rarely did interviews and avoided all things PR as much as I possibly could. My teammates were better at it, anyway, so it worked out for all of us.

The intern knocked on Gloria's door and Gloria called out, "Come on in."

She opened the door and said, "Hi Gloria, I have Mr. Jansson here. He's eager to get the meeting started."

"Perfect!" Gloria stood up from behind her desk as I walked into the room. "Have a seat, Lars."

"I am hurried," I told her. "In hurry. I can't remember, but you know what I am saying."

"I understand, and I'll make this quick." She leaned back against the front of her desk and I sat down in a chair along the wall. "I had no idea you were dating Sheridan Lee. I mean, I knew you went on one date with her, because of the charity auction, but the photos and videos I've seen online today seem to indicate there's something more between the two of you."

I just looked at her, waiting for her to actually ask me a question. She lowered her brows, looking frustrated.

"Lars, the PR department needs to know these things. We were totally unprepared to respond to the questions we've had coming in all day about you and Sheridan."

Still, she hadn't asked me a question. I folded my arms across my chest and said, "My contract does not say I have to do that."

"No, I imagine it doesn't," Gloria said, giving me a pointed look. "But I'm telling you that, as a courtesy, we need to know these things."

"My coaches tell me things. And my GM. You do not." I stood up, giving her an expectant look.

"Really? You're going to make me go through Coach Gizzard?"

"I am a personal man," I said with a shrug.

Gloria rolled her eyes. "The word you're looking for is *private*, Lars. You're a *private* man. And I respect that. But you only get a limited amount of privacy when you're dating one of the biggest celebrities who has ever called St. Louis home, and when you yourself are also a public figure."

"What do you want from me?" I asked her. "I am in a hurry."

"A few details about you and Sheridan would be a great help. Just how long you've been dating, any upcoming appearances together, and—"

"No."

Gloria glared at me in silence.

"It is in my contract," I reminded her. "No PR unless my coaches tell me so."

"Fine." She threw her hands up in resignation. "But I'm not the enemy, Lars. I'm here to help. If the time comes that you need help managing media requests, my door will always be open to you."

I nodded. "I will remember that. I need to go now."

"Thanks for stopping by."

I didn't even need Nash to confirm it for me this time—she was being sarcastic.

"You are welcome," I said, hustling out the door.

I still had a lot to learn about women, but I knew I'd fucked up by leaving Sheridan's apartment last night, and I needed to get over there as soon as possible to make it right. I jogged back to the other side of the arena and exited through the team entrance to our private parking lot.

I'd just made it out the door when a guy with a big camera started taking photos of me. I looked over and saw that there were two more guys getting their cameras ready to take photos.

"Lars," the first photographer called. "How's Sheridan? How long have you guys been dating?"

I scowled at him, put my head down and ran to my SUV, opening the door with my key fob and getting in quickly. I made it out of the parking lot before any of them caught up to me.

The only attention I wanted to draw was for hockey. And even then, I kept reporters at arm's length. I wasn't good at interviews like Wes, Nash, or Drew. I let my performance on the ice speak for itself.

Any photographers looking for information about Sheridan would be in for a rude awakening. What we did was no one's business but ours.

I looked in my rearview mirror and then did a double take. What the hell? The photographers were following me.

This wouldn't end well for them.

CHAPTER ELEVEN

Sheridan

THE TEXT from Lars saying he was coming over after practice had totally caught me off guard. The bouquet of pink and purple flowers that arrived about an hour later was breathtaking and even more surprising. The knock on the door thirty minutes later had me fighting back a smile despite the shitty morning I'd had.

"Hi," I said as I opened the door.

"Hello." Lars looked like breakfast, lunch, dinner, *and* dessert, all rolled into a tall, muscular god in a tight black Henley and...gray sweatpants. Sweet Jesus, what was I supposed to do with all of this?

Apparently, let him brush a kiss across my lips

and take a Starbucks coffee from him. He was carrying a big bag of food too, so I led him to the kitchen, where he set everything on the counter.

"What are you doing here?" I asked as we unpacked lunch.

"I shouldn't have left you alone last night," he said quietly, one hip against the counter.

"No, you shouldn't have," I agreed. "But the flowers—and all of this—" I made a sweeping motion with my hand. "Weren't necessary."

"I like you," he said slowly, meeting my eyes. "But I am not good at…this."

"This? You mean dating?"

He shrugged. "Relationships. Dating has no expectation. This…is different."

"Well, the media obviously thinks so."

He grunted. "There were three of them behind me as I drove."

"You led them here?" My eyes widened in dismay. "I better warn Barney and—"

He was shaking his head. "No! It's okay. I took them on a chase."

I paused, cocking my head. "You led them on a wild-goose chase?"

"Yes. I drive to Starbucks, then to get food, then to gas station. At gas station I call nonemergency police number and give them license plates. I told police they were driving erratic. Police arrived. I left."

I stared at him for a moment and then burst out laughing.

"Oh, you're good," I said, getting out two plates.

"Thank you. I do not like them following me. I will tolerate at games, and maybe when we are out because we cannot control public places. But to follow me home? Or to your house? This is not okay."

"You're right. And you handled it brilliantly." I set out plates, utensils, and napkins, along with serving spoons. "This smells delicious."

"You like Chinese food?"

"Love it." We settled on stools side by side at the counter and dug in.

"How is your back?" he asked after a moment.

"It's better. My physical therapist is coming over at three to stretch me out and make sure nothing else is going on."

"Do you work today?"

"I'm working from home. Sometimes when my back spasms like that, it'll come back again and I don't want to deal with it at work."

"This happens often?"

"It used to, right after the accident, but it's been

better lately. I have to remember to sit down more often."

"I will remind you in the future."

Our eyes met and the fire lurking behind his did things to me. He was an awkward, quirky mess, but he was so damn good-looking. And strong. And rich enough to not be after my money. Which was a big thing for me. I'd already learned that lesson the hard way, so anyone I let into my life had to be financially secure.

"I was mad this morning," I admitted after a moment.

He looked so uncomfortable it made me uncomfortable, and that took a lot.

"But you've made up for it nicely," I added quickly. It wasn't that I was trying to let him off the hook so soon, but I already understood that Lars didn't take social cues like other people did. Maybe it was the language barrier or maybe it was just his personality, but there was no doubt his quirkiness wasn't an act. He was genuinely unsure how to handle situations like this, and though I longed to ask him why, this wasn't the time. Not yet. Until I decided whether or not I was going to pursue things with him, I'd keep those questions to myself.

"Sometimes I don't understand...dating rituals. Or women. I understand sex, but the other stuff..."

He shrugged. "I never want to upset you, but you have to tell me what you need from me."

"Okay." I smiled. "I can do that."

"I would like to spend time with you, get to know you better." His eyes sought out mine again. "But I do not want to impose if you are busy."

"I have a few things going on, and my three o'clock session is very important, but other than that, we can hang out. I don't mind at all. I'd like to get to know you better too."

"Okay." He went back to eating and I did too. What an interesting turn of events this was. Of course, I had to bring up the press we'd been getting.

"So I'm sure you've seen the pictures from last night online."

He nodded. "The team's PR department called me in. They wanted details."

"What did you tell them?"

"My contract says I do not have to do any press unless directed by one of my coaches or the general manager."

"So…?"

"I told her nothing."

"Well, at some point, we're going to have to say something," I said thoughtfully. "I don't talk about my personal life either, but I've never dated someone as famous as you before, so this kind of changes things."

"What will you say?" he asked.

"Basically, that we've gone out on a few dates and it's none of anyone's business."

"This is okay for me also."

We smiled at each other and he pushed his plate away.

"What would you like to do now?" I asked, arching a brow playfully.

He narrowed his eyes a little. "This is trick question?"

I laughed. "No. If we could do anything today, what would you want to do?"

"If I tell the truth, you will be mad."

My face fell a little. "You want to leave?"

His eyes narrowed as he reached out a hand to me. "No! Not even close. I would want to spend the day making love to you."

"Oh." I stood up and took a step toward him. "Why would that make me mad?"

"Your back?" He pulled me between his legs and I leaned against his solid chest.

"My back is fine. We just can't get too crazy. No twisting or wild positions so I don't irritate it."

"This is okay." He wrapped one arm around me and dug the other into the hair at the back of my neck, pulling my face down to his. His lips parted, his eyes closed, and I was lost. This guy did things to me. For all his idiosyncrasies, my body understood the pleasure that was on the horizon, and I forgot everything else.

His kiss was gentle but firm, showing me how much he wanted me while simultaneously taking it easy because of my back.

"Can I undress you?" he whispered against my mouth.

"Let's go to the bedroom," I said. "The bed is easier for me."

"Yes." He reached down and scooped me up, carrying me to my room.

I didn't give it a second thought this time, because I knew he wouldn't drop me.

He set me on my feet and tugged my T-shirt over my head. I wore a simple sports bra beneath it and he cocked his head. "This is not a regular bra. I do not want to hurt you."

"Just lift it straight up, like a shirt. It doesn't have an opening like a regular bra."

He tugged it over my head and then paused, staring at my chest. A moment of insecurity flashed through my subconscious, but I refused to let it show. He had to want me—all of me—or this wouldn't go anywhere anyway.

"So perfect," he said finally, his voice gruff. He reached out his hands and lightly squeezed my breasts, lifting them and then running his thumbs over my nipples until they were hard little peaks of aching need. "You are so beautiful. I love your body."

"And I love yours." I motioned to his chest. "Off."

He smiled and slowly pulled his shirt over his head. Fuck, he was beautiful. That abdominal V would be the end of me. I ran a finger down one side, my mouth watering. His erection was huge and hard, even through his sweats, and I couldn't wait for it to be inside me again.

"Soon," he whispered, as if he'd read my thoughts. He slid my yoga pants down, his lips turning up as he realized I didn't have panties on.

I stepped out of them and he ran his hands down the curve of my hips, my thighs, and then up to cup my ass.

"This," he growled. "I fucking love your ass."

I frowned. "You don't think it's too big?" I almost kicked myself; I never, ever voiced my insecurities in front of anyone but Vanessa and I couldn't believe it slipped out.

He'd dropped to his knees and gazed up at me in confusion. "Too big? For what? A much smaller man maybe. But for me? Your ass is heaven. Someday, if you trust me, I would very much like to make love to your ass."

I'd never done anything like that before, but I might with Lars. "You're huge," I said with a faint smile, "but I'd be willing to try."

He smiled just before nuzzling my crotch, his tongue sliding between my folds as he continued massaging my ass with his hands.

"Fuck, that feels amazing," I murmured, resting one hand in his long hair, stroking it softly as he stroked me.

"You can bend over?" he asked. "Because of your back, I mean."

"I could probably bend over the edge of the bed, but I need that support."

"Yes." He let me get into position on my own. I couldn't see him but I felt him behind me, his lips on my ass cheeks, hands all over my thighs and then his mouth between my legs again. "Legs closed," he said. "Is nice this way."

I clenched with longing as he pushed my knees together and moved behind me. His tongue was hot and wet against my most sensitive parts, and the groan that left me was loud as he licked from my clit to my ass. Thank God I'd showered before he came over.

His mouth was truly the most wicked thing I

could have ever imagined touching me there. He went from soft and teasing to rough and gritty, letting his teeth graze my clit and then tongue fucking me just the way he'd promised when we'd texted. He took me right to the edge and then held back, doing it again and again until I was panting with need.

He nibbled my clit and then sucked it hard just as I felt a finger press into my ass. I gasped and came at the same time, my body exploding with pleasure and sensations I'd never felt before. He hadn't been kidding about coming hard because it was so intense I momentarily blacked out. The aftershocks made me shiver and his finger was still in my ass. I was a willing prisoner and I never wanted this to end.

"Was okay? The ass play?" he asked, slowly getting to his feet.

"Mmm, yes." I smiled up at him.

"Come." He helped me up and I sprawled across the bed, still on my stomach because turning over felt like too much work.

"One minute," he said, disappearing into the bathroom.

"M'kay." I closed my eyes, still reveling in how good it had been.

Then he was next to me, one hand stroking up and down my back. We rested in silence for a while.

I knew more was coming but what we'd just done had been intense and I had a feeling everything we did would be.

I tensed a little when his fingers caressed the scars on my back.

"This was painful?" he asked quietly.

"Yeah. Very."

"Was it a car accident?"

"The scars are from multiple surgeries," I said, turning my head to look at him. He was on his side, staring down at me intently, as if he were genuinely curious about what had happened. "And no, not a car accident." I swallowed. "I was at a rehearsal for a fashion show in New York for a new designer. They had me arrive onstage in the air, suspended by cables, to make it look like I was flying. The cables held just fine, but the wooden beam they were attached to at this old theater gave out. I fell about twenty feet and landed on my back. My spine was broken in two places. By the grace of God, my spinal cord wasn't severed, but it was damaged."

"You broke your spine?" He looked shocked, as if he'd had no idea what had happened.

"You didn't know? It was all over the news for weeks. They didn't think I would walk again."

"I don't watch news or social media. Sometimes for sports, but anything else, no."

"Oh. Well, now you know."

"How long did it take you to walk again?"

"Eight months."

"And when did this happen?"

"About fourteen months ago."

"You have only been walking again six months?"

"Yes. That's why my back spasmed the way it did the last time we were together—my muscles and spinal cord are learning to work again."

"You are very strong," he said quietly. "Also very brave." He leaned over to kiss me and, once again, I was swept away.

CHAPTER TWELVE

Lars

Mavericks Group Text

Wes: Hey guys, I got a heads-up from my agent that an article by that sleazebag sports reporter Ronnie McIntyre will hit the news wires soon. Whatever it says, no one respond. Not to calls from reporters, not on social media, not even to your grandma. We'll discuss it further this morning at practice.

Beau: It's 5:15 bro! I thought this was an emergency of epic proportions.

Wes: Define emergency. Because this isn't good. It looks like Keegan is giving us all the middle finger on his way out the door.

Nash: Fuck him.

Wes: No one responds. And get to practice early. My agent hasn't seen the article, but from what he's heard, it's a smear piece about us.

Drew: We'll handle it as a team. We've got your back, Wes.

Wes: Thanks.

I SET my cell phone on the table beside Sheridan's bed, rubbing my eyes. I hadn't expected any texts when I woke up for my morning workout. When I scooted over to Sheridan's side of the bed and curled my body around hers, kissing the back of her head, she moaned softly.

"Too early," she murmured. "Still sleepy."

"I have to go," I said softly. "For my workout and practice. I'll text you when I'm done."

"Mmm, okay."

"It isn't leaving if I tell you I am going…right?"

She rolled over and I could see a hint of a smile on her lips.

"Right, you're good. Thank you, Lars. It was really nice having your company yesterday, and I liked that you stayed the night."

I brushed the hair away from her face. "Your bed feels good. I like it."

"And your body feels good, so it works out for both of us." Her smile grew wider.

I moved to kiss her, but she turned her face to the side and said, "I'm not ready for you to experience my morning breath yet."

"I heard you snore and fart last night, though. Morning breath is not that bad."

She gasped. "I did *not* snore or fart."

"You did. And how would you know since you were asleep?"

"Lars." She sighed with exasperation. "Go do your workout. Let's pretend this conversation never happened."

"It didn't smell bad."

"Oh my God." She covered her face with a pillow. "End this humiliation and go. I'll talk to you later."

I slid out of bed and got dressed, smiling in the near darkness. Sheridan was cute when she was embarrassed. I didn't see what the big deal was, though—I farted all the time.

Instead of going to the gym, I went for a run in Sheridan's neighborhood, which was silent and still at this hour. I wondered what Keegan had said that Wes's agent was so concerned about.

Keegan was just an asshole with a grudge. He'd stolen our teammate Konstantin's girlfriend, the two of them cheating behind Kon's back for months before he found out, and burned his bridges with the entire team. All of us were on Kon's side. We'd been hoping since it happened that Keegan would get traded, and figured he'd prefer that, too.

Why would he and Svetlana want to be here, where everyone disliked them? They could start fresh in a new place, and Konstantin wouldn't have to see them anymore.

I finished a three-mile run and drove my SUV home, where I found Rosalina cleaning the floor in my guest bathroom. She was an early riser, like me.

"Mr. Lars?" she said as I walked past the open bathroom door.

"Good morning," I said.

She looked up, her brow furrowed. "Do you want breakfast?"

Loki approached me, rubbing against my ankle until I picked him up and petted him.

"I can get my breakfast," I said.

"No." Rosalina pulled off her rubber gloves, glaring at me. "I make breakfast."

When I wasn't on the road, she made me the same breakfast every day—four eggs over easy, two pieces of bacon and two pieces of whole wheat toast. I nodded my thanks, because I wouldn't have been able to make it the way she did.

After breakfast and a shower, I said goodbye to

Loki and Rosalina and headed to practice. Wes had said to be early, so I arrived about forty-five minutes earlier than usual. When I walked into the locker room, I was surprised to see my entire team there. Everyone looked at me, and a wave of unease passed through me.

"What?" I said.

"Did you see it?" Wes asked me.

"See what?"

His face fell, and I looked at Nash, whose expression was equally somber.

"What's going on?" I asked him.

Nash took a deep breath and met my gaze. "Keegan talked some shit to get attention since he can't get any from playing hockey. He's a fucking douchebag and I'm going to beat his ass next time we play Nashville."

"What did he say?"

Every man in the room looked away from me. I took out my phone and said, "Where is it?"

"Don't read it," Nash said. "Just trust me—you don't want to read it."

I looked up from my phone screen. "I want to read it."

"Keegan doesn't know shit," Wes said. "He's got an axe to grind."

The locker room was silent and my irritation

flared. It seemed everyone here except me had read this article.

"Where is it?" I asked, my fingers ready to type into my phone.

Coach Gizzard walked into the locker room, his expression as sullen as everyone else's.

"Kirby, Volkov, and Jansson, come with me," he said.

Wes, Konstantin, and I followed our coach out of the locker room. He didn't say a word as he led us around to the suite of offices the Mavericks' administrative staff occupied. When he walked into a conference room and I saw who was sitting there, I knew things were bad.

Our team's general manager, Mitch Levoie, was sitting at a long conference table with Gloria from PR. Mitch stood, shook all of our hands, and asked us to sit down.

I rarely met with Mitch. Was I being traded? Or was this about the article?

"I know this came as a shock to all of us," Mitch said. "But it's important that no one lashes out in response. I'll be discussing things with the Nashville GM later this morning."

"What is going on?" I asked, out of patience.

Mitch exchanged a look with Coach Gizzard, but it was Wes who answered.

"Lars hasn't read it yet," he said.

There was a moment of uncomfortable silence, and then Mitch looked at Gloria and said, "Will you send him a link?"

"Of course."

She picked up her phone and typed into it, and my phone dinged with a new message.

"We'll give you a moment, Lars," Mitch said.

Next to me, Wes sighed heavily.

I read the headline of the article. "Miller: Mavericks locker room toxic."

So it was going to be Keegan Miller running his mouth about his former teammates now that he'd been traded. What was the big deal? I read on, and saw that he'd started with Wes.

"Wes Kirby is no Ben Whitmer, I'll just say that," Miller said. *"Wes isn't a leader. It's almost like he enjoys conflict among the team. He feeds it. But without Ben holding him up out on the ice, he's constantly worried about his spot on the team, and he'll sabotage anyone to keep it."*

Not one word of that was true. I looked up at Wes, my fury escalating. But there was more to the article, so I decided to finish it first.

Konstantin Volkov, Miller said, is a hothead who gets into physical altercations with teammates about everything from his salary to where to eat for dinner.

"He thinks management is screwing him," Miller said. "He's always talking about how he's better than most of the guys who make more than he does. He thinks it's because he's not American, and he's always saying our GM has it out for immigrants."

Another teammate, Miller said, made him fearful for his physical safety for other reasons.

"Lars Jansson is like a brick wall, and he's mentally unstable. He's a complete weirdo, and I never knew when he was going to explode over nothing. That guy's got some serious issues. He could keep a team of mental health professionals busy around the clock. Everyone around him knows he's autistic, but everyone's afraid to say it."

My heart was beating fast as I looked up at Wes.

"It's a bunch of bullshit," he said. "Don't—"

"What does that mean? What is autistic?"

There was an uncomfortable silence around me before Wes said, "It's a developmental disability. But listen, Keegan's no doctor. He's got no business running his mouth like that."

Coach Gizzard spoke up then. "Lars, none of us give any credence to what Keegan said. He's disgruntled and looking for attention."

I nodded, squeezing the armrests of my chair to ground myself. I was dizzy. If what Keegan had said was untrue, why had all my teammates been looking at me that way? Why didn't Nash want me to read the article?

"I'll be consulting with the team attorneys and Rosa later today, too," Mitch said, the mention of our team owner reinforcing how serious all this was. "We may pursue legal action. But that stays in this room. Everyone needs to be tight lipped. No comments to anyone whatsoever. Gloria will release a generic statement and that's all we're putting out for public consumption at this point, okay?"

Everyone in the room either nodded or muttered their agreement. I was still lost in my own thoughts about what Keegan had said. He thought I was disabled? And unstable?

"Lars, you are a very important member of the Mavericks family," Mitch said. "I'm deeply sorry Keegan chose to say these things, and you will always have our full support. If legal action is viable, you bet your ass we'll be pursuing it. Don't let this get you down, okay?"

"Yes," I said. "Okay."

Mitch, Gloria, and Coach Gizzard talked some more about what would be included in the team's official statement before we were all dismissed. Wes clapped a hand on my shoulder as we left the room and I tried to relax.

I tried, but I couldn't. I had a giant tangle of

emotions inside that I couldn't unpack right now. Because I'd heard what everyone said about Keegan's accusations being bullshit, but something just wasn't sitting right with me.

If the things Keegan had said about Wes, Kon, and me were all untrue, why had Mitch only apologized to me?

CHAPTER THIRTEEN

Sheridan

Even before I'd gotten involved with Lars, my morning routine usually included a cup of tea, oatmeal or a couple of eggs, and meditation to start my day. On days I didn't go into the office, I'd follow it up with yoga or stretching, and have a second cup of tea while I caught up on news and media releases online. Since I had season tickets, I always checked the sports pages to see how the Mavericks had done the night before and if any of the guys were in the news. Especially now that I knew many of them.

I almost missed the interview with Keegan Miller but my gut clenched painfully as I read his nasty commentary on his old team. Obviously, I didn't know Wes or Kon as intimately as I knew Lars, but I couldn't believe the things he said about them either. And Lars was the furthest thing from dangerous. He was huge and strong and a beast of a man, but kind and gentle. Awkward, sometimes unpredictable, but I wasn't even a little bit afraid of him and as a victim of abuse, I'd recognize it anywhere.

I'd never seen his temper in any way, shape, or form, and while the autism comment might have a twinge of truth to it, it seemed irresponsible for someone with no medical training to say something like that publicly.

It also had to be hurtful as hell.

Could Lars be autistic? I truly had no idea but even if he was, it was no one else's business and certainly not Keegan Miller's. I was furious on Lars's behalf and immediately called him. He was at practice, but I wanted him to know I was here for him.

"Hey, handsome, it's Sheridan. I saw that awful article and just want you to know Keegan Miller can fuck right off. I don't know who he thinks he is, but I hope the Mavericks' PR people have something to say about it. Believe me, if anyone knows what it's like for the press to print hurtful things about you, it's me. Anyway, I'm working from home today so I'm here anytime if you want to talk. Okay, bye."

I lost myself in work and the next time I looked

up from my computer, my neck was stiff, I was starving, and the clock read six thirty. We'd had a mishap with a large shipment of fabric today, so I'd been putting out fires all afternoon. I had staff who normally handled these things, but a shipment this large represented tens of thousands of dollars, and I'd been on the phone making sure we got to the bottom of it.

I stood up and stretched, my back screaming in protest from sitting for so long. I slowly bent over and let my arms fall freely in front of me. It was a good, gentle way to stretch out, and I held the pose for ten seconds before slowly lifting up. I should have gone for a walk this afternoon, but it was dark and cold now, so it was safer to stay home. Maybe tomorrow I'd walk to the office. It was exactly one point one miles from my apartment, and my physical therapist had said it was time for me to push myself more. The harder I pushed, as long as I did it properly, the quicker I'd get those stupid spasms to stop and my back to fully heal.

Opening my freezer, I perused the frozen meals I had delivered twice a month and nothing appealed to me. They were low-fat, low-carb, high-protein meals made specifically for both my health and dietary needs, but spaghetti squash lasagna just wasn't cutting it for me tonight. Mostly, I wanted ice cream and maybe a big slice of chocolate cake.

Sigh. Food had been the enemy most of my life. I'd come to terms with my bad eating habits and learned to compromise, but it was so damn hard sometimes. I closed the freezer and opened the fridge. There was fresh watermelon and low-fat cottage cheese, so I scooped some out, dumped watermelon in the bowl and carried it to the couch. I turned on the TV and sank down, taking a bite. I didn't mind cottage cheese and loved fruit, but a burger with all the fixings sounded so much better.

"Next time," I silently promised myself.

I picked up my phone and realized Lars had never called me back.

That was odd.

I was a little worried about him after this morning's media bullshit, so I typed out a quick text.

Sheridan: Hey, just checking in to see if you're okay. Call me when you get a chance.

THE DAYS I went into the office usually started at six thirty so I'd have time to meditate and stretch, but I got up at six since the plan was to walk to work, which would take longer. Vanessa had called last night and offered to walk with me, but this time I wanted to do it on my own. I'd worked hard the last year to get where I was and had gotten a little tired of always needing help. Normally, I'd have Flynn follow me since I did get recognized sometimes, which could create a scene, but I lived in a pretty safe neighborhood, all things considered. And today was just for me. A personal goal.

It probably sounded stupid to other people, the idea that walking to work on my own was something to aspire to, but they didn't know me and they definitely didn't know what had gone on in my life the last fourteen months. Hell, even longer than that when it came to my personal life. Getting away from my prick of an ex had proven much, much harder than anything, other than learning how to walk again, and even that was going better these days. But now I'd met Lars and that was a bright light in my somewhat dim existence.

Being a supermodel had its perks, but there was a dark side too. Especially as a *plus-size* supermodel. People said such unkind things, sometimes without even realizing what they were saying.

"Wow, you're so beautiful. Even at your weight!"

"I bet if you exercised, you'd lose it all!"

"You should try keto—and then you'd be like regular models."

As if there was such a thing. A *regular* model. What the fuck did that even mean? Granted, I was blessed to be able to do what I did, make the kind of money I did, and hopefully show the women of the world that you didn't have to be a stick to be beautiful. Beauty came in all shapes and sizes and, before my accident, I'd been active and healthy. Not everyone was that lucky, so I did my best to be a positive role model, especially for teenage and preteen girls. I spoke at middle and high schools, gave empowerment speeches whenever I was invited, and was in the process of creating body-positive messages to go with each of our lines of lingerie. But there were only so many hours in the day and I was tired.

My ex had almost broken me; the last year had come close to finishing the job.

I'd risen above it, but much of my charity and outreach work had fallen to the wayside out of sheer self-preservation. Now I was antsy to get back into everything, which was part of why I wanted to walk to work today. Alone. Free. No Vanessa, no Flynn, no anyone. Just me and my thoughts and dreams.

I'd just rounded the corner to my office building

when I spotted a familiar figure standing outside and my chest instantly tightened.

What the fuck was Hugh doing here?

Dammit.

I slowed down and took a moment to breathe, but he spotted me and gave me a smarmy smile as he approached. "What? You don't have your hockey boy toy walk you to work?" He was chewing gum and made a loud smacking noise as he popped a bubble.

"What do you want?" I asked, scowling as I stood a couple of feet away from him.

"What I've always wanted. You."

"That ship has sailed."

"Not from where I stand."

I didn't respond, merely waiting for him to say whatever he was going to say.

"You know I'm never going to sign those papers, right?"

I sighed. "That's up to the lawyers and the judge."

He took a step closer, his face twisting into a snarl. "That's up to *me*. Every fucking thing is up to me. You'd be smart not to forget that. I've owned you since you were fifteen years old, and you will always be mine. No matter who you fuck, where you go, what you do. Mine, Sheridan."

"Go away, Hugh. Please just leave this to the lawyers."

"You'd still be that chubby little whore who didn't know how to suck a dick." He reached out and gripped me by the arm.

"Take your hands off me," I hissed under my breath. I really didn't need him to make a scene for someone to record that would go viral before lunch.

"Sheridan." Vanessa came running out the front doors with one of our security guards behind her.

Hugh immediately let go of my arm and I walked toward the security guard, my gaze meeting Vanessa's. Hers blazed with anger as she squinted at Hugh.

"This is the last time," she said to him. "Next time, we get a restraining order."

He laughed. "Good luck with that, mamacita."

I could practically hear the growl in Vanessa's chest and I tugged her arm. "Let's just go inside."

"Mr. Archman, you need to leave the premises," the security guard said.

"It's a public sidewalk, my man."

I didn't hear the rest because we went inside and got on the elevator.

"What were you thinking?" Vanessa demanded.

"Nothing," I said, leaning back and closing my eyes. "I need to walk more so I decided to walk to work. He's never been out front before, but I suspected he was either following me or having me followed, and now I know."

"I'm going to send Nellie to get us coffee," she said as we stepped off the elevator. "Go to your office and decompress—I can see you're ready to jump out of your skin. Then call your fucking lawyer. This has to stop, Sheridan. You can't keep living in fear."

I nodded. "I know."

"Go."

I turned and went into my office. I shut the door and sank down at my desk, noting that my hands were shaking and I was a little nauseated. God, why did I let him affect me like this, even after all this time? I hated feeling vulnerable and afraid, and he knew it, which was why he did the things he did. He hadn't touched me in a long time, though, so things might be escalating. Again.

Dammit.

My mind immediately went to Lars. I never felt afraid when I was with him; that was for sure. I knew without a doubt he would protect me physically from anyone or anything that tried to get near me.

Why hadn't he called me back?

Normally, I wouldn't reach out to a guy this many times in a row without a response, but I was worried, so I grabbed my phone and texted him before I called my attorney.

Sheridan: Hey, just checking in. I've had a rough morning and I'll probably be in meetings all day, but if you want to talk, or even just get lunch or something, let me know and I'll make the time.

I was surprised when my phone buzzed with a text notification a few seconds later.

Lars: I have the morning skate soon. And I must nap before tonight's game. Are you coming?

Sheridan: I was planning to.

Lars: We can get together tonight after game?

Sheridan: Sure.

Lars: I can have a pass left for you to join me in family lounge after.

Sheridan: Okay. Then I'll see you tonight.

I put down my cell phone and pressed the intercom button on my desk phone to call Nellie. "Nel? Are you there?"

"Yes, Ms. Lee. What can I do for you?"

"Can you get my personal attorney on the phone, please?"

"Absolutely."

A minute later, the desk phone rang, and I picked it up. "Marian?"

"Hi, Sheridan. What's going on?" My attorney was smart, efficient and badass as hell, but this whole situation with Hugh was taking too long.

I told her what had happened this morning. "I

don't care what you have to do. I don't care what I have to give up. I don't care what it will cost me. Get him to sign those fucking papers."

CHAPTER FOURTEEN

Lars

Mavericks Group Text

Wes: Hey Sawyer, I'm adding you to our group text. We talk about team stuff mostly, but there's some personal stuff too. Ready for your first home game as a Maverick?

Sawyer: Yes.

Wes: A bunch of us will be going out after the game. You and your wife are welcome to join us. It's Annie, right? I think that's what Mitch told me her name is. Apologies if I got that wrong.

Sawyer: We're not really late-night people, but thanks for the invite.

Wes: Sure, and tell Annie my wife Hadley will save her a seat in the family box. Any other family coming to the game with her?

Sawyer: No one's coming, actually. Just me.

Wes: Okay, cool. See you at the arena.

I WAS TRYING. I was doing everything in my power to act like I didn't care about the bullshit Keegan had said about me. I was in the locker room, having my pregame ice bath, trying to stick to my regular routine.

My head wasn't in it, though. Since the article had come out, I'd been holed up in my apartment, avoiding the media. At least, that's what I told my teammates and Sheridan when they called. The truth was, I was avoiding everyone.

I'd spent hours researching autism on my phone, and what I'd found was sobering. I didn't exhibit every symptom of autism spectrum disorder, but I had several. My whole life, I'd known I was different. My mom had told me when I was growing up that people are made differently and I'd figured that was why people thought I was strange. I was just different from them—a loner who valued quiet and order in my life.

What if Keegan was right, though? What if, this

entire time, I'd had a disorder that affected the way I interacted with the world?

Nash walked past the tub I was sitting in without saying a single word. He didn't even look at me. It was a far cry from the last home game, when I couldn't get my teammates to leave me alone.

I rose from the icy water and grabbed my towel, stepping out. Turning my phone off before the timer had gone off, I walked over to Nash's locker.

"Hey, man," he said. "I ordered our food. Got one of the front office interns getting the delivery for us."

"You paid for it?"

He shrugged. "Yeah, you paid last time."

Though he was right, I couldn't help wondering if he felt sorry for me. I was wondering if my entire team felt sorry for me, actually. Same with my coaches. The only person I'd encountered since the story came out who treated me the same was Rosalina. I had a feeling she didn't keep up with the news and had no idea what was going on.

I'd be seeing Sheridan tonight, and I was looking forward to it and dreading it in equal measure. What if there was pity in her eyes when she looked at me? I didn't think I'd ever be able to see her again if she felt sorry for me.

Agitated and eager to resume my usual vibe with Nash, I blurted out, "You're a dick."

He cocked a brow. "Because I paid for your food, I'm a dick?"

"No, just…you just are."

"Go eat your Reese's Peanut Butter Cups, dipshit."

"It is not time for that."

He looked up at me. "Sit down."

I sat on the bench next to him, both of us sitting with our elbows resting against our spread knees. Nash looked over at me.

"How you doing?" he asked.

I shrugged. "Fine."

"You don't need to bullshit, Lars. It's me. Tell me how you're really doing."

I looked at the ground and exhaled hard. "I don't know."

"How do you feel about what Keegan said?"

Glancing side to side to make sure no one was within earshot, I sat up straight and spoke to him in a low tone. "You are confused about how I feel?"

"Yeah, I don't want to assume I know. I want you to tell me."

I scowled. "I do not like talking about feelings."

"Do it anyway."

I narrowed my eyes and said, "Fucking pissed."

"Why?"

"Why?" I snapped.

"Because you think he made it up or because you think he might be right?"

Nash was my closest friend. Not just in St. Louis, but anywhere. If he ever needed an organ, I'd donate one in a heartbeat, but right now, I wanted to punch him.

Instead, I got up from the bench and stalked into the weight room. Fuck him. Nash was shit at making me feel better. I went over to a heavy bag, which was suspended from the ceiling by a chain, and started punching the shit out of it. Jab. Jab. Uppercut.

"I'm not the enemy," a voice said from the other side of the room.

I looked over to see Nash, who had just walked in.

"Fuck off," I clipped, still punching.

"Why does it matter?" He walked closer to me. "Keegan was way off about a lot of what he said. You're not dangerous. But that's not what's bothering you, is it?"

I pushed the bag out of my way and advanced on him.

"Everyone is being different to me. They do not want to look at me. What Keegan said changed how they think of me."

Nash shook his head. "No, it didn't. It changed how *you* think of you. Keegan said a lot of shit because he wanted to stir the pot on his way out the door. But if he's right, and you have autism, so what? It doesn't change a damn thing, Lars."

"It does!" I yelled and shoved his shoulders. "It changes everything!"

He covered the few steps of distance I'd created between us, unfazed. "How?"

"People feel sorry for me now."

"I don't feel sorry for you."

"No one will look at me!" I pointed in the direction of the locker room. "And I…" I closed my eyes and sighed heavily. "I do not know what to say. What should I say?"

Nash put his hands on my shoulders and spoke in a level tone. "You don't need to say anything to us, Lars. We're your teammates. We've got your back, same as before. Just go out there and play. You're the same person you were the day before that article came out. Nothing has changed."

I hung my head. "I am…the things that are true about autism…I am some of those things."

"So what? One of my best friends in high school had a brother with autism. He just processed things differently. It's not that big of a deal, man."

"Was he like me?"

Nash shrugged. "He was quiet. A little awkward. But a good dude, and I consider him a close friend."

"I know I am different, but…"

"Hey. You're *you*. You're Lars Jansson, a pro hockey player who looks like Thor and gets more ass than a toilet seat. Trust me, lots of guys would kill to be you."

"I like Sheridan," I admitted. "She knows about the article."

"So what? If she deserves you, she'll feel the same way about it that your teammates do. It changes nothing."

"But what if there is something I can do to be normal? There is no medicine for autism, but what if—"

"Dude, listen. You need to talk to a therapist about all this. My sister's a therapist. I'll ask her for a recommendation."

"They can help me get better?"

"They can help you understand how you're feeling about everything. But you don't need to get better, man. You're a great guy, just as you are."

"I am…awkward."

"Yeah, so? You must be doing something right; you're dating a supermodel."

I nodded. "I just want everything to be like it was before. When you called me an asshole."

"Oh, you're still an asshole. Like I said, nothing's changed."

He grinned at me, and despite the dread I still felt in the pit of my stomach, I smiled back.

———

"G REAT GAME!" Sheridan beamed at me as I approached her after the game.

I'd just walked into the family suite with a few teammates, all of us freshly showered and dressed in suits. We'd won the game 3–2, and Sheridan had been the first thing on my mind when it ended.

"Thanks," I said, putting a hand on her hip and leaning down to kiss her.

She gave me a sexy smile, reaching up to touch the end of a lock of my hair. "This damp hair and suit thing is working for me, Mr. Jansson."

"Is it?" I gazed into the ever-changing color of her hazel eyes, my heart pounding with excitement.

"I may need to bring you home with me after we go out."

I shifted, uncomfortable.

"What?" she asked.

"Would it be okay if we don't go out?"

Her eyes brightened. "Even better."

"Really?"

"Absolutely. I'd love to spend some time alone with you."

There was no pity in her eyes. The only thing I saw when Sheridan looked at me was a sexy gleam, and she hadn't looked at anything but me since I walked in the room.

"My place this time," I said.

She hesitated a moment before saying, "Sure. I'll just need to send Flynn your address so he can take the proper security measures and take me home in the morning. That is, if you want me to stay the night?"

"I do, and tell Flynn whatever you want, but I will take you home tomorrow and anyone who tries to bother you at my place will have to get through me first."

She tilted up and I leaned down. We met in the middle for a kiss.

"Get a room, you two," Wes said in a joking tone. "You guys want to ride with us?"

"We are going home instead," I said.

Sheridan and I both turned to face Wes and Hadley, and I put my arm around her waist, sliding my hand down to the ass I'd never be able to get enough of.

"You guys suck," Wes said, rolling his eyes. "We're the ones who have to get up with our kids in the morning, but you don't see us pussing out."

"See you in the morning," I said, not wanting to waste any more time.

Sheridan said goodbye to Hadley and the other wives and girlfriends that she knew, and we made our way toward my SUV.

"I have to stop for food," I told her.

"Sure. Where are you thinking?"

"Taco Hut."

"Yeah, a taco sounds good."

"I will be eating ten."

She gasped and turned to look at me. "Are you serious? Ten tacos?"

I nodded. "Also, two orders of rice and beans. Games make me hungry."

"I'm not judging. You do you."

I gave her a warning look as we approached the arena's exit doors, taking her hand.

"There will be photographers," I said. "Maybe I should call security to help."

"Or we could make a run for it."

I looked down at her high-heeled boots. "You can run in those?"

"Hang on." She put a hand on my arm for balance and reached down to unzip one boot, then the other.

Reaching down, she picked up the boots and said, "Let's go."

"You are sure? Your feet will hurt."

"Nah, it's all good. I can see your car from here."

"Get on my back."

She laughed and shook her head. "Then you'd rip your suit jacket and I'd cry. That jacket fits you perfectly."

I took my jacket off and passed it to her, then unbuttoned the sleeves of my dress shirt and rolled them up. Sheridan watched me, her chest rising and falling a little faster.

"I do want to ride you," she said playfully. "But I had something else in mind."

I reached into my pants pocket and took out my keys, passing them to her. "Unlock it on the way."

"Are you sure? You have to be so tired from the game."

"I am sure." I turned and bent slightly. "Get on my back and we will call Taco Hut on the way to my place to order our food. Hurry, or I may eat my suit jacket before we get there. I am starving."

"Lars Jansson, you just made a joke!" Sheridan's smile was so perfect and genuine that warmth radiated throughout my body.

"Get on," I encouraged.

"Okay, so all I have to do is climb on and hold on for dear life while also holding on to my bag, my coat, my boots, your jacket, and your keys." She got on my back and gave a little squeal as I grabbed her legs. "I guess let's go?"

So we did. Snowflakes swirled through the night sky as I sprinted through the parking lot, Sheridan laughing and holding tightly to my neck as several photographers followed, shouting questions.

I took a picture of the moment in my mind, wanting to remember the glow of Sheridan's rosy cheeks, the warmth of her body against mine in the chilly winter air, and most importantly, how right it all felt.

CHAPTER FIFTEEN

Sheridan

THE FIRST THING I noticed about Lars's apartment was the lack of color. It was huge, with an open concept floor plan and expensive furniture, but there was almost nothing that might give a visitor a clue about the man who lived here. It was clean, modern, and very much a bachelor pad. His kitchen was pretty nice, though, with black quartz counter-tops and the biggest refrigerator I'd ever seen in my life. I mentioned it as we opened the bags of food we'd picked up.

"My housekeeper, Rosalina, does most of the cooking but I thought it important to have a good kitchen." His eyes met mine. "And bedroom."

I chuckled. "I'm fond of a good bathtub myself."

"I do not take baths often. Not at home. I do at the arena, before games, but at home I usually take showers."

"I love a good bath," I said, nibbling my chicken ranch taco. "It relaxes me and it's good for the muscles in my back."

"Does massage help?" he asked. "When it hurts?"

"When the spasms come, nothing helps but the meds. For everything else, I use a variety of techniques. Massage, yoga, stretching, and now walking. My physical therapist said I have to move more so I've been trying. I want to try some new things, but it makes me nervous because I don't want to have another episode like I did at the restaurant."

"In the summer, when I don't have hockey, I'll help you. We can work out together. I take time off early in the summer to give my body a chance to rest and heal, so I can do less strenuous things with you and show you some moves the team trainers show us after injuries. If you would like this."

I smiled over at him. "Very much. Thank you." I looked around. "So where is this cat I've heard so much about?"

Lars rolled his eyes, something I'd never seen him do before. "He is not so friendly. I do not even like cats."

"So why do you have one?" I asked, chuckling.

"Annalise, she wanted him for me, and now I am attached. Even though he is an asshole." He looked around and let out a low whistle. "Loki, come! I have food."

We both sat there for a moment, waiting, and to my astonishment, a gorgeous, gray, green-eyed cat came walking around the corner, tail swishing indignantly, as if horrified that he'd been summoned.

"You are a good boy," Lars said, reaching down and scooping him up. "But do not scratch Sheridan."

I reached out my hand and let Loki sniff it. Then he turned up his nose and wiggled free of Lars's grasp, jumping back onto the floor.

"I've never had a pet," I said, watching him sit at Lars's feet while he fed him a piece of chicken.

"Me either," Lars said. "My schedule is difficult, but he is very independent, and Rosalina comes to feed him. She thinks he's an asshole too."

I couldn't help but laugh. "So tell me something about you I don't know. Do you have any hobbies? You have a cat, you work out almost every day, and hockey is pretty much your life. What do you do for fun?"

"Not so much during hockey season," he said slowly, a frown on his face. "I am very focused."

"I noticed. But you must do something to relax?"

He shrugged. "Sometimes I do things with my teammates, but not so often. I see Annalise a few times a month. And you."

Our eyes met again, and I felt a shiver of desire so strong he probably saw it.

"You were just thinking about sex," he said, a faint smile playing on his lips as he looked at me.

Oops. Busted.

"It's been a few days," I said, shrugging. "And I'm kind of spoiled with how good it is."

He downed the second half of his fourth taco in one bite and then took a long drink of water. Without another word, he wiped his mouth with a napkin and slowly got to his feet.

"Will your back be okay if I put you on the counter?"

My heart rate instantly kicked up a notch because I had a feeling I knew what was coming.

"As long as you don't twist me in any weird way."

Before I could move, he'd swept everything aside and had me up on the counter.

"I have eaten enough food," he murmured, moving between my legs as he bent his head to kiss me. "Now dessert."

THREE GLORIOUS ORGASMS LATER, we finally made it to the bedroom and I nestled into Lars's arms as we got under the covers. He had a massive California king bed and the kind of furniture that reminded me of something Vikings would have slept in a thousand years ago, including a huge stone fireplace that was currently the only light in the room.

"I think I like your bed almost as much as mine," I murmured, the side of my face resting against his wide chest. I heard the faint beat of his heart and it made me smile because it was such a simple thing after the crazy shit he'd just done to me. I wasn't a prude, and I was learning a lot about what I did and didn't like in bed, but after sleeping with no one but Hugh until now, it still took a little getting used to.

"Yours would be good if it was bigger," he said, stroking a hand down my back.

"I can buy a bigger bed," I murmured.

"Your apartment is very close to arena," he said, resting one of his hands on my ass. "So I don't mind staying there."

"Nice to know," I said, chuckling. "The only problem with me staying here is you have to drive me home in the morning and you get up so early."

"Is already almost two," he said. "I cannot get up at five thirty to work out on three hours of sleep after a game. Tomorrow I will go later. We can both sleep."

I tipped up my head. "Are you sure? You don't like changing your routine and I don't want to be the reason you do."

"Is okay." He leaned down to kiss my lips, his mouth hovering over mine. "Was worth it."

"I'd say let's go again but I don't know if I have another orgasm in me. That last one…" My voice trailed off because it had been the strongest one I'd ever had. "Well, I've never gotten off like this. Like I do with you."

"No? Were your other lovers so selfish?"

"I told you—I've only ever been with one other guy."

"You have really slept with only one other man? How is this possible? A woman as beautiful as you?" He sounded genuinely confused.

"I met him when I was sixteen. He became my agent, then my boyfriend. He was my first and only. He was verbally and emotionally abusive, taking advantage of the fact that I was overweight to make me feel bad about myself. Then, when I started making money, he became controlling and manipulative because he didn't want to fall off the money train. And finally, when I found out he'd been lying, cheating, and stealing from me for essentially our entire relationship, he hit me and called me names." I felt his arms stiffen around me.

"I will hurt him," he growled under his breath. "Tell me his name."

"Don't worry. It was the first and last time. I walked away and never looked back. Unfortunately, I've been trying to break the contract between us for two years now and haven't gotten very far."

"Contract?"

"Technically, on paper, he's still my agent. He gets fifteen percent of every penny I make."

"This is why you don't model now?"

"It's why I haven't been in a hurry to get back to it since the accident. Eventually, I have to find a way to get rid of him, but the amount of money he wants is…insane."

"He is large?"

I wasn't sure what he meant at first. "You mean could you take him? Oh, yeah. You'd snap him in half. He's not big. I weigh more than he does. I'm also an inch taller than him."

"This was your first love?"

"I was so young and stupid," I said, sighing. "I thought…well, it doesn't matter. But I've been trying to get away from him for so damn long, and he still scares me. Sometimes it feels like I'll never be free of him."

"You are safe in your apartment?"

"I think so. He showed up at work yesterday but—"

"Work? He came to your *office*?"

"He was outside but—"

"This is not okay!" He started to sit up, but I put a gentle hand on his chest.

"Hey. Everything is okay. He can't get inside the building and I'd walked to work, so he caught me at a vulnerable moment, but nothing happened." I didn't dare tell him Hugh had grabbed my arm.

"Why didn't you tell me? I could have come after the morning skate."

I smiled to myself because that was as sweet as it was ridiculous. "You've had a lot going on and I was worried about you," I reminded him. "Keegan and that stupid article."

He made a sound that was a cross between a sigh and a grunt. "He's such a fucking asshole. None of those things he said about my teammates were true."

"And what about what he said about you?" I asked gently, since he hadn't mentioned it yet tonight.

"I don't...know. Do you think I am...autistic?"

"I'm in no way qualified to answer that," I admitted. "But does it matter?"

"To me, yes."

"Why? It doesn't change who you are. It certainly doesn't change who you are to me. You're the biggest, strongest guy I've ever known and I'm not even a little bit afraid of you."

"But I am weird, right?"

"What does that even mean? We're all weird in our own way."

"You know exactly what I mean." He was staring up at the ceiling now and I lifted my head so I could see him better. "You see it. Everyone sees it. Even I fucking see it. I just did not know it had a name."

"Lars. Look at me."

He shifted slightly, his eyes meeting mine in the semidarkness.

"When I'm with you, I feel safe. Not because you're physically strong, but because of the man you are. I could hire a bodyguard your size if that was the only thing I needed, but that's not what's happening between us. When you touch me, I don't flinch, waiting to see if you're going to hurt me. When you look at me, I'm not instantly worried that you're going to criticize how I look or what I'm wearing. You're a good man. A strong, sexy, athletic one, but also kind and gentle, which means so much to a woman like me. You have no idea how many people have tried to hurt me—both physically and emotionally—because of my size, my job, my looks."

"Never." He shook his head slowly. "I am far from perfect, but I will never purposely hurt you." He paused. "Maybe sometimes you have to tell me things, like not to leave in the morning, because I don't know so much about relationships."

"Is that what this is?" I whispered. My breath practically stuck in my throat as I struggled to say the words.

"I think so. Yes. If you want this. With me." He reached out one of his big hands, putting it on the side of my face. "You are special, Sheridan. When I'm with you, I feel almost…*normal*."

"You *are* normal."

He narrowed his eyes a little, as if he were thinking about something serious, but then he kissed me. Except this kiss wasn't filled with passion and hunger like the kisses we'd shared earlier had been. This kiss was something new, something I hadn't ever experienced with anyone else, and my gut told me he hadn't either. This was the beginning of an emotional bond, of something that went beyond the amazing sex we'd been having.

I was nervous, because there were so many things I still needed to tell him, but I just wanted to bask in his attention, his body, everything that made him the man he was and how it felt when we were together. Later, after we'd had time to get used to this new stage of our relationship and there was less chaos surrounding us, I'd tell him the rest.

CHAPTER SIXTEEN

Lars

Mavericks Group Text

Nash: Who the fuck put up those pictures of me in the locker room?

Wes: What pictures?

Nash: It's a picture of me and that old lady from the Golden Girls and it looks like she's holding a whip.

Wes: Can you send us a pic?

Nash: Can you kiss my ass?

Drew: Nash, I just want you to know I'm completely on your side. This is ridiculous.

Nash: Thank you.

Drew: No, thank you.

Nash: For what?

Drew: For being a friend.

"AND HOW DID you feel about spending last Christmas alone?"

I shrugged and glanced around the office of psychiatrist Dr. David Chiou, only eleven minutes into our first session and already bored out of my mind. How would I manage to sit here and talk to him for an entire hour?

"Fine," I said, my gaze stopping on a row of bobbleheads on one of his bookshelves. "You like the Avengers?"

"Yes, how about you?"

"Some people say I look like Thor."

David smiled. "I can definitely see why."

I shifted in my chair, uncomfortable. David seemed nice, but I wasn't used to being around anyone like him. He was a middle-aged Chinese man about half my size who had told me at the start of our session that he'd never watched a hockey game. His office was full of plants and oversized, but comfortable chairs. A small fountain gurgled in one corner of the room. The room offered a soothing vibe, but I was off balance here. I was used to being around athletes who often communicated in grunts and profanity.

"Do you like being alone, or do you prefer to be in the company of others?" he asked.

"Both." I looked over at the clock on his wall, wanting to speed things along. "Do I have autism?"

"I don't know."

I scowled. "I thought this was your job, to tell people what is wrong with them."

"Well, Lars, I can assure you there's nothing wrong with you. There might be things you struggle with, but that's true for most people."

"What do you struggle with?"

"We're here to talk about you, Lars, not me."

I sat up straight in my chair, giving him my most imposing glare.

"So I don't have autism?"

David smiled. "You may. It will take several sessions and some testing for me to tell you more about that. It's important to remember, too, that autism spectrum disorder affects people differently. There's no one-size-fits-all diagnosis or treatment plan."

"I want to know." I rapidly tapped my fingertip against the arm of the chair I was sitting in. "I will pay extra to find out fast."

"Can I get you some water?" David asked.

"No, I am fine."

He cleared his throat and paused before speaking again.

"It's going to take some time, Lars," he said. "And whether or not you fit the criteria for an autism diagnosis, I'm more interested in how you're feeling overall. You said at the beginning of this session that you suspect you have autism. Can you tell me more about that?"

My armpits were sweaty and I couldn't seem to stop tapping my finger. I imagined that I was about to skate out onto freshly resurfaced ice, stick in hand, but it only calmed me a little.

"I do not like talking," I said.

"Why not?"

I shrugged. "Sometimes…it is hard to know what to say."

"Is that an uncomfortable feeling for you? Talking to someone one-on-one?"

"Sometimes. But sometimes that is easier for me than lots of people listening."

David nodded. "Sure. So it's easier when there's just one person?"

"Yes. As long as that person is not a reporter."

He smiled. "I hadn't even considered that. Tell me about what makes you feel pressured. What situations do you find yourself in that you wish you could just escape from?"

I tried to think about what really bothered me before answering. "Questions. How do I feel, what do I think…whether the questions are about hockey or me or anything else does not matter."

"And what situations make you feel most comfortable?"

"Being alone. Being with Sheridan. Being with my teammates, other than the newest one. He is a dick."

David wrote something on the notebook he was holding in his lap, and I wondered what it was. I didn't like being analyzed. I'd thought I could come in here, pay this psychiatrist and get a diagnosis, but so far it wasn't like that at all. I was planning to bitch Nash out later for talking me into doing this.

"My other teammates think Sawyer is a dick, too. That is not just me. Did you write that down?"

"Nope." David turned his notebook toward me so I could read it. "I wrote down the people you feel most comfortable with. But why do you feel the way you do about this new teammate?"

"He does not smile. He is not friendly."

"When we started this session, you told me people thought you weren't friendly. Is that true?"

I thought about it, and…shit. He was right. The things my teammates and I disliked about Sawyer, like his attitude and how he interacted with us, sounded a lot like me. He was cold, abrupt, and disinterested in getting to know anyone.

"It is true," I admitted. "Acting friendly is…for me, it is…" I sighed, frustrated. "I don't know the English word."

"Would you say it feels unnatural?"

"Yes. I am bad at what Americans call chitchat. And I do not want to get better at it. I think it is okay to have quiet."

"So if someone said they didn't like you because you aren't friendly, how would you feel about that?"

"Fine. I do not need everyone to like me."

I stood up, unable to just sit and talk any longer. I walked over to one of the bookcases along the wall so I could look at something other than David. He kept talking while I took in the books and trinkets lining the shelves.

"Who is Sheridan?"

"My…girlfriend." I swallowed hard after saying it, because I'd never called a woman my girlfriend before.

"And how long have the two of you been together?

"Not long. A month or so."

"And when was your last relationship prior to Sheridan?"

I pointed at a framed photo on the shelf. David

and another man were standing in a place so beautiful that it hardly looked real. There were mountains covered in lush, green foliage and brilliant blue water in the background.

"This looks like Sweden," I said.

"Is that where you're from?"

"Yes."

"That was taken very close to Sweden, in Norway. My brother and I took a two-week trip to Sweden, Norway, and Denmark a couple years ago."

I cocked a brow and gave him a smile. "There. You told me something about you and now I will tell you something about me. I have never had a relationship before Sheridan."

"Why is that?"

Shrugging, I walked back over to my chair and sat down. "I never wanted one."

"And why do you want one now?"

"Because Sheridan is…special. And I have seen my friend Wes with his wife and wished I could have someone like her."

"Do you think Sheridan is like her?"

"Yes."

"Tell me what she's like."

I wrapped my hand around the back of my neck and exhaled hard, trying to find the words to describe Sheridan.

"She is...different from me." I waited, briefly hoping that would be enough of an answer for David, but he simply looked at me with a frustratingly patient expression, like he had all the time in the world to listen. "Beautiful. She is very beautiful, but also she does not find the things hard that are hard for me. Everyone likes her. She makes people feel...comfortable. And me—she makes *me* feel comfortable. And happy. She does not say she thinks I should change."

"Have other women made you feel like they wanted you to change?"

I shrugged one shoulder. "Women have tried to get me to be in relationships. They have told me I would be happy if we were...what is the word for just the two of us?"

"Exclusive?"

"Yes, exclusive. That I needed a wife to have my children and make a nice home for me."

"You didn't agree with them," David said.

I shook my head, adamant. "I have Rosalina, my housekeeper. And I do not want children yet. It seemed like..." I paused, frowning. "Those women did not want to know me. They wanted to be married to a professional athlete with lots of money, and it did not matter which one."

"Sheridan is different, though?"

"Much different. We watch movies in sweatpants, and she cleans off her makeup before we start the movie if it is nighttime. She…likes who she is. She does not try to impress me, even though she could try because she is much richer than I am."

"Really?" For the first time since our session began, David sounded genuinely surprised.

"Yes. She is a supermodel."

"Oh, wow. Right here in St. Louis?"

"Yes."

"Hmm. Can I make an observation, Lars?"

I waved my hand, prompting him to continue as I stated the obvious. "We are in your office. You do not need to ask me."

He smiled. "That's a fair point. I just wanted to point out that you've talked far more about Sheridan than anything else. It seems like when you are interested in something, and you *want* to talk about it, you're insightful and engaged. So even though you told me you're not good at talking, I don't think that's true across the board."

"So I don't have autism?"

After a single note of laughter, David said, "I don't know yet. But we'll begin with one session a week and schedule you for testing. I'll need some time before I can give you an accurate diagnosis. Does that sound okay?"

"Yes. But I travel much for hockey, so it can be hard to schedule appointments."

"We'll figure it out. You took the first step by coming today."

I sighed heavily. "Patience is hard for me."

"Give me about a month, okay? I don't want to rush things. And if you need to talk to me in between our weekly sessions, just call my office."

"For extra talking?" I shook my head, not liking that idea at all. "That will not happen."

CHAPTER SEVENTEEN

Sheridan

I'D JUST FINISHED a session with my physical therapist when my phone rang and I saw Hadley's name on the screen. I wrapped a towel around my neck and answered as I headed to the locker room to change and get my things.

"Hey, Hadley!" I hadn't talked to her in a week or so.

"Hi. How are you?"

"I'm good. What are you up to?"

"I'm about to go read to Annalise's preschool class, but I was wondering if you were free this afternoon to do something with me."

"Sure, what do you need?"

"There's a new guy that just got traded to the team…Sawyer Cain."

"I read about that. Lars hasn't said much about him, though."

"Yeah, he's not very friendly, according to Wes and the others. So I was thinking we'd go over to his house and introduce ourselves to his wife, Annie. The guys are out of town and maybe she's lonely? And since you're the newest WAG on the team, it might be nice for her to have someone to talk to who isn't a veteran. I mean, Sawyer's been in the league for a while, but obviously not here in St. Louis. You're also a native, which might be helpful for her. You don't have to. I totally understand if—"

I interrupted her. "No, I'd love to. I just finished working out, so I'm going home to shower and work for a little while. What time were you thinking?"

"I could pick you up at three, if that works? Nina's coming too and we're bringing a homemade red velvet cake and flowers."

"Should I bring something?"

"Nah, we've got it covered. Just text me your address and I'll pick you up at three."

"I live in a building downtown, so I'll just meet you downstairs because parking is a nightmare."

"Perfect. See you then."

I waved goodbye to my therapist and headed

down to where Flynn was waiting in my Mercedes. The physical therapist's office was too far to walk to and after my run-in with Hugh last week, I wasn't willing to risk it.

I was excited about hanging out with Hadley and Nina, though. I hadn't had a chance to see them much between the team's travel schedule and how busy things were at the office, so this would be nice. I liked everyone I'd met so far and felt like I fit in, despite the newness of my relationship with Lars.

For most of my adult life, Hugh had kept everyone but Vanessa away from me, and then less than a year after filing for divorce, I'd had the accident and there hadn't been an opportunity to make friends. I had my mother, of course, and a few aunts, but that wasn't the same. I'd had friends on the modeling circuit, but I was in a different class, both because of my plus-size status and how in demand I was. Other plus-size models were jealous, some didn't have relationships with the same designers, and a handful had gotten close enough to see how manipulative Hugh was and eventually kept their distance.

With the Mavericks' wives, I had the opportunity for a fresh start, which was an incredible feeling. Coupled with my growing feelings for Lars, I'd never felt as content as I did right now. The thing with Hugh was still hanging over my head, but I was going to push Marian to offer him anything he wanted to get him out of my life for good. I didn't care about money, and I'd started squirreling it away just in case things didn't go my way, so I had a little nest egg no one knew about or would be able to trace. Even if I had to start over with nothing, it would be worth it to never see or deal with Hugh again.

———

HADLEY PULLED up right at three and I slid into the back seat of the minivan she drove. Nina was in the passenger seat and we exchanged greetings as I put on my seat belt.

"I really want to hate you," Nina said, glancing over her shoulder at me. "How do you always look so good?"

I laughed. "I've been having my makeup professionally done for more than a decade and eventually you pick up some tips."

"Maybe you could do my makeup before the next home game," Nina said. "Then I won't look like the old lady in the group."

"You absolutely don't look like an old lady!" I

said, shaking my head. "But I'd be happy to do your makeup. And yours too, Hadley."

"Thank you." Hadley smiled at me in the rearview mirror.

"So do we know anything about Sawyer and Annie Cain?" I asked. "I googled them and didn't find much. College sweethearts, married five years, no kids. In fact, they haven't done a public appearance together in a long time. The most recent photo I could find was from two or three years ago."

"All I know is that this is his third team in four years," Nina said. "And his play is inconsistent. Like he'll have an amazing game and score four goals and then not even a shot on goal for weeks."

"I wonder if there's trouble at home?" I mused. "Oh my God—what if we get there and there's a houseful of sister wives?"

Hadley snorted. "What if they're *Amish* sister wives?"

"I don't think that's how that works…" Nina said, frowning.

Then the three of us cracked up.

"Maybe she's shy," I said after a moment. "Not everyone is an extrovert like us."

"True."

"Where do they live?" Nina asked. "They're closer to the city, right? Not in the 'burbs like we are."

"Yeah, they're actually just a few miles from Sheridan. It looks like it's one of those newly renovated old townhouses off the beaten path. Oh, right there." Hadley pointed as she pulled into a spot right on the street.

We got out and Hadley got a cake carrier out of the back, Nina was holding a bouquet of beautiful red, white, and pink flowers, and we headed up to the front of a row of townhouses.

"Here goes nothing." Hadley rang the doorbell and we waited.

"If she's not home, can we still have cake?" Nina murmured.

"Heck yeah." Hadley raised her hand to knock again as a pale woman wearing a pink turban opened the door a crack.

"Can I help you?"

"Um, hi." Hadley and Nina looked as startled as I felt. "Are you Annie Cain?"

"Yes?" The woman opened the door another inch.

"I'm Hadley Kirby. My husband, Wes, plays with Sawyer. We came to welcome you to…the team."

"Oh." The woman blinked a few times and slowly opened the door. "I, um, I've not been feeling well so I'm not dressed or anything." Her voice was a whisper, as if speaking took more energy than she had.

"We won't stay long," Hadley said, smiling. "We

just brought you a cake and wanted to say hello, but we'll let you rest."

"Oh. No. Please. Come in." She stepped aside and Nina, Hadley, and I exchanged a glance before walking into the foyer. The living room still had a stack of boxes that had obviously not been unpacked from the move, and the coffee table was littered with what appeared to be pill bottles, water, and tissues.

"Should I put this in the kitchen?" Hadley asked, motioning to the cake in her hand.

"Yes. Th-thank you." Annie sank down in a chair. "Please excuse the mess…like I said, I'm not feeling well and Sawyer's on the road."

"I'm Sheridan," I said, smiling at her. "I'm dating Lars Jansson. Is there anything we can do for you? Maybe get you some soup or something?"

"I haven't been able to keep anything down the last two days," Annie said. "But thank you."

"I'm Nina. I'm married to our starting goalie, Drew—" She cut herself off as Annie jumped to her feet, hands covering her mouth as she practically flew into the powder room in the hall.

We heard the sound of her vomiting and looked at each other.

"Maybe we should go," Hadley whispered.

"What if she needs help?" I whispered back.

We stood there, unsure what to do, when Annie came back in.

"I apologize." She held a towel in her hand, her pale blue eyes a little watery and her voice raspier now. "This round of chemo has been kicking my ass."

"Oh, I'm so sorry." Hadley glanced at us. "What can we do? Do you need anything?"

"There really isn't anything. The meds help with the nausea but anytime I eat, it comes back up. It's an ugly cycle." She sank onto the couch and closed her eyes.

"Would you rather we left?" Hadley asked. "We just wanted to welcome you to town. We had no idea you were sick. If Sawyer had said something…" Her voice trailed off.

"He doesn't say anything because I asked him not to. I don't want my illness to be the focus, instead of hockey. And the last three years, at home anyway, it's all about my illness."

"I'm so sorry." I sat down beside her. "What can we do while we're here? Really, anything at all. Get groceries for you, load the dishwasher…anything that might help while he's away."

"We get groceries delivered and someone comes to clean. Mostly I just sleep or watch TV. I don't have the energy for anything else." She paused, her eyes meeting mine with a look that was almost embarrassed. "It's nice to have company, though. If you don't mind me running to the bathroom and falling asleep mid-sentence."

"We don't mind at all." Hadley sat in a chair across from her.

"I'll put these in the kitchen." Nina went to put the flowers somewhere and I turned to find Annie watching me thoughtfully.

"You're Sheridan Lee," she said after a moment.

I nodded. "Yes."

"Oh, wow. I'm a huge fan of the red bathing suit."

I grinned. "Thank you. Me too."

"Don't know that I'll be wearing one ever again now that…" Her voice trailed off and she blew out a breath. "Sorry. Cancer has been hard, but the double mastectomy was harder in some ways. No matter what your intelligent mind says, no matter how much your husband promises he doesn't care, you still mourn the loss of your breasts. Your femininity."

"Once you're better, you can get fake ones," Hadley said gently.

"I know." Annie raised a trembling hand to her head. "It's not just the breasts, though. It's also the loss of every hair on my body, from the ones on my head to my eyelashes to my unmentionable parts. It's the scars. It's…everything." She leaned back and closed her eyes. "And the worst part is what it's doing to Sawyer. My illness has dominated his entire life and it's awful to watch him suffering with me. It's like he punishes himself so I don't feel as bad, like if he can be as miserable as I am, it will somehow help me. And of course it doesn't, because watching him suffer just makes it worse." She swiped at her eyes.

I reached out and put a hand on her arm because none of us knew what to say.

"I want him to live," she whispered. "And keep living, but he's in such a dark place now that it's back…" She got a tissue and dabbed at her eyes. "We thought it was going to be okay, that the surgery and aggressive chemo and radiation would get rid of it. But it's back. And it spread, and this is essentially my last chance. If this doesn't work…"

"There are new treatments coming out every day," I said softly.

"Thank you for listening," she said after a moment, sitting up a little straighter. "I apologize for rambling. And please don't tell your husbands the things I said about Sawyer…he's already a private guy, so he cringes when I talk about him."

"Lips are sealed," Nina said solemnly.

"Word of honor," Hadley added.

"Lars doesn't talk much anyway," I said, chuckling.

"Would you guys like some tea? It helps my stomach and you guys can have some of that cake you brought over. Just, you know, fair warning, that I might fall asleep halfway through." Annie's eyes glittered with the first sign of life since we'd been here.

"Absolutely." Hadley got up. "You sit in the kitchen and tell us where everything is so we can do the work and you can chat."

"Thank you," Annie whispered. "Thank you for coming. It's been a long time since I felt like I belonged in his world."

"You're one of us," Hadley said.

My eyes got a little misty as I watched her walk into the kitchen. Suddenly my problems with Hugh and everything else going on in my life had new perspective. And Annie had just given me a great idea.

CHAPTER EIGHTEEN

Lars

Mavericks Group Text

Wes: Ross, where the fuck are you? The bus was supposed to leave five minutes ago.

Ross: Is Coach there? Did he get my text?

Wes: He's standing outside the bus waiting for you, looking pretty pissed.

Ross: Tell him to read my text.

Wes: Do you need help with something?

Ross: No. I locked myself out of my room earlier and it took forever to get the front desk guy to get me a new room key.

Wes: But you're back in your room now?

Ross: Leaving my room now. Anyone have socks I can borrow?

Wes: I have socks. Just get your ass down here.

"IT SMELLS LIKE ASS IN HERE," Boone grumbled as we all found seats on the bus that would take us from our hotel to the arena in Toronto.

No one seemed to care enough to respond. It *did* smell like ass, but the trip was short and I had much more important things on my mind.

The wait to find out if I had autism felt like forever. I had reporters and photographers on my ass every time I left the house these days. And I missed Sheridan.

"What the hell?" Sawyer demanded as we waited for the bus driver to start driving.

No one asked him what he was talking about. We'd all gotten used to him being a sullen, grumpy fuck. It worked for me, because my teammates used to say that about me, but I seemed like a ray of sunshine in comparison to our newest teammate.

"You need to tell your nosy wife to mind her own business, Kirby," Sawyer said.

Wes, who had been talking to Beau, looked over

at Sawyer. "What the hell are you talking about, dude?"

Sawyer's eyes flashed with anger. I'd never seen him look so pissed off, and my muscles twitched in unconscious response. When someone was coming for one of my teammates, I wanted to protect them.

"What the fuck?" Sawyer's voice had risen. "Your wife and two other wives went over to my *house*. Uninvited, obviously. How did they get my address? Did you know about this?"

"That doesn't make sense," Wes said dismissively. "Why would Hadley go over to your house?"

"My wife just texted me that she did. She and two other wives stayed at my house for more than an hour."

"How dare they?" Drew said sarcastically. "I'm sure Nina was one of the other two. She's prone to bullshit, like being welcoming and other nice things. Probably brought a cake over, too."

Sawyer stood up then, and all eyes were on him. The tension on the bus seemed to be rising by the second.

"Where the fuck did they get my address?" he asked Wes.

Wes shrugged. "No idea. I don't expect my wife to run stuff by me. She does what she wants."

The ice in Sawyer's tone made my skin prickle

with awareness as he said, "She better not come anywhere near my house again. She'll be sorry if she does."

"Are you threatening my wife?" Wes demanded, standing up.

"Cut the shit," Coach Gizzard said from the front of the bus. "We've got a game to prepare for."

Wes gave Coach an incredulous look. "Did you hear what he just said about my wife?"

Coach stood up, turned around and looked at Sawyer. "What's the issue with a few wives stopping by to meet your wife?"

Sawyer was silent for a few seconds, clearly at a loss. I squinted, almost certain I saw tears shining in his eyes as he spoke. "My wife is medically fragile. Exposure to germs or viruses means actual life or death for her."

Wes's expression changed in an instant, the anger sliding away.

"Well why the hell didn't you tell anyone?" Coach asked. "That's the kind of stuff we need to know."

"Annie didn't want people to know," Sawyer said, the fight gone from his tone. "I wanted to respect that."

Coach nodded and said, "Let's talk when we get to the arena, Cain."

My phone buzzed with a text and I looked down at the screen.

Sheridan: I just went to meet Annie Cain with Hadley and Nina. She's so sweet but it was very sad because she has cancer and it seems pretty serious.

I glanced at Sawyer, and then back down at my phone screen. It made sense now—why he was so private and why he was always in such a shit mood. Who wouldn't be if their wife was seriously ill?

Me: It was nice of you to go.

Sheridan: She said she appreciated it, and she gave us all her number. My heart is broken now, though. The poor woman is desperately ill, and it's so damn unfair.

Me: It is. It must be very hard for both of them.

Sheridan: Can you fly home right now and give me a hug?

Me: No, but I would if I could.

Sheridan: How's the road trip going?

I considered telling her about what had just gone down on the team bus, but then she'd probably feel bad about going over to Sawyer's house. Probably best to just leave it alone.

Me: Boring.

Sheridan: I'm working from home the rest of the day, mostly boring meetings. Hopefully we'll both get to do something more exciting soon...

Me: There are many exciting things I want to do with you.

Sheridan: Such as...?

Me: I have been thinking since waking up about burying my tongue in you. Then burying my cock in you. Would you like that?

Sheridan: God yes. I have a Zoom call starting in one minute and I'm not wearing a padded bra, so stop saying things that make my nipples hard.

Me: It's bad your nipples aren't in my mouth right now.

Sheridan: Not helping. I'm not going to look at my phone again until after this meeting is over...

Sheridan: Good luck with your game tonight.

Me: Good luck in your meeting.

Sheridan: xoxo

I stared at my phone screen for a second, arching a brow. I wasn't a "xoxo" kind of guy, but I didn't want to ignore her way of saying goodbye and not reply. I sent a thumbs-up and put my phone away.

SEVERAL HOURS LATER, my mind was finally focused entirely on something other than Sheridan.

I'd reviewed the stats of my opponents and watched a little film, but not as much as I would have liked. I'd been in a mood before the game started.

The pregame pasta I'd gotten from a local Italian restaurant had fucking sucked. It was cold and the chicken was dry. Our equipment manager, Clint, was back in St. Louis with his wife, who had delivered their son last night, and the assistant who had sharpened my skates wasn't as good at it as Clint.

But here I was, on the ice, even though my mojo was off. It was the second period, and we were down 2–1. I was no longer pissed off about the pasta or my skates—now my anger was focused on Tony Gruen.

Tony was the first line center for Toronto, and he played dirty. He'd just come skating out of the penalty box, running his mouth at Wes before the door was even opened. It was instigating a fight with Wes that had landed him there in the first place, and I wasn't letting him get another crack at my captain.

"Shut the fuck up and play," I said, glaring at him.

He gave me a disgusted look. "Was I using words too big for you, Jansson? You need a special ed teacher to come out and hold your hand?"

Tony immediately turned his attention back to the game after his comment, but I wasn't having it. I dropped my stick and barreled into him, slamming him against the boards and taking my gloves off.

I didn't have the words to fight back, but I had

my fists. I let Tony have it, punching him relentlessly as the crowd roared in response.

"Enough, man." I heard a voice calling out to me to stop, but I couldn't.

I kept hitting Tony, and he groaned in response. Several of my teammates tried to intervene, but all my attention was focused on Tony. Two of my teammates finally put themselves between me and Tony, and two others forced me to back away from him.

It wasn't until I was sitting in the penalty box and catching my breath that I started to calm down. If my teammates hadn't pulled me off of Tony, I didn't think I ever would have stopped punching him. I'd never felt so out of control before.

I was used to trash talk—I was a hockey player. I'd been called a caveman, a goon, and a dumbass before. But now that my mental health was being discussed on blogs, in newspapers, and even on Twitter, it cut deeper.

"Hey, Jansson!"

A Toronto fan standing right next to the penalty box pounded on the glass. He looked like he weighed about a buck fifty, with beady eyes and coffee-stained teeth.

"You suck!" he yelled. "You want to hold up your fingers and tell me your IQ? You'll only need one hand!"

I flinched, like I was going to lunge toward him, only moving a few inches before I sat back down and smiled. It had been enough to make him jump about a foot in the air before scurrying away.

This day had sucked so hard. I wanted to go back to being the invisible member of our team instead of the one most talked about. I wanted to fall asleep in Sheridan's bed, her nails gently grazing my scalp as she ran her hands through my hair.

Not tonight, though. Tonight I had to suck it up and play hockey.

The lamp lit up behind our goal. Tony fucking Gruen had just scored on the power play and I slammed my hand against the bench in the penalty box. He gave me a shit-eating grin as he skated past the penalty box and I gripped my stick, eager to get back out there.

CHAPTER NINETEEN

Sheridan

I slid behind the wheel of my Mercedes and took a minute to enjoy the feeling. I was driving again, walking every day, and having the best sex of my entire life. Not to mention my Swedish hunk of a boyfriend who made me so freakin' happy. He was quirky, introverted, and quiet, but gentle, kind, and trying so hard to please me. Not because he had to, but because he wanted to. And that was all that mattered to me, that he cared enough to try. Hugh had never given a shit about my needs, especially not in bed, and it was refreshing to know not every man out there was a manipulative prick who was after my money.

I'd just pulled up in front of Sawyer and Annie's townhouse when my phone rang and I saw Hugh's name on the screen. I'd avoided his last two calls, so I figured I'd better answer this one or I wouldn't be able to enjoy myself tonight.

"What do you want?" I asked abruptly, putting the car in park and engaging my Bluetooth.

"What the hell are you doing?" he demanded. "You think you're just going to ride off into the sunset with some new guy?"

"Not that it's any of your business," I replied. "But maybe."

"Everything to do with you is my business. Now, then, forever."

"I repeat. What do you want?"

"First of all, I'm not signing that piece of garbage your attorney sent over. You can forget it. Second, if you continue with this bullshit, believe me when I say I will ruin your boyfriend."

"Lars can take care of himself," I said quietly, though my chest tightened with worry.

"I have two women ready, willing, and able to come forward with accusations of sexual assault."

"What?" One of my hands balled into a fist. "Dammit, Hugh, this has to end. It's not good for either of us."

"It's fine for me." He chuckled. "And don't forget —I still have that video."

"I'm calling my lawyer." I disconnected and dropped my forehead to the steering wheel. I was going to have to give him everything I had to make him go away, and even then, I wasn't sure he would. The video he had would destroy my reputation and my life, not to mention what he'd threatened to do to Lars. I needed to call Marian first thing in the morning, but it was four thirty now and I was bringing Annie over to Hadley's, where I was going to do everyone's hair and makeup before the game.

My hands were shaking and I was nauseated, though, so I was in no condition to drive yet.

Damn him to hell.

I hated Hugh with every fiber of my being.

A knock on the window made me jump and my hand flew to my chest as I noticed Annie standing there watching me curiously. I quickly unlocked the door, and she got in.

"Hey, are you okay?" She looked worried.

"I...no." I took a deep breath. "But I will be. If you can just give me a minute."

"Of course." Annie put on her seat belt and turned to me. "Can I do anything?"

"Can you make my nasty snake of an ex go away and leave me alone?"

"Probably not, but I can listen if you want to talk. And I won't tell a soul. Not even Sawyer, if you ask me not to."

I blew out a frustrated breath. "We've been together since I was fifteen and he's been my agent since I started modeling. Because I was so young when we got together, the contract I signed is stupid. Beyond stupid. And so far, my lawyer can't get me out of it. He doesn't want to give up anything, and on top of that, he threatened to go after Lars too."

Annie winced. "How?"

"By having female friends of his say that Lars assaulted them or some such bullshit." I slammed my fist on the steering wheel. "I fucking hate him!"

"Make sure you document all this stuff," she said softly. "Tell your attorney everything. Like, write down the date and time of the call, along with the duration. I was prelaw in college."

"Thanks." I pulled a tissue out of my purse and dabbed at my eyes. "I appreciate it."

"Do you still want to go to the game? We can go inside and just hang out instead?"

I shook my head. "You're sweet to offer, but I promised Annalise and some of the WAGs I'd do their hair."

She peered at me. "Oh, I just noticed what you did. That's pretty." She patted her purse. "I have a wig in here…do you think you could do a little bit with that?"

"Sure." I took a deep breath and pulled back onto the street. "Sorry to vent to you with my problems. How are you feeling?"

"I'm drugged up on anti-nausea meds and we're done with chemo for three weeks, so I should have a good week or two until we start the next cycle."

"That sounds awful. I'm so sorry."

"It's okay. But I don't want to talk about that tonight. I just want to feel normal. That's why I was hoping you'd help me with makeup and to get my wig on right, so people don't see me and immediately think, 'oh, shit, cancer.' It gets old. Anyway, tell me who Annalise is."

I filled her in as best I could on the drive to Wes and Hadley's place in the suburbs and by the time we got there, I was in control again. Hugh always sent me spiraling, and I was going to have to find a way to keep from letting him upset me. Marian was hoping to get a restraining order, but it was hard to get a judge to sign off on one when we never knew what to expect from him.

"Hi, Sheridan!" Annalise opened the front door. "Are you doing my hair? Oh, will it be like yours? It's so pretty." She reached for my hand, which shocked me, but I gave Annie a grin as I let Annalise pull me inside.

"Someone's excited," Hadley said as I walked into the room.

There were half a dozen women already there, including Nina and Hadley. Introductions were made since I only knew a couple of them and Annie didn't know any. Hadley had explained to everyone sitting with us tonight that Annie's health was fragile, without going into any details, and that she would be wearing a mask during the game. We'd figured it would be better to mention it ahead of time rather than have Annie face a dozen questions, and so far, it was working.

I wove red, black, and white ribbon into Annalise's two braids and then put a little blush and lip gloss on her. Her eyes shone as she twirled around the room in her Mavericks jersey.

"Mommy, look!" she said to Hadley.

"I see, baby."

"Will you do braids like me so we can be twins?"

"Sure." Hadley met my gaze and I nodded. I braided her hair, added the ribbon, and she went to finish her makeup while I worked on Nina.

"So, blond or brunette?" Annie asked, coming out of the bathroom. She had on a wig that gave her a short dark bob, while she held another wig in her hand that was honey blond and a little longer.

"Maybe the blond," I said thoughtfully. "The dark is such a contrast to your pale skin and eyes. I think it emphasizes how tired you are."

"Blond it is." She disappeared back in the bathroom and Annalise watched her curiously.

"Why is she wearing hair?" she asked.

"Because the medicine she takes made her real hair fall out," Hadley told her. "So until her hair grows back, she doesn't want to be bald."

"But the medicine will make her better, right?" Annalise asked hopefully.

Me, Hadley, and Nina exchanged glances before Hadley said, "Absolutely. Now go eat your snack."

I finished everyone's hair and makeup, laughing and joking as we had a glass of wine. I left Annie for last so I could focus on her. She was so pale and the bags under her eyes were huge and dark, but I was prepared. I took her into the bathroom and covered her face with the heavy foundation I often used for photo shoots, adding false eyelashes that attached with magnetic liner since she didn't have any eyelashes left of her own.

"There," I said, smiling. "What do you think?"

"Oh, Sheridan." Her eyes filled with tears. "Thank you. I haven't looked...normal in forever. Thank you so much." She threw her arms around me and I hugged her tightly, reminding myself how much worse things could be.

"Miss Annie, you look so pretty!" Annalise breathed from the doorway.

"Thank you, sweetheart." Annie said. "You look pretty too."

"We all look pretty!" Annalise grabbed our hands and pulled us back into the family room. "Look, Mommy! Doesn't Miss Annie look pretty?"

I winced, hoping Annie wouldn't be embarrassed, but she wasn't. She took a little bow as everyone clapped and gave me a little wink.

"More than anything, I can't wait to see Sawyer's face," she whispered to me.

"Are you a natural blond?" I whispered back.

She nodded.

"He's going to love it!"

THE MAVERICKS HAD A GOOD GAME, beating Tampa 4–2, but Lars went in the penalty box twice; once for roughing and the second time for fighting. I had a feeling the guys on the other teams were saying dumb shit and he was letting it get under his skin, but I didn't know how to help. Luckily, the mood in the family lounge was rowdy and boisterous, so I didn't have time to worry about Lars's on-ice woes.

Annie was practically bouncing with excitement as she waited for Sawyer to see her.

"Wait here," I told her, just inside the door. "I'll keep an eye out for him. When he's close, take off your mask and step into the hallway so he can see your whole face. Then you can put it right back on."

Annie nodded, squeezing my arm. She'd been so happy during the game, whistling louder than the rest of us put together when Sawyer scored. We'd watched from the back row, instead of our usual seats at the front of our section, since there were fewer people in the back. She was desperately trying to find a balance between staying healthy and living a little bit.

"Here he comes," I whispered to her.

She took the mask off and stepped into the hallway just as Sawyer came around the corner. His step faltered for a minute and then his eyes widened.

"Annie." He reached out his arms and she practically flew into them as he lifted her off the ground and whispered to her.

"I'm not crying, you're crying!" Hadley whispered in my ear as we watched them together.

"I've done my good deed for the week," I whispered back.

"Hey, babe." Wes came over and wrapped an arm around Hadley, kissing the side of her face.

"Have you met Annie?" she asked him. She tugged him over to where Sawyer was holding her against him, and I looked around for Lars.

"He's coming," Nash said to me, when he caught my eye. "Coach had a few words with him."

I grimaced. "Bad?"

"I dunno, but probably."

He went to greet someone I didn't recognize as Lars came down the hall and I grimaced at the black eye that was visible even from here.

"Hi." I lifted my face as he leaned down and kissed me.

"Hi."

"Does it hurt?" I reached up and trailed my fingers along the rapidly swelling skin around his eye.

"Not so much." He seemed aggravated. "I will put ice at home."

"Coach chew you out?" I asked.

He shrugged. "I will tell you later." He wrapped his fingers around mine. "You are ready?"

"You want to go?" I asked, disappointed.

"Thor!" Annalise came running over to him and Lars instinctively reached out to catch her, lifting her up. "Look what Miss Sheridan did to my hair? Isn't it pretty?"

"Is very pretty," he said, nodding. "You will not be sad if I go home, yes?"

She made a face. "But I thought we were going for ice cream."

"I am sorry. Another time. I promise."

Annalise's lower lip protruded a little. "But Lars—"

"Remember? We talked about this. Sometimes I am tired. Another day. I already promised."

"Okay. Bye." With a completely crushed expression, she walked away.

"You're too tired for ice cream?" I asked him, frowning. "She and I have finally made friends and now you want to go home?"

"You don't understand," he muttered.

"I understand that you've been in a bad mood since the psychiatrist told you it would take weeks to get a diagnosis, and it's not fair that you take it out on Annalise."

"I didn't!" He grunted, giving me a look.

"You kind of did. But fine. Let's go. Just let me say good night to Annie."

I said my goodbyes to the ladies and Annalise, and then Lars and I walked to his car. I'd left mine at Wes and Hadley's, so we were going to have to go there and pick it up. The plan had been for him to follow me home, but I was annoyed now.

"You are mad." He said it as a statement when we'd been in the car for a while without speaking.

"Not mad, disappointed."

"I am sorry. This game was difficult, and I am tired."

"Not everything is about you, you know," I said, staring straight ahead. I had all kinds of shit I was dealing with that he knew nothing about, and while that was partly my fault, he never even asked. He knew I had issues with my ex, but it never came up, as if the only thing that mattered was him.

"Your back is okay?"

He glanced at me and while I appreciated the sentiment, I just didn't have it in me to point out that my back wasn't the only problem in my life.

"Yeah, my back is okay."

He pulled up in front of Wes and Hadley's and I got out my keys. "Are you still coming over?"

"Do you want me to?" He met my gaze questioningly.

"Yes, but I think we need to make it an early night. I'm tired too."

"Okay. I will follow you."

I got into my Mercedes and started the engine.

I was falling in love with Lars, but I needed him

to be there for me the way I was always there for him. The problem was that I didn't think he had a clue what I needed, and I wasn't sure I had it in me to fight with both Lars and Hugh at the same time. Something had to give, and right now it felt like it was going to be me.

CHAPTER TWENTY

Lars

Wes: Everyone's invited to my house for Thanksgiving. We're having it catered, so no one needs to bring anything. RSVP by a week before so we order enough food.

Boone: Will there be any single chicks there?

Wes: Stay away from Hadley's friends. I don't need that headache.

Boone: Ouch.

Wes: You can find hookups on Tinder, dude.

Boone: You were more fun before you got married.

Nash: Hey Boone, I know someone you can hook up with. She's older, but you should give it a try.

Boone: It's Mistress Sandra, isn't it?
Nash: It might be.
Boone: Fuck you.

"We could go shopping," I suggested to Sheridan as we ate omelets and cinnamon rolls for breakfast at her kitchen table. "For Christmas."

Her eyes widened and she broke into a grin. "Really?"

"Yes. It takes long time for packages to arrive in Sweden. I need to buy gifts for my family now so Rosalina can mail."

"I love shopping. You have no idea. It's one of my favorite things to do."

I looked over at her. She was wearing a fluffy white robe, her face was clean of makeup, and her hair was still a little tousled from sleep. And I couldn't help but stare. I thought she was most beautiful this way. Probably because she looked so happy. Lazy Sunday mornings were rare for us—this was only the second one we'd spent together in more than two months of dating.

"I did not know that," I said, getting up to refill my coffee.

She shrugged. "I never mentioned it because I figured shopping wasn't high on your list of fun things to do."

"You are right. But I do like Christmas shopping. Annalise said she would like an Avengers necklace, so we must find one."

"I want to get my mom new living room furniture, but I don't need to look for that today." She cleared her throat and said, "Which reminds me, my mom wants to meet you."

"I would like that."

Nodding, she said, "I'll tell her we can come over for dinner soon. She's pretty excited."

"Why?"

"Um, because my boyfriend is a pro hockey player who looks like Thor?"

"I am your boyfriend?"

She grinned at me. "I think so? If you're okay with that?"

I smiled back. "I am, because that means you are my girlfriend."

"Now that that's settled, let's go shopping. As soon as I finish this cinnamon roll, I'll go get ready. This is going to be so much fun."

I smiled, glad that she liked the idea. I owed her one for being so grouchy lately. The pressure just kept building—it wasn't just the media hounding me nonstop now. An autism advocacy group had also targeted me with a campaign on

Twitter. According to them, I had a responsibility to address the speculation that I had autism, and not sweep it under the rug like I was ashamed.

There was nothing to address, though, because I still didn't know. I had an appointment with David at the end of next week to finally get my test results. I wasn't nervous about it; I just wanted to know one way or the other.

Sheridan and I dressed in warm clothes, coats, hats, and gloves. The winter cold had set in, and we were heading to an outdoor shopping mall.

"You know what's nice?" she said, breaking the silence on our drive.

"The way you sucked me off last night," I answered. "That was *very* nice."

One corner of her mouth quirked up in a smile and she gave me a look. I'd noticed that it made her happy when I commented on how great she was in bed. She said her ex had never had a single nice thing to say in that area, and I wanted her to know how wrong he was.

"Thank you, but I was thinking that it's nice that people don't recognize me much anymore. Before my accident, when I was doing a lot of ad campaigns, people stopped me when I was out. A lot of the time, they didn't know my name, but they knew I looked familiar. Now, though, I'm just another anonymous person, and I really like that."

I looked over at her and smiled. "I do not think you could ever be another anonymous person, Sheridan. You are too beautiful."

"Not today," she said, wrinkling her nose and laughing. "In my puffy parka and stocking cap, with no makeup on. I look like an Eskimo."

"You are sexier than Eskimos."

She busted out laughing. "That might be the best compliment anyone's ever given me."

The car was quiet again, but when I was with Sheridan, the silence never felt uncomfortable. There was always something warm and peaceful in the air between us when we weren't talking, and it was something I'd never felt with anyone else.

I reached over and covered her hand with mine, just as she let out an excited gasp.

"Are you serious? There's an outdoor ice rink over there!"

"Do you want to skate?" I asked.

Sheridan turned to me, her eyes bright. "I do, but would it be boring for you? You ice-skate practically every day."

"Not like that," I said, trying to figure out if I needed to take the next exit to get to the outdoor rink. "Not with you."

"So skating and then shopping?"

"Sure."

I'd skated outdoors before, mostly when I was a kid. This rink was crowded and loud, but I made sure not to cringe, because this was something Sheridan wanted to do.

The skates we rented were old and worn out. The only pair they had that was big enough to fit me had a hole in the toe area, but I made myself laugh about it with Sheridan instead of bitching.

"Let's go check some kids," I said, grinning. "This is going to be fun."

"Oh God, please tell me you're joking."

I arched my brows and laughed. "Of course I am."

"Well, you usually don't joke, so I never know for sure." She looked up at me from the bench she was sitting on. "Did I mention I'm not very good at ice-skating?"

I reached for her hand and helped her up. Her expression was panicked as she struggled to get her footing.

"I won't let you fall," I assured her.

"Are you sure? I'm exceptionally good at falling. I probably should have thought this over more. I could end up having a back spasm and then you'd have to drag me off the ice."

"Relax. Hold on to me, however you feel most comfortable."

She felt most comfortable clinging to me for dear life, both arms locked tightly around my waist. Kids were flying past us, even the ones using the little walkers with wheels that helped hold them upright.

"We cannot move this way," I told her. "Only one arm around my waist."

She took a deep breath and released her hold with one arm, tightening her other. We started slowly, a smile spreading across her face as we made it ten feet and then twenty.

"It feels weird balancing on this little blade," she said. "I can't believe you skate the way you do."

"Hockey skates are different," I said. "Better."

"Are you saying your toes don't poke out of your hockey skates?" she teased.

"They do not."

"Is your toe cold?"

"No, it is fine."

"I think you're pretty amazing, in case you didn't know that."

I looked down at her face, warmth blooming in my chest. "I think you are very amazing, too. The amazingest, but that is probably not an English word."

"It is now. You just made it up."

We both laughed until Sheridan slipped, one of her skates sliding out from beneath her. She was just starting to cry out in distress when I caught her.

"See?" I smiled down at her. "I won't let you fall."

———

A FEW HOURS LATER, we dropped off a load of shopping mall purchases at my SUV and were heading back in for round two. I usually hated shopping, but I was having fun. Sheridan was taking the lead, deciding which stores to go to based on what we were looking for. She'd helped me pick out designer sunglasses and soft scarves and stocking caps for my mother and sister, and science experiment toys and clothes for my nieces. My sister had sent me their sizes, and that was all Sheridan needed. She mixed and matched different items, completely in her element.

"I will start chewing on my fingers if we do not eat soon," I said as we walked hand in hand back to an outdoor patio area of the shopping mall.

"Next time, you might want to mention how hungry you are *before* you reach the point of eating your own fingers," she said playfully.

"I will try."

"Do you like ramen? There's a ramen place not far from here."

I wrinkled my nose, saying, "I like it, but I want a cheeseburger."

"That sounds amazing. Oh, and a milkshake, because it's never a bad time for a milkshake, no matter how cold it is. Let's find a map and see where we can go."

We found one of the mall directory maps and while she looked for a place to eat, I went to a nearby bathroom. After I was done, I took out my phone and typed out some notes to myself about things Sheridan had seen and liked while we were shopping. I planned to come back and buy them for her for Christmas.

As I neared the directory kiosk where Sheridan was waiting for me, I saw a short, dark-haired man talking to her. Instinct made me pick up my pace, and I walked faster.

"Jesus, you've gotten even fatter, Sheridan," the man said. "You make the other plus-size models look thin."

"What the fuck do you think you're doing?" I asked him, standing beside Sheridan and putting an arm around her waist.

"Just catching up with the woman I made famous."

Sheridan looked like she was about to be sick as she said, "This is Hugh, and I'm sure it's no coincidence he's here at the same time as us."

Everything clicked into place then. This was the man who had abused her. He'd taken advantage of her personally and professionally, and was the reason she didn't feel as good about herself as she should. And now he was *following* her. Hugh held out a hand and grinned at me.

"Nice to meet you, Lars."

"I cannot say the same, Mr. Jasshole."

He scrunched up his face in confusion, before finally getting it. "Ah. Hugh Jasshole. I see what you did there."

"You have three seconds to get the fuck out of here before you end up bleeding on the ground," I said, narrowing my eyes and pulling Sheridan closer.

"Lars, don't," Sheridan said, pulling on my arm and trying to direct us away from Hugh.

"No one will talk to you that way ever again," I said to her. "I will not have it."

Hugh laughed and said, "I guess I see the appeal, Sheridan. The big, dumb caveman you can just lead around by his dick."

"I will knock you unconscious," I said, clenching my fist and taking a step forward.

Sheridan turned to block me and placed her

palms on my chest. "Lars, no. This is what he wants. He can't get what he wants from me so he plans to get to me by ruining you."

"I got everything I wanted from you a long time ago, fat ass," Hugh said, spitting in Sheridan's direction.

His spit landed on her coat and a fury I'd never felt before overtook me. Whether Sheridan liked it or not, I would never stand by while someone spoke to her that way. I smashed my fist into Hugh's face, feeling satisfaction when my fist stung from the contact. He stumbled backward, yelling and covering his face with his hands.

"Call the police! I'm being assaulted!"

"Lars!" Sheridan whirled to face me with an accusing look. "What the hell have you done?"

CHAPTER TWENTY-ONE

Sheridan

LIKE HE'D BEEN DOING since the day I'd met him, Hugh was ruining my life. Not only was he an abusive prick, he'd fucked up my wonderful evening with Lars. Instead of ending a great night of ice-skating, shopping, and laughter with lovemaking, we'd argued. Then he'd gone home instead of sleeping over like he usually did. He'd been adamant no one would ever spit on me, much less say the things Hugh had said—and I loved him more than ever for it—but he had to understand how much was at stake. The cops had been called, chances were the whole thing had been recorded by onlookers, and I had to talk to my attorney as soon as I was coherent enough to have a conversation.

So I was in a bad mood when I got to the office Monday morning, brushing past Nellie as I locked myself in my office. It was early, not even eight thirty, so Vanessa wasn't in yet and I had a little time to come up with a game plan.

I hit the intercom to talk to Nellie. "Nel? Can you put an executive staff meeting on the calendar for ten thirty?"

"Yes, ma'am. But I don't know if everyone is in today."

"Then tell them to come in." I wasn't usually a bitch at the office—that was more often Vanessa's job—but I had neither the time nor the patience for any bullshit today.

A few minutes later, Nellie hesitantly came into my office, a pad in her hand. "Ms. Lee, do you need anything? You seem stressed."

I managed a small smile. "I'm totally stressed."

"I saw the video online," she whispered.

"Is it everywhere?" I asked.

She wrinkled her nose. "No, but the sports sites are playing it and it's on Instagram."

I rolled my shoulders, trying to relax. I probably should have gotten up and worked out, which was what Lars had inevitably done, but I wasn't that energetic in the morning.

"Thanks for letting me know," I told her.

"You want links?"

I hesitated. Normally, I did, but I didn't want to replay it over and over, whether it was on social media or not.

"No." I shook my head. "The press will probably start calling, but just tell them I have no comment at this time."

She opened her mouth but closed it again. "I'm so sorry he's doing this to you," she said.

"Me too." Nellie knew about almost everything in my life because she'd been with me since the start of the company. She'd been a freelance assistant I'd used on and off when I needed help during charity events and such, and when I'd started the lingerie company, she'd been my first choice for a personal assistant. "Hey, Nel?"

"Yes?"

"Things might get ugly going forward, so I totally understand if you want to cut your losses."

She frowned. "And abandon you to the big bad wolf? No way. Fuck him." She nodded and then turned and left my office, letting the door close softly behind her.

I smiled, even though there wasn't much to smile

about today. Nellie's loyalty made me feel good, and I made a note in my personal log to give her a larger-than-usual Christmas bonus. Then I sent Marian an email telling her I was done fucking around with Hugh and what I wanted her to do.

There was a knock on the door and Vanessa stuck her head in. "Hey. You got a minute?"

"For you? Always."

She came in and sank into the chair across from me. "What the hell happened yesterday?"

"You mean how Hugh spit on me and Lars lost his mind?"

She grimaced. "He *spit* on you? Jesus, it's escalating."

"Yeah, well, not for long. I'm done with this bullshit."

"What do you mean?" She furrowed her brows. "Sher, don't do anything crazy. It always makes things worse, and you said your lawyer is handling it."

"I'm not letting him go after Lars. This is my shit and I have to deal with it. Which is exactly what I'm going to do."

"Does it have anything to do with this ten thirty board meeting?"

"Yup." I drummed my fingers on my desk. "I had an idea and I'm going to run it by all of you."

"Care to share?"

I smiled. "I'm going to sell you the company."

"What?" She gaped at me. "What are you talking about? And I don't have that kind of cash anyway."

"I'm not going to sell it for what it's worth," I said, leaning back in my chair. "You can totally afford it. And the best part is, not only does Hugh only get half of what little I make from it, that's it. He gets nothing else. Ever. I will literally work at Walmart before I give him what he wants. I won't work another day until he signs those papers."

Vanessa chewed her lip. "Girlfriend, I know you're mad, but maybe the best thing to do is give him at least part of what he wants. I mean, we both know you're not going to work at Walmart or whatever."

I arched my brows. "Bet me."

She looked startled. "Is it worth it? I mean, I know he's been nothing but awful to you, but half of everything you make is better than not making anything."

"Not to me." I turned to my computer. "I have a few things I need to get done, but I'll see you at ten thirty, okay?"

Vanessa frowned but got to her feet. "All right. I'll see you then."

———

I loved Sheri Lee and had handpicked everyone that worked here, with the exception of some of the warehouse crew. In general, though, I knew everyone sitting at this table, but the problem was that I had to be careful. I'd spoken to Marian earlier, and she'd warned me that I couldn't trust anyone. Not completely. So while she was drawing up the papers for Vanessa to sign, she'd added some things I hadn't thought of.

No matter what happened, Vanessa couldn't fire me. As CEO, Vanessa could technically force me out, but whether I resigned or was asked to leave, I'd get a year's worth of severance and my health insurance would be paid for two years. I didn't care much about the severance, but the health insurance was important because of my ongoing back issues. I trusted Vanessa but Marian trusted no one, and when it came to health insurance, I hadn't argued with her. Besides, Vanessa wouldn't care about what was put in the contract because the sale was only intended to keep Hugh from getting anything else from me.

I wasn't playing around anymore. This legal battle had to end before it cost me things that were far more important than money, like my dignity. And Lars.

God, I didn't want to lose Lars.

Deep down, I loved the overprotective Neanderthal that came out when anyone so much as looked at me wrong. I couldn't let him know that I liked it, because he had to knock it off until he understood how much was at stake, but it still made me feel good inside. No one had ever cared about me like that. Hugh probably would have laughed if someone had spit on me while we were together. Lars, on the other hand, would protect me, no matter the cost. It was probably time to tell him everything, but I was afraid. Everyone except my mother and Vanessa had used me or abandoned me over the course of my career, and Lars wasn't just some guy. He was the man I'd fallen in love with.

"All right, everyone." I raised a hand to quiet everyone down as my executive staff gathered around the conference table. "Here's what's going on." I gave them an abbreviated version of my plan to sell Vanessa the company for far less than it was worth. "I just don't want my ex to get anything more from me."

Ian Coulter, my chief financial officer, didn't look pleased. "That looks terrible on paper," he said slowly. "As if there's dissention in the ranks. It could hurt us going forward."

"No one has to know. This isn't a publicly traded company so I can do whatever I want. I understand it's a little uncomfortable for all of you, but the contract specifically says she can't fire anyone for six months."

"So what will your role be?" Marnie asked.

"On paper, I'm a design consultant. And I've got lots of plans for next year, but I'm not going to throw anything else into the mix until my personal situation is handled. Once that's settled, and I'm legally in the clear, Vanessa will sell me back the company for the same amount of money, and everything will go back to the way it was."

"I don't like it," Ian said, shaking his head.

"I know." I sighed. "And I'm sorry to do this to everyone. I just have to get through this legal battle I'm in. Until I do, it's impacting every part of my life. I'm exhausted and stressed, so the sooner this is done, the sooner things can get back to normal."

"Vanessa, what do you think?" Our chief technology officer, Lenny Katzenburg, asked.

"I just want Sheridan to be okay," she said softly. "I'll do anything she asks of me."

"So we don't get a vote?" Bernie asked.

"Not with this, no. I'm sorry." I met his gaze

guiltily, but this wasn't negotiable. "But I promise, nothing is going to change. This is simply to stop my ex from continuing to make money off of me."

"He sounds like a low-life prick," Marnie muttered.

"Believe me, he is." I got up and gathered my things. "Thank you for meeting on such short notice, everyone. I'll be in touch once the papers are signed."

"Sheridan, wait up." Vanessa followed me back to my office.

"Hey." I sank into my chair. "What's up? I think I'm going to work from home the rest of the day."

"Seriously? You just dropped a bomb on everyone and you're just going to cut and run?"

"I'm not running anywhere," I said, scowling. "I work from home all the time."

"Well, today you should be worried about morale."

"What's wrong with you?" I demanded. "I thought you were on board with this?"

"I am…I just want to make sure you know what you're doing."

"I do. Believe me, I have a plan."

"Are you going to share?"

"I did. I'm going to sell you my company for a ridiculously low amount so dickhead only gets half of a pittance. Then Marian is going to go to the judge and demand we get a court date to get this over with."

"You think that'll work?" Vanessa looked doubtful.

"Marian thinks it will."

"What does Lars think?"

"About what?"

"All of it."

I hesitated. "I haven't told him."

"You haven't…" Her voice trailed off. "What do you mean? You haven't told him all of it or you haven't told him any of it?"

I leaned back in my chair and stared up at the ceiling. "I haven't told him anything. I'm scared."

"Why?"

"What if my mess of a life scares him off? Especially with the shit going on in his life right now."

"I think you're taking a big risk."

"I know. I'm going to come clean this week. It's time. I'm in love with him and I can't keep such a big secret now that it's getting serious."

"Is it?"

"What, serious?"

"Yeah."

"Yes, I think so. I mean, we're officially together and exclusive."

"You'd better hurry up, girlfriend. It won't be pretty if he finds out on his own."

"I know. Let's just get through the sale of the company and then he and I are going to have a heart-to-heart."

"Good luck."

I wasn't sure why, but I suddenly felt like I was going to need it.

CHAPTER TWENTY-TWO

Lars

Mavericks Group Text

Beau: Lars, everything ok?

Lars: Yes.

Beau: My brother's a police officer, and he told me two officers were on a call involving you.

Lars: I am fine.

Wes: Anything we need to let the PR people know about?

Lars: No.

Wes: Can you give me a little more information?

Lars: I punched someone. He deserved it. I did not get arrested.

Wes: Call me. We need to talk about this.

Lars: I am busy. I will call later.

"How are you, Lars?" David asked me as he led the way from the waiting room into his office.

"I am fine."

I wasn't fine, really. Sheridan was pissed at me and I was at the top of Coach Gizzard's shit list for almost being arrested. They'd written up a report, but hadn't actually arrested me. When Sheridan told them her attorney had lodged multiple complaints to the police about Hugh stalking and harassing her, the officers had told Hugh to just go home and not come looking for her again. I had to put all that out of my mind, though, and focus on the reason I was here.

"Have a seat," David said. "Can I get you anything? Water? Coffee?"

I shook my head and sat down in the same chair I'd occupied for each of my three sessions with David so far. This was our fourth week, and today was the day I'd been waiting for since the first time I'd called David's office.

"So tell me what's been going on with you since we last met," David said.

"I would rather get right to the results. Do I have autism?"

There was a knot in my stomach as I waited for his answer. I'd spent hours taking tests on computers and even longer answering David's endless questions. I'd done everything he asked of me and now I had to know.

"We can talk about the results first, but I'd still like to have a regular session with you after we discuss your diagnosis. Would that be okay?"

"Yes." I squeezed the arm of the chair I was sitting in, bracing myself. "Tell me."

He took a folder out from behind the clipboard he was holding and cleared his throat.

"I want to preface this discussion by reminding you that autism spectrum disorder is so named because there's a wide spectrum of how people are affected."

I leaned forward in my chair and exhaled hard. "What is the answer? Yes or no?"

I couldn't wait another second. My whole life was hanging in the balance right now, but David didn't seem to get that. Probably because it wasn't *his* life we were talking about.

"Yes, Lars. I believe you have autism spectrum disorder, and you are on the very high-functioning end of the spectrum."

I buried my face in my hands. Deep down, I'd known. From the first time I'd googled autism and read the list of signs, I'd known I fit the description. But I'd been hoping that somehow, through the sessions I'd had with David, I could somehow convince him I was normal and get the diagnosis I'd hoped for.

"Talk to me, Lars," David said.

I slid my hands away from my face and looked at him, defeated. "What else is there to say?"

"This diagnosis is just the beginning. We still—"

"The beginning?" I gave him an incredulous look. "This is the *end*. It is over. I have autism, and there is no cure."

"What is it the end of?"

David's neutral tone was fucking offensive. No matter what we were talking about, he was always so deliberately reasonable. Approachable. Detached. Unshockable.

"I would like to piss in your fountain," I said, glancing at the gurgling water spilling over a rock formation in the corner, before looking back at him.

"Why?"

I sat back in the chair and looked up at the ceiling, groaning in aggravation.

"*Why?*" I echoed. "If I do piss in your fountain, will you get mad?"

His lips tipped up in a small smile as he said, "No,

but I would ask the cleaning service to change the water."

"What if I pissed on *you*?"

"Are you feeling angry about this diagnosis, Lars? Because if you are, that's completely normal."

"I don't know. I am feeling…a lot."

"That's understandable."

"Why am I feeling all these things when I have autism? I thought autism meant I had no emotions."

I felt a twinge of hope that maybe, now that David knew I was having a rush of feelings, he'd reconsider his diagnosis.

"It doesn't mean that at all. People with autism have the same feelings as everyone else, but they sometimes have trouble expressing them."

Damn. I felt…beaten, like Keegan had won. It didn't matter if the world knew about this diagnosis or not—I knew. And I'd never see myself the same way again. I was flawed. Broken. Different. *Disabled.*

"I don't know what to do," I admitted to David.

"That's okay. You don't have to do anything right now. If you have questions about your diagnosis, I'll answer them to the best of my ability. I have books I can give you so you can learn more about autism. But I want you to remember, Lars—you're the same man who walked into my office that first day. This doesn't change who you are."

I shook my head. "I am not who I thought I was."

David looked down at his clipboard. "I disagree. In our sessions, you've told me you're quiet, hard-working, and devoted to the people you care about. Has that changed?"

After a moment of silence, I said, "No."

"Do you remember how you told me you study film more than any of your other teammates? How you can remember small details and memorize statistics?"

"Yes."

"That's the kind of thing many high-functioning people on the spectrum also excel at."

"Excel?"

"It means to be very good at it. Much better than average."

"But I am disabled."

David gave me an earnest look. "Look at it as being differently abled, Lars, and not disabled. Look at the life you've made for yourself. Most people who want to play professional sports never make it. But you did."

I nodded, staring at my lap. "Autism is why I don't know what to do for Sheridan sometimes."

"Not necessarily. But if you read about autism, and learn how it affects you, you'll be able to identify the things you struggle with and work on them. You can tell her what's hard for you and why, and she can help you work through it."

I rubbed my hands over my face, feeling unsure about everything. "This is like I am buried by a big pile of rocks. And I cannot get out."

"It's overwhelming."

"Yes."

"Let's talk about something else," David suggested.

I looked up at him, surprised. "Something else?"

"Yeah. How was your weekend?"

"It was…good. And then bad."

He smiled. "Tell me the good part first."

"I went Christmas shopping with Sheridan. I bought gifts for my family in Sweden. We went ice-skating at an outdoor rink."

"That sounds like a nice way to spend time together."

"Yes. I am happy when we're together. There is no other…" I stopped, correcting myself. "There *are* no other thoughts or worries. I spend all our time just looking at her and laughing with her. Nash is my best friend, but Sheridan is also becoming my best friend."

"What happened to make it bad?"

I scowled and said, "Hugh. Her ex."

"You mean she brought up her ex while you were together?"

"No, he came to the mall and upset her. He was an asshole to her and I punched him in the face."

"I see."

"He deserved it."

Another small smile came and went quickly as David said, "Even if he did, is it worth getting into trouble for?"

"Yes."

"How did you feel after you punched him?"

I met David's gaze. "Like I wanted to punch him again."

He nodded. "And how do you feel about it now?"

"Like I want to punch him again."

"So no regrets?"

"No. This is how we do it in hockey. If you hurt someone on purpose, you will get hurt back. He hurt her on purpose. I think it's not right for her to have to be hurt again and again, and no one ever stands up for her. No one ever stops it. I stopped it."

"Did she appreciate it?"

I scoffed. "No. She is mad at me. She did not return my calls or texts yesterday."

"Why is she mad?"

"She said I created more trouble for both of us by hitting Hugh."

Her expression after I punched Hugh flashed through my mind for the thousandth time since Sunday. Instead of appreciating that I'd stood up for her, she'd been angry. She'd cried on the way home and ended our day together, and I'd been confused as hell.

"You disagree, I assume."

I shifted in my chair, aggravated. "Yes. I will not let anyone treat her that way. He spit on her. He is a bully. I cannot stand bullies."

"Can she get a restraining order against him?" David asked.

"She said her attorney is working on things."

"Maybe she just needs some time to cool down."

I grunted in disagreement. "There is nothing for her to be angry about."

"But she is."

"Is it hard for me to understand her because of autism?"

David smiled. "No, Lars. Countless men have made their wives or girlfriends angry and had no idea why. The important thing, when she's ready, is for you to listen to her and not tell her she has no right to feel the way she does."

"So I should lie?"

"It's not really lying. She gets to feel how she feels and you get to feel how you feel."

I sighed heavily. "I have to decide if I am going to tell her I have autism."

"What concerns do you have about telling her?"

"I don't know." I shook my head. "I am still under all the heavy rocks."

"I understand. You might want to take some time to process things. And if I can help you come up with a game plan for that conversation with Sheridan, I'd be happy to do that."

"Is this the last time I will see you?"

"That depends. Do you feel like talking to me helps you?"

I nodded. "It is hard, but...I don't know the word."

"Necessary?" David offered.

"Yes."

"I really think we can get you to a place where you not only accept how autism makes you different, but where you can start to embrace it. Your rigid training regimen and hyperfixation on things like statistics have helped you get where you are."

"English is not my first language," I reminded him.

He grinned. "Sorry. I need to work on not using words like hyperfixation."

David walked over to one of his bookshelves and studied the titles, pulling three books out by the spines and walking back over to hand them to me. He retrieved a folder from the table and passed that to me, too.

"Give these a try. These are a few books I recommend and also the written reports on my findings. Feel free to seek a second opinion if you'd like, but the testing I did is an industry standard. And remember, I'm here every day and you can call the office if you have a question or need to get in an extra session."

"I am not doing extra sessions."

He put his palms up and said, "That's fair. Just letting you know the option is there."

"I want to leave now. I want to call Sheridan."

"Sure thing."

I stood up and David walked with me to his office door. As I reached for the handle, he turned to me.

"You got through the hard part. I'm proud of you."

"The sound of that fountain is making me have to pee."

He laughed and stepped aside. "Go ahead, Lars. I'll see you next time."

CHAPTER TWENTY-THREE

Sheridan

AFTER A FEW HARROWING days at the office, I was so ready for date night. Lars and I hadn't spoken the day after the incident with Hugh, but then I'd texted him and asked if he wanted to get together. Then Annie had texted me and asked if Lars and I would be interested in a double date, so that's what we were doing tonight. Lars would be here any minute and I adjusted the lingerie I wore beneath my gray leggings and silver tunic. Lars and I had a full evening planned, and while I wanted to end it with him seeing me in some sexy new lingerie, we had to have a serious talk before that could happen.

It was time to come clean about everything and

let him know just how precarious my situation was. Hopefully, he wouldn't freak out. That had been my hesitation for a while now, since Hugh complicated almost every portion of my life. Lars deserved the truth, though, so after we had dinner with Sawyer and Annie, I planned to invite him up so we could talk in private.

He always waited for me right outside the doors of my building and I loved seeing him standing there. In black slacks and an emerald green button-down shirt with a long leather coat, he looked good enough to eat. I hated that we'd been at odds the last couple of days, but I intended to make things right tonight. I hoped so, anyway.

"Hello." He smiled at me, and I leaned up to press my lips to his. I let them linger a little longer than I usually did standing on the street, but I'd missed not talking to him every day. His eyes crinkled a little as he looked at me. "You are okay?"

"I am. I will be. Let me tell you on the way."

"Okay." He opened the passenger side door and held one of my hands as I climbed up. Then he shut the door behind me and went around to the driver's side.

I leaned back in the seat and reached for his hand after he'd pulled into traffic. "I was hoping later tonight, after dinner, we could come back to my place and talk. I've had some stuff on my mind and after what happened the other night with Hugh, I want to explain why it upset me so much."

"Yes, I'd like some time for us to be alone. I have something to discuss with you as well."

"I'm not mad anymore," I said, glancing over at him. "I just…well, I don't want to talk about it now, but I feel like we've reached a point where we can trust each other with the things that are most important to us."

He hesitated what seemed like a beat too long but slowly nodded, squeezing my fingers. "I feel this too."

We drove the rest of the way to the restaurant in silence and I snuggled against him when he put an arm around me as we walked inside. Annie had texted me that they were already seated, so we found the table and joined them.

"Hi!" Annie wore her blond wig tonight and the magnetic lashes I'd given her, and she looked like she was feeling better than she had the last time I'd seen her. She wore a thick wool sweater dress that gave the illusion she'd put on a little weight, and while I knew it wasn't true, it was nice to see some color in her cheeks.

"Hello!" I hugged Annie while Lars shook Sawyer's hand and we settled at the table.

"I'm starving," Lars said, picking up the menu.

"You realize you say that at least once every time we're together?" I said, chuckling.

"I am a very large man," he said. "I require many calories."

"I am a very small woman but the doctor says I require many calories too," Annie said, her eyes twinkling with mirth.

"When does the next round start?" I asked her, referring to her chemo treatments.

"Not for two weeks. Two glorious weeks of no nausea."

"Then it starts again?"

She nodded. "Yeah, but this is the last round. Then radiation, which is draining but doesn't make me sick. But let's not talk about me tonight. What are you guys doing for Christmas?"

Lars and I glanced at each other. I knew his family wasn't coming for the holidays so I'd assumed we'd spend it together. "Are you coming to my mom's with me?" I asked him. "On Christmas Day?"

He nodded. "Yes, if you would like this."

"It'll just be us, one of my cousins and her family, and sometimes Vanessa comes."

"Both sets of our parents are coming," Sawyer said, sliding his arm along the back of Annie's chair.

"They all want to cook, feed, and mother me,"

Annie said, smiling. "But it's nice that they all get along so we don't have to choose which family to celebrate with."

"You have family in the States?" Sawyer asked Lars.

Lars shook his head. "No. My mother and sister are in Sweden. I see them only in summer."

"How fun. Are you going to Sweden with him this summer?" Annie asked me.

"We haven't gotten that far," I admitted. "We've only been dating a couple of months."

"Is it true you met at a charity bachelor auction?" Sawyer asked, looking from me to Lars and back again.

"Yup." I grinned. "But the money was for a good cause and it turned out to be a good thing for the two of us, too."

"Very good," he said, leaning over to kiss the side of my face. I smiled at him and we exchanged a long glance. There was something different in his eyes tonight and I wondered what it was he wanted to talk to me about, because there was a sadness surrounding him that I didn't understand.

"I don't know who's cuter," Annie said to her husband, cocking her head. "Us or them?"

"Definitely us," he said, gently running his knuckles across her cheek.

"You're such a romantic," she said.

We talked and joked through dinner, and I was glad to see Lars and Sawyer found things to talk about. Not just hockey either, but they seemed to have a similar workout routine and decided to meet up once a week at the gym at six in the morning.

While the guys were talking, I noticed Annie hadn't really eaten anything. She'd taken a few bites of the soup she'd ordered, but her pasta was mostly untouched, and she seemed to be sagging a little.

"You okay?" I asked softly. "You look tired."

"I just got a little dizzy," she whispered.

"Babe?" Sawyer turned, immediately in tune to his wife. "What's wrong?"

"Just a little dizzy."

"You want to go home?"

"Let me sit here a minute," she said, reaching out to put her hand on his arm. "Maybe it'll pass."

"Are you dehydrated again?" Sawyer asked her, covering her hand with his.

"I don't know."

Lars and I exchanged a glance. It was hard to know what to do or say in these kinds of situations. Annie had been looking forward to tonight and had texted me half a dozen times today, so I hated that we might end the evening early. She got to go out so rarely, but she'd said she felt good today.

"I'm going to the bathroom," Annie said, looking at me. "Will you come with me?"

"Of course." I immediately got up, but the moment Annie tried to stand, she sank back down in her chair.

"Babe." Sawyer quickly reached for her. "What is it? Do we want to go to the ER?"

Annie's eyes filled with tears. "No. I hate the hospital." She buried her face in her husband's shoulder as they whispered to each other.

I nodded at Lars and he surreptitiously took care of the bill since none of us were hungry anymore.

"I think we're going to the ER," Sawyer said after a few minutes of whispering with his wife. "She doesn't want to, but she's too fragile to risk going home if she's dehydrated or having a reaction to one of her meds."

"Of course. We'll come too." I looked to Lars, who was already out of his chair.

"Yes, whatever you need."

"You don't have to," Annie whispered.

"We want to," I replied. "And this way, we'll be nearby if either of you needs anything."

———

THE WORST PART about situations like this was not knowing what was going on. Lars and I were in the waiting room as the ER doctors evaluated her and tried to see what was wrong. They'd taken her right in, and Sawyer had gone in a few minutes later. Now it had been over an hour and we hadn't heard anything at all.

"I do not like this feeling," Lars muttered.

"I know. No one likes to feel helpless."

"Maybe she should not have come to dinner," he said.

"She's dying," I said softly. "Her cancer is advanced and it's spread. I think she's afraid every one of these opportunities might be her last."

He looked down at me. "It's so bad? The cancer?"

I nodded. "She doesn't want people to know how bad it is, so please don't repeat it, but yes, the doctors only gave her about a twenty percent chance that she'll make it two years."

"Twenty percent..." His voice trailed off and he slid his arm around my shoulder. "I cannot imagine."

"Me either." I rested my head on his shoulder.

"Hey." Sawyer came out a few minutes later, his face tight and drawn. "They're going to admit her. She's not just dehydrated, but possibly severely dehydrated, and maybe malnourished. They need to run a bunch of tests to see why she's not able to keep anything down. It's going to be a long night. You guys should go."

"No way." I shook my head. "We'll stay at least until she's settled. And if you have to stay with her overnight, we can go get you some things."

Sawyer managed a tight smile. "I appreciate it. Really. But I keep a bag in the truck for exactly this kind of thing, since this isn't the first time it's happened."

"We will stay," Lars said firmly.

"I…" Sawyer nodded. "Thanks. I'm going to get back there but I'll let you know once she's in a room."

He disappeared down the hall and I rested against Lars. "I feel so bad. I wish there was something I could do."

"Cancer sucks," he murmured, kissing the top of my head.

"It does."

"Is this comfortable for you?" he asked. "Maybe you should sit somewhere with a better chair for your back?"

"I'm okay. But thank you." His concern made my entire body tingle with happiness. Between my father taking off and so many years with Hugh, I'd begun to wonder if there was such a thing as a good, kind man. And now I knew there was.

We sat there until midnight and then I finally got up to stretch and walk around. Lars came with me as we paced the halls and sometime close to one in the morning, I looked at him.

"Babe, maybe you should go home."

He shook his head. "No way. If you stay, I stay."

"You have a game tomorrow and you're very strict about your routine on game day. You need to rest. I'll stay here until we get news about Annie and then I can Uber home."

"No." He met my eyes. "Not happening."

I couldn't help but chuckle. "This isn't the same as when you sneak out while I'm sleeping. This is about Annie, and maybe even about Sawyer. Assuming it's nothing more than dehydration, I'd like him to go get some sleep too, but I'm sure he won't leave her here alone. Maybe if I stay with her, he'll be able to get some rest so he can play. It really upsets Annie when he misses games because of her, so I'm trying to see if I can do something for both of them."

He hesitated. "If Sawyer leaves, then I will go, but until then, I stay with you."

I smiled up at him. "Have I told you lately how awesome you are?"

"Maybe." The lazy-but-oh-so-sexy smile he gave

me warmed me from head to toe. "But maybe you can tell me again."

"You're fucking amazing and I'm crazy about you." I'd just wound my arms around his neck when Sawyer came back to us.

"Hey, guys. I'm so sorry it took this long, but she's finally in a room."

"Did you get any test results?" I asked.

He nodded. "Yeah, she's severely dehydrated and has already gone through two bags of saline. The good news is that she's not really malnourished, just very underweight, so they're going to try and give her some IV nutrients." He let out a long breath and closed his eyes. "Sorry, it's been a long day."

"Why don't you go home?" I suggested gently. "I'll stay with Annie so she's not alone and so there's someone here to make sure the doctors are on top of things. She told me how much it bothers her when you miss games because of her, how you've gotten a reputation for being a prima donna because you're supposedly out if you so much as stub your toe. But that's not really why."

He sighed. "I told her I don't care what the guys think of me, but you see how she is. She's as protective of me as I am of her."

"Exactly. So why don't you guys go? You can rest, go to the morning skate, and then swing by here when you're done. I can Uber home in the morning to shower and change. I don't mind. Really."

Sawyer seemed hesitant. "I don't like to leave her."

"I know, but she won't be alone, and I promise I'll call if anything changes."

"You sure?" His eyes sought mine, almost as if begging me to tell him everything would be okay.

"You're not any good to her if you're exhausted and stressed about the game."

He blew out a breath and nodded. "You're right. Let's go back and tell her the plan."

I turned to Lars. "You go ahead and go. Text me in the morning."

He frowned. "I'll go when Sawyer goes."

I smiled. "All right. Come on. You can both say good night to Annie and then head home."

CHAPTER TWENTY-FOUR

Lars

Wes: Sawyer, I'm sorry to hear Annie is in the hospital. If there's anything you need—seriously, anything—you've got it.

Sawyer: Thanks.

Drew: Cancer fucking sucks. Nina said Annie is a beautiful, kind soul. We're so sorry you guys are going through this. If you need to be with her instead of playing hockey right now, we get it. We've got your back.

Sawyer: I appreciate it.

Boone: Is she at Barnes?

Sawyer: Yes.

Boone: What's her favorite color?

Sawyer: Purple, why?

Boone: Lots of purple flowers heading her way. You guys know what to do.

Sawyer: That'll make her happy. Thank you.

I WAS able to order Annie's flowers from my phone. The bouquet was called "Purple Paradise" and included flowers in every shade of purple. I would have sent her a hundred of them to brighten her day, but I knew the other guys were on it, too. So was everyone in the Mavericks' front office and all of our coaches and trainers. Annie's room would look like a floral shop by late afternoon.

My pregame routine just didn't feel as important today. I sat in the ice bath for more than ten minutes, lost in thoughts of Sawyer and Annie.

It was so fucking unfair that she was dying. Seeing her shrunken body last night had shaken me. It had to be hard as hell for Sawyer to see his beautiful wife slowly being robbed from him.

"Food's here," Nash said as he walked past the tub.

I nodded, standing up and grabbing my towel. The locker room was nearly silent, because we were all down about Annie and none of us knew what to say to Sawyer.

What could anyone say? It didn't matter that any of us were sorry. It wouldn't help anything.

He sat on a bench, elbows on his knees and face buried in his hands. I knew from the way he'd looked at his wife last night that he'd trade places with her in a heartbeat right now, if only he could.

I felt the same way about Sheridan. She'd quickly become the most important person in my life. All my reasons for not wanting a relationship seemed stupid now. It had never been that I didn't want a relationship; I just hadn't met Sheridan yet. With her, there was no choice. I couldn't even look at other women now. She was the one I'd been waiting for, without even knowing it.

As a team, we dressed, listened to Coach Gizzard's pep talk—which was shorter and more subdued than usual—and took the ice.

Sawyer had spoken to Annie on the phone right before we left the locker room. She was feeling a lot better. His whole demeanor had softened during the call, and when he'd hung up, he'd told us that she loved all the flowers and wanted us to win tonight's game. She was watching it from her hospital bed, and Sheridan and Hadley were there with her.

The fans roared as the puck dropped, and it felt a

little surreal. I couldn't stop thinking of Annie, and the way Sawyer's eyes had teared up in the locker room earlier when his wife sent him a picture of the manicure Sheridan had given her.

A teammate had once said in an interview that he loved playing hockey because it made people happy. It gave people an escape when they needed it most and made them feel part of something bigger than themselves. Tonight, I thought of that during every play. I pictured Annie in her hospital bed, proudly watching her husband play in this game.

Tampa didn't have a shot. Every man on our team was playing for Sawyer and Annie Cain tonight, and we won 3–0. Between that and the news that Annie was feeling better, the mood in the locker room was a little lighter after the game.

"You want to go out?" Nash asked me after we'd both showered.

"Not tonight. I'm going over to Sheridan's."

"Pussy."

I ignored his jab, eager to get over to Sheridan's apartment. Not only were we overdue for time alone, I planned to tell her about my autism diagnosis. I wasn't ready to tell anyone else yet, but I wanted Sheridan to know. I didn't think it would change the way she saw me, but still, I was nervous.

I nodded as I passed people I knew on the way

out of the arena, walking quickly so hopefully no one would try to stop me to talk.

I hadn't been inside Sheridan in more than a week; the last thing I felt like doing right now was making small talk. She'd sent me a selfie right after my game of her dressed in lingerie that had my blood pumping hard.

As soon as I opened the door to the players' lot, photographers descended on me. I put my head down as flashes went off and questions were yelled.

"Lars, are you being charged with assault and battery for the attack at the mall?"

"Is it true that Sawyer Cain's wife is terminally ill?"

"Does it bother you that your girlfriend is married?"

My head automatically snapped up, searching out the face of whoever had asked that last question. One photographer in particular was wide eyed, looking like he was in the process of pissing his pants.

"What did you say?" I asked him.

"I'm sure you already know Sheridan Lee is married," he said. "How do you feel about that?"

"She is not. I dare you to say one more word about her." I narrowed my eyes at him and he stared back silently.

I stormed off toward my SUV, fucking done with the vultures that stalked me these days. Didn't they have anything better to do?

I'd made it about twenty feet when someone yelled out from behind me.

"She is married, though! She's been married to Hugh Archman for the past ten years."

I turned to face the group of photographers, who immediately stopped approaching me. A couple of them started backing up.

My instinct was to defend her against the lie. Something stopped me, though. Whichever photographer had just said that had Hugh's name. That gave me pause.

Either they were trying to provoke a reaction, or...I couldn't even wrap my mind around the alternative.

Was it true? Was Hugh not just Sheridan's former agent, but also her husband?

———

"HEY, YOU," Sheridan said, smiling and reaching up to hug me in the doorway of her apartment. "Mmm, you smell amazing."

I hugged her back, thoughts racing through my mind. All of them ended the same way, though.

Would Sheridan really lie to me about being married?

"Annie fell asleep as soon as the game ended," she said, locking the door and then walking toward the kitchen. "We had a nice girls' evening. I've got food if you're hungry; do you want something?"

Beating around the bush wasn't my thing. I had to know, so I just came right out with it.

"Are you married?"

The happiness melted away from Sheridan's expression. She locked eyes with me from across the room and we just stared at each other for a couple seconds.

She walked into the living room area, looking ill. My heart raced as I waited for her to say no.

Say no, Sheridan. *Fucking tell me the woman I love isn't married to another man.*

"What did you hear?" she finally asked.

"Yes or no?" I demanded.

"Yes."

She didn't flinch or look away as she said it. The ache in my gut felt like I'd just been punched.

"You are Hugh's wife?" I asked, incredulous. "And you never told me?"

"I was planning to tell you last night."

I scoffed. "Bullshit."

"Lars, I was."

Narrowing my eyes, I asked, "What about all the times you could have told me? The night we met?" I ran a hand through my hair, fury building in my chest. "I have been sleeping with a married woman."

"Stop saying that!" Sheridan came toward me, her eyes flashing angrily. "We've been legally separated for two years."

I felt a spark of hope as I asked, "What does that mean? Are you married or divorced?"

She hesitated before saying, "We aren't divorced."

"What are you, then?" I demanded.

"We are married but legally separated. We haven't been able to agree on a divorce settlement. I'm working on it as fast as—"

"Fuck!"

I stormed toward her apartment door, needing to put distance between us. I was still reeling from my diagnosis and from Annie being so sick, and now this? My girlfriend was married, but hadn't thought to let me know.

"We're legally separated," she repeated. "Lars, you don't know how hard he's made it. I want this divorce to go through more than anything, but he won't—"

"You should have told me," I said, unable to look at her.

"You're right. I should have."

"I am a fool."

"Don't say that, you didn't—"

I turned to lock eyes with her, fire running through my veins.

"A photographer asked me about it after the game. I said you are not married. I look like a fool now."

She hung her head. "I'm sorry. I never meant for this to happen. I just sold my company to Vanessa and I'm donating as much as my attorney allows me to charity and giving as much as I'm allowed to my mom. I've offered Hugh half of everything many times, but he won't take it. I'm hoping that when he sees our shared assets getting lower and lower, he'll realize I'm willing to give away everything if that's what it takes."

I looked away again, so pissed off I could hardly see straight. My life had taken a nosedive off a cliff in a matter of an hour.

"You lied to me."

"I guess if lying by omission is a thing…then yes, I did." Her voice broke with emotion. "I'm ashamed, Lars. Ashamed of everything Hugh has done to me and ashamed I married him."

The anguish in her tone tore at my heart. I'd fallen in love with her, and a part of me wanted so badly to protect and comfort her.

I couldn't, though. My mother had raised me to be honest and hardworking. She loathed deceit, and I did, too. I liked to think that if my father could see the man I'd become, he'd be proud of me. But a man who'd carried on a relationship with another man's wife was nothing to be proud of.

"I cannot do this, Sheridan," I said, my heart cracking in two as I looked down at the floor.

"What do you mean? You can't do what? Our *relationship?*"

She was crying, and I knew I'd break if I looked at her. I was back under the pile of rocks, but this time, the rocks were larger and heavier. The weight was oppressive, like I couldn't escape.

"I cannot be with someone who is not honest with me."

I unlocked the front door and threw it open, wanting to bolt but waiting to see if she had anything left to say.

"Fine," she finally said, her voice tearful. "I'll never be with a man who doesn't want me again. Fuck you for making me believe you were better than that."

Without another word, I slammed the door behind me, taking the stairs instead of the elevator. This was a kind of betrayal I'd never experienced. All I wanted was to be alone.

Tonight.
Tomorrow.
Forever.

CHAPTER TWENTY-FIVE

Sheridan

With a heavy sigh, I turned away from the bathroom mirror after a brief glance. I didn't look like a woman who'd ever made a living on my looks. My skin was a wreck and dark circles drew attention to my puffy eyes. Was there enough concealer in the world to cover up the devastation on my face?

I didn't know how I was going to get through the first day of Vanessa owning the company. It felt like I'd been carrying the weight of the world on my shoulders with everything going on with Hugh, but I'd had Lars's massive shoulders to lean on. Now I had no one.

On top of everything else, Thanksgiving was in

two days, and I was coming up short on things to be thankful for at the moment.

God, this sucked.

I managed to make myself presentable and walked to work, since the fresh air was supposed to be good for me. I hadn't felt so lost and alone in more than two years, since the night when the accountant I'd hired had told me how much money Hugh had been funneling out of our joint accounts. My suspicions about his financial dishonesty confirmed, I'd gone home early and caught him with a petite blond who'd been giving him a golden shower. I'd been mortified, humiliated, and heart-broken to know that my husband was that much of an asshole. I hadn't even liked Hugh anymore at that point though. This time around was much worse because I was still crazy in love with Lars.

Not anymore, I told myself firmly as I walked into the building.

"Ms. Lee." One of the security guards at the front desk was staring at me. "Good, um, morning."

"Good morning, Chet." I frowned at the weird look on his face but got on the elevator.

I really didn't want to be here today but Vanessa and I needed to show a united front so the staff wouldn't panic, so I had to be here for at least half a day. Maybe I'd cut out early and head over to my mom's when I was done. I could pack a bag and spend the weekend there, let her spoil me a little after I told her about Lars.

"Hey." Vanessa was standing there when I got off the elevator, her brows lowered with concern.

"Hi."

"I don't want you to get upset. Just go home and let me handle everything."

"What are you talking about?" I asked in confusion, frowning at her.

Her eyes met mine. "I'm on it, okay? I promise. But you don't want to be here right now."

"Vanessa, what's going on? You need to tell me, and then I'll decide if I want to be here."

Dread swirled through my chest as she hesitated.

"The video," she finally said.

"What video?"

"Sheridan. The *video*."

I narrowed my eyes and then froze. "Oh my God."

"Let me handle it, okay? Everything is going to be okay."

"How?" I managed, my voice a little shaky.

"I don't know, but we'll find out. Just go home and—"

"Where?" I cried. "Everywhere? Did he release it online?"

"We don't know yet."

"Oh, God." *We.* Who did that mean?

"Please, just—"

"I'm not going home!" I hissed, tears welling in my eyes.

I turned toward my office.

"Sheridan, you don't need to see it!" Vanessa said, hurrying after me. "Really. Just go home and get a massage or something. I'll handle things here at the office."

I walked into my office and turned on my computer, Vanessa on my heels.

"Why are you doing this to yourself?" she asked. "Come on, it's not worth getting upset over. I'll—"

"It's not worth getting upset over?" I met her gaze as pain and humiliation shot through me. "Have you seen the damn video? Of me and Hugh—" I stopped abruptly. I knew every second of that fucking video and it haunted me.

"It was eleven years ago, hon." Vanessa perched on the side of my desk. "No one is going to think much of it."

"Hugh videotaped me without my permission!" I said, clenching my fists. "And he's held this fucking video over my head for years. This is the whole reason I haven't been able to divorce him, because he won't give up that video and I've been afraid he'd—"

My hands shook and my vision blurred as I sank down into my office chair.

"Right, but if it's out there now, you can't change it, so let me do damage control while you go home and relax. Freaking out here at the office isn't going to help anything."

"Burying my head in the sand won't either."

"You trusted me with your whole company. Why don't you trust me to handle this?"

"It's not about trust." I swiped at my eyes. "What if it was you in that video? How would you feel knowing the whole world is going to see you like that?"

"We don't know the extent of it yet. Let me dig into this, okay?"

"I'm not going home." I clicked on my keyboard and my biggest nightmare was looking me in the face. Right on the home page of the company's intranet.

"What the fuck..." I stared at the still photo in horror. Even without clicking on the video, I knew what viewers would see and just the thought of it turned my stomach. Thank God I hadn't eaten anything yet today or I would have heaved up my breakfast. Fury raced through my veins for the second time, bringing tears to my eyes, but I was stronger than this. I'd been just shy of my seventeenth birthday when that video had been taken, and Hugh was the asshole for taking advantage of me that way. I'd let him, of course, but back then I'd been sure he would be the only guy who'd ever love me.

"Is this just on the intranet, or is it posted publicly?" I asked. "Did Hugh hack us somehow?"

"So far, we haven't found it posted publicly, but we're calling in some IT support to help us investigate more thoroughly, and to get it off the intranet. This just blew up a little bit ago."

I nodded numbly.

"I called a meeting with the executive staff," Vanessa said after a moment. "I really think you need to go home."

"No." I swiped at my eyes and stood up, absently turning off the computer. "This is still my company and I should explain."

"Sheridan." Vanessa crossed her arms and gave me an imploring look. "You're the one who taught me to separate my head from my heart when it comes to business. You're all heart right now. It's not going to help anything. Let me handle this."

She was right. I hated it, but she was right. I would have said the same thing if the tables were turned.

"Okay," I conceded. "I'll go home."

I CRIED a lot more when I got back to my apartment, but when I was finally cried out, I called Marian and updated her. Then I packed a bag, threw it in the back of my Mercedes, and headed for my mother's. She lived in an upscale suburb of St. Louis, in a gated community where we both felt safe. The house was in her name and paid for, and the front gate understood that Hugh was never, ever allowed in.

I pulled into her driveway and took a breath. It had been a brutal day and now that I was away from my apartment, the office, and the city itself, I already felt a little calmer. I got my bag out of the back and wheeled it up to the front porch. I had a key, but I liked to knock, just in case, and Mom answered the door in surprise.

"Sheridan? Hi, honey!" She reached out and hugged me.

To my horror, the tears came right back, as if I hadn't been crying for almost twenty-four hours at this point, but I couldn't seem to help myself.

"Oh, honey, what's going on?" Mom pulled my suitcase inside and kept one arm around my waist as she led me into the family room. "Sit. I'm getting you some water." I buried my face in my hands and tried to figure out how I'd gotten to this point.

I'd lost Lars, my company, and my dignity in a span of twenty-four hours. Even though the sale to Vanessa was temporary, it still scared me to know I didn't own Sheri Lee right now. We'd been closer than sisters for more than a decade but it was still uncomfortable for me to hand over the business I'd poured my soul—and a substantial amount of money—into.

"Here. Blow your nose. What's going on?" Mom sat next to me, handing me tissues and a bottle of water.

"You have no idea what a clusterfuck my life is right now," I said mournfully.

"Well, I kind of do."

"No, you really don't. This goes way beyond that abusive prick I can't seem to get rid of."

"Is it Lars?"

I nodded, dabbing at my eyes with a tissue as I told her what had happened.

"You never told him you were married?" She grimaced. "I don't blame him for being mad, but to break things off…he'll probably cool off, you know? Did you tell him the things Hugh used to do to you? The things he made you do? I think that would explain a lot."

I shook my head. "No. I can't even think about those things, much less say them out loud to Lars."

"But if you love him and he loves you, you should be able to talk to him about anything."

"Well, after last night, I'm pretty sure he doesn't even like me, much less love me."

She took my hand and squeezed it. "You're smart and beautiful and successful. There are lots of men out there."

"Not like him." I rested my chin on my hand.

"Give him a few days to cool off and then call him. Maybe you two can talk it out."

"I don't think so. But really, as much as it hurts to lose him, he's not my main concern." I told her about selling the company to Vanessa and the upcoming court battle with Hugh.

"Fucking Hugh." Mom tapped her foot impatiently. "I'd really like to smack him into the middle of next week."

"I don't know whether to just give him whatever he wants or play hardball and tell him to go fuck himself. At this point, he's already cost me the thing I loved most, which was Lars. I don't know if I'm coming or going right now."

"You need to get your fancy lawyer to fuck him up the ass without lube."

I nearly choked on the sip of water I was taking.

"I'm serious, Sheridan. He's going to get half of the marital assets; that's just the way it is, but going forward? Fuck him. Do whatever you have to do to beat him at his own game."

"I'm trying, but so far, nothing is going according to plan. It's like he knows what I'm going to do before I do it. It's pissing me off that he's always a step ahead of me."

"I've never known you to be a quitter." She smoothed my hair back. "You've kicked and clawed your way to the top, even with a deadbeat dad, an abusive husband, and a mom who couldn't support you the way she wanted to."

"You've always been there for me, Mom."

"And I always will be. I just wish I could be more help."

"Thanks, Mom." I had no solutions, but I wasn't going down without a fight. The problem was, I didn't know how much more fight I had left.

CHAPTER TWENTY-SIX

Lars

Mavericks Group Text

Wes: Happy Thanksgiving, guys. It's the first one without Ben and Lauren, so it's a bittersweet day for me. It's been almost a year since we lost them, and I'm grateful to every one of you for your support. You've rallied around me, Hadley, and the kids, and I'll never forget it. If you're not coming over for Thanksgiving, have a great day off wherever you are. And if you are coming, get your ass over here. The bar is stocked and ready!

"I made this for you," Annalise said, grinning and holding up a mass of multicolored feathers.

"Wow." I took it and nodded with appreciation. "Thank you."

"Aren't you going to put it on?"

I studied it, stepping inside since I'd literally been standing in the doorway of Wes and Hadley's home when Annalise handed me my gift.

"Where should I put it?" I asked Annalise, stumped.

She laughed and said, "On your head, silly. We made pilgrim and Indian hats at school and you're an Indian. I made pilgrim hats for me and Sheridan."

My heart sank as she ran to a nearby table and picked up two hats made of construction paper, complete with yellow square buckles.

"You did a great job," I told her. "Sheridan won't be here today, though."

"What?" She made a grumpy face. "You're supposed to bring your girlfriend to Thanksgiving, you know."

"Hey, peanut, go help in the kitchen," Wes said, rescuing me.

"But I'm helping Lars with his hat."

"You can help him later. Go." He hiked a thumb in the direction of the kitchen.

"But Mommy said the best way I can help is to leave her alone."

Wes smiled at that. "Ask her if you can please have a job, okay?"

She nodded glumly and reached for my hand. "Let's go, Lars."

Wes arched his brows, amused. "Lars is staying with me. Now beat it because today is the first day Santa gets serious about the nice and naughty lists for Christmas."

Annalise's eyes widened and she took off. Wes shook his head and smiled at me.

"Let's get you a drink, man," he said.

We walked to the room on the main level of their home that he'd turned into a bar and lounge area, complete with a large TV, a couple leather couches and matching club chairs, and a wooden bar that ran along the wall adjacent to the TV. This was the area the guys would be congregating in now that it was too cold for cookouts.

"You have become a good father," I said to him as he drew me a beer from one of the taps behind the bar.

"I don't know about that," he said, "but thanks."

"You are good with them," I assured him. "If I am ever a father, I want to be like you."

Wes passed me the glass and said, "Thank you. That really means a lot."

I took a long sip of my beer. "I hope that keg is full, because I am going to be drinking more than my share today."

"I heard you and Sheridan broke up. You okay?"

I shrugged. "Not really. I had just found out I had autism and then I found out she'd been lying to me. It has been a very shitty week."

"Oh wow." Wes came around the bar and sat down on a stool next to me. "How did you find out about the autism?"

I hadn't planned to tell Wes—or anyone—but the words had just come out. And as much as I'd thought I didn't want to discuss it with anyone, it felt good to admit the truth out loud.

"I had testing done by a psychiatrist."

"Because of what Keegan said?"

I nodded.

Wes frowned and shook his head. "Fuck that fucker, Lars. None of us give a shit what he says about anything. He thinks I'm a shitty captain? I'd like to see him do better."

"He was right about me, though."

"So what? You've made it pretty damn far in life just the way you are. I'd trust you with my life, or my kids' lives."

"Thank you."

Wes nodded toward my glass and let out a single note of laughter. "You've already finished half your beer. You weren't kidding, were you?"

"No."

"Well, I bought a couple of kegs, so drink up. But you're staying in our guest room if you do."

"I miss Sheridan."

"Do you want to talk about it?"

"The more I drink, the more I'll want to talk about it," I cracked.

"Well, if it makes you feel any better, lying is a hard limit for me, too."

I looked over both shoulders to make sure no one else was in earshot before I said, "She is *married*, Wes."

His brows shot up. "What? How?"

"She said she was planning to tell me, but I found out when a photographer asked me about it."

"Wait, seriously…how? How could someone as famous as Sheridan have a husband at home that you knew nothing about?"

I shrugged. "They do not live together because they are legally separated."

Wes gave me an incredulous look. "Way to bury the lede, dude."

"What does that mean?"

"It means you left out the most important part. Being legally separated is a lot different than being married. Is their divorce pending?"

"She says she has been trying to get a divorce for more than a year, but he will not cooperate. He used to be her agent, since she was a teenager and she started modeling."

Wes nodded knowingly. "So she's his meal ticket."

"What is meal ticket?"

"Sorry," he said. "It means he relies on her for his income. He doesn't have his own gig to make money. I'm sure he doesn't want to let that go."

"He should have to," I said, aggravated. "The law should not allow him to just not give her a divorce."

"I don't think the law is set up that way, actually. I think if one person stalls long enough, a judge can decide it. Maybe there's more to the story than you know."

"Probably," I said, finishing my beer. "More she should have told me."

"But if her estranged husband is that dirtbag you punched in that video, she's probably ashamed of ever marrying him."

"She said that," I admitted. "And he is very strange. Can I get more beer?"

Wes laughed and clapped me on the shoulder.

"You don't need to ask. Help yourself to anything. And try to see where Sheridan's coming from, okay? She's good for you and I really like her."

I nodded and rose from my barstool.

"And Lars?"

"What?"

"Prepare yourself, because when Hadley finds out you broke up with Sheridan, she's going to have some choice words for you."

"PLEASE TELL me I didn't hear what I think I just heard," Hadley said to me a couple hours later.

We were standing at the kitchen sink, where she was washing pots and pans and then passing them to me to be rinsed and dried.

"I cannot be in a relationship with a woman just because you like being friends with her," I said sternly.

Hadley dropped the pan she was scrubbing into the large stainless steel sink, and a few soap bubbles flew up in the air.

"Lars, I'll be friends with her either way," she said, glaring at me as she put a wet hand on her hip. "I want you to be in a relationship with her because she's positive, sweet and compassionate and I've never seen you happier than you were with her."

My heart raced nervously because she was right about all those things. And following Wes, Nash and Drew and Boone had all told me I'd acted rashly by breaking up with Sheridan over finding out she was married but legally separated. I didn't like being filled with self-doubt while surrounded by my teammates and their families.

"Let's just wash the dishes," I said. "I have talked about this enough today."

"You clearly *have not*," Hadley said, shaking her head. "Or else you'd be running out my front door without even grabbing your coat to beg that woman to forgive you for being such a callous, stubborn, overreactive jackass."

"I did not ask for your opinion."

"Yeah, well, you're my friend, so I don't need your permission to tell you when you screw up spectacularly."

Glowering, I set down the dish towel I was holding and said, "I found out she was married from one of the crazy photographers who follow me everywhere. She never told me, Hadley. She let me be humiliated."

Hadley shrugged. "And she owes you an apology

for that. But have some compassion, Lars. It sounds like this guy is an absolute maniac. You'd known him for about ten seconds when you punched him in the face, remember?"

"Pie?" Nash interjected, sticking a pumpkin pie between me and Hadley. "Who wants some pie?"

"We're having a discussion, Nash," Hadley said. "If you want to be helpful, grab a dish towel. Otherwise, leave us alone."

"I want some pie," I muttered.

"Can we finish the dishes first?" Hadley asked.

"If we talk about something besides Sheridan."

Hadley stiffened, reaching back into the dishwater. "That's fine. I've said everything I need to say."

"Dude," Nash said under his breath. "When a woman tells you something is fine, it is so not fine."

"Really, Nash?" Hadley challenged. "Advice on women from the guy who licks senior citizens' boots and hasn't had a real girlfriend in years?"

"What the hell, Wes?" Nash yelled out, aggravated. "I guess nothing is private around here, is it?"

"I tell my wife everything," Wes replied, talking loudly from the dining room.

"Are they talking about Mistress Sandra?" Boone called out from the living room. "Because I posted about that on Reddit."

"I hate you all," Nash muttered.

As Hadley passed a clean pot to me for rinsing, she turned to Nash. "But I bet you agree that Sheridan is the best thing that ever happened to Lars and it was a huge mistake to break up with her, right?"

"Oh, yeah. I totally agree with that."

I threw the towel I was holding at Nash's face and said, "You dry the dishes. I'm going to get a drink. And some pie."

"Hey, will you cut me a piece of pumpkin?" Nash asked.

"No."

I skipped the drink and just got a piece of pie, sitting down in the only open seat in the living room, which was a spot on the couch next to Annie.

"How's the pie?" she asked me.

"Very good. Can I get you a piece?"

"No." She smiled. "I've already eaten more today than I have in the last week. It was so good, though."

She wore one of her wigs, and her red sweater hung on her small frame. But there was more color in her cheeks than there had been the first time I met her. Sawyer was on her other side, their clasped hands resting in Annie's lap.

"I'm sorry about you and Sheridan," Annie said softly.

I gave her a wary look, not in the mood for another lecture. But all I saw in her eyes was sincerity.

"Thank you," I said shortly.

"You're a very good man, Lars."

If she hadn't used my name, I would have thought Annie was talking to someone else. Pretty much every other person in the house today thought I was the worst.

"I don't know about that," I muttered.

"Cancer is a bitch, but it's also taught me a lot. I know for sure we all make mistakes, and sometimes forgiving ourselves and moving on is our only choice if we want peace. I won't bore you with a thousand life lessons, but that one is really important. You're a good man and you don't have to be perfect to be worthy, just remember that."

"What makes you think I am a good man?"

Annie smiled. "Everything I've seen and heard about you, and also the fact that you're wearing that hat."

I'd forgotten Annalise's feather hat had been perched on my head for the past couple of hours.

"Thank you, Annie," I said, just as Sawyer leaned closer to say something to his wife.

I was even more miserable than before. My

stomach churned, and I lowered my plate of pie to my lap, unable to finish it.

Annie was absolutely right—you didn't have to be perfect to be worthy. It was true for me, and it was also true for Sheridan.

I'd made a terrible mistake.

CHAPTER TWENTY-SEVEN

Sheridan

GETTING BACK TO MY COLD, empty apartment on Monday was a stark reminder of the wasteland my life had become. No light, no laughter, no anything. I'd done my best not to mope over the weekend, hanging out with Mom and a few of my cousins, but deep down I'd just wanted to curl up in bed and cry myself to sleep.

The only good news, if you could call it that, was that the video of me and Hugh having sex had only been released on the company's intranet, so it hadn't gone completely public. Vanessa had it taken down within an hour of it going live, but knowing that everyone I worked with had undoubtedly seen me doing…*those things*…made me shudder with distaste. Bile rose in my throat and I took a moment to breathe.

When I was finally in control again, I started to unpack, throwing in a load of laundry and wondering if I should call Vanessa to tell her I was home. We usually talked every day, but I'd needed time with family and to be away from everything that represented my shit show of a life right now. I'd told her I would call her when I got back into the city, but I didn't feel like talking to anyone. Besides, she was at the office and everything about the office made me uncomfortable right now.

I'd placed an online order for groceries yesterday and it had just arrived, so I mindlessly put it all away. I was still reeling from everything that had happened. It had barely been a week, but I missed Lars so much it was physically painful. I missed the feeling of his strong arms around me, the way he palmed my ass whenever he had a chance, and more than anything, the quiet strength he exuded. Everything about Lars made me feel safe. Wanted. *Loved.*

How had I fucked up so badly?

My phone rang and I looked down, ready to send the call to voice mail, when I saw it was Barney.

"Ms. Lee, there's a gentleman here to see you—Mr. Katzenburg."

Lenny.

Great.

"Ask him if this can wait until tomorrow," I said quietly.

"He says it's urgent, Ms. Lee."

"All right." I got up and walked to the door warily, unlocking it as I waited for him to come up the elevator.

"Hi, Sheridan." He stepped off the elevator and met my gaze directly. "I'm sorry to bother you at home but this is extremely urgent."

"Come on in." I motioned him inside and shut the door behind us. Lenny was the second person I'd hired after Vanessa. I'd met him at a business conference where he'd given a speech about the shortage of women in IT, how it was a male-dominated field but that as a part-time professor of computer science at one of the local universities, he hoped to change that. I'd liked his directness, his sense of humor, and his incredible knowledge about IT in the business world. I'd approached him a week later with an offer he hadn't been able to refuse and that had been just about a year ago.

"How are you?" he asked as he settled in a chair in my living room.

"I've been better." I cocked my head slightly. "What's going on?"

"Vanessa asked me to look into how the video got onto our system, and to strengthen our system against another hack like that."

"I'm sure Hugh hired someone to do it; he's not tech savvy enough to have done it himself."

The look in Lenny's eyes when he met my gaze worried me.

"I can confirm it wasn't Hugh," he said.

I sat down and put my palms on my thighs, nodding. "He wouldn't have let it be traced back to him. Will we ever be able to find out where this hack originated?"

Lenny had dark circles beneath his eyes. Everything about his expression was weary. He'd probably been working around the clock on this since it happened—even on Thanksgiving.

"Hey," I said softly. "I know hacks can come from other countries and be just about impossible to trace. Only one person had access to that video, my agent and I know he was ultimately responsible. Don't keep running yourself into the ground trying to figure out exactly where it came from. We'll probably never know."

"That's the thing, though, Sheridan—I do know."

"You do?" Anticipation swirled in my stomach.

"I'm sorry. I hate having to tell you this, but you

need to know the truth." He paused. "It was uploaded from Vanessa's IP address."

"Vanessa's?" I would have laughed if he didn't look dead serious. "Are you sure?"

"I double- and triple-checked. There's no mistake. She signed in to the back end of our site and uploaded it from her personal laptop at exactly 6:54 that morning. Her computer required her fingerprint in order to sign in. She either posted it herself or she allowed someone to by telling them how to log on to her computer."

I was too stunned to move, my heart hammering painfully against my ribs. It didn't make any sense. Why would my best friend do that to me?

"You're one-hundred-percent certain?" I asked Lenny, my voice breaking.

"I am. I'm sorry."

This might have been almost as painful as losing Lars. Except I'd known Vanessa longer and had trusted her with everything. I'd fucking sold her my company, thinking she'd keep it safe.

"Oh my God." I got up and started to pace, hands on my hips.

"So I decided to do a little more digging, just to see if I could find anything else and…it's not good."

"What do you mean?" I whirled around.

"I found legal documents on her computer…

correspondence with an attorney…" He coughed as he handed me a stack of papers. "It's *a lot*."

My hand shook slightly as I took the papers from him.

My vision blurred as the depth of Vanessa's betrayal hit me right between the eyes.

"She's already done the paperwork to have everything put in her name. Not just the business, but all the assets, your holdings, everything."

"Son of a bitch." I hissed.

"And the last page, well, you need to brace yourself."

"Fuck." I flipped to the last page and I must have gotten pale because Lenny was instantly at my side, nudging me into a chair.

"I know," he said. "I fucking know. I came as quickly as I could. To warn you."

"Did you hack her computer?"

"Yes." His eyes met mine.

"What else? Tell me everything."

He laid it out for me in excruciating detail and all I could do was listen as my world crumbled around me.

Vanessa had done this.

My best friend had betrayed me in the most awful way possible.

And the hits just kept coming.

I WALKED to work in the morning because I needed the time to get myself together. I hadn't slept last night. I'd talked with Lenny until nearly eight thirty, and then spent the next several hours on the phone with Marian. I'd called my mother to warn her, just in case Vanessa tried to get any information out of her since they'd always been close, and then I'd gone up to my studio to draw. I'd been hurt, humiliated, angry, frustrated, and so many other emotions it was hard to articulate the pain I'd been in. Sleep would have been impossible, so I'd painted, giving my hands something to do while my brain raced on overdrive and my heart shattered into tiny pieces.

I'd never dreamed Vanessa was buyable. Hugh had gotten to her just like he'd gotten to almost everyone else in my life, and there was nothing left for me to do. Nothing left for me to fight for.

Fuck Vanessa, I thought to myself. I didn't know what she thought she was doing, but I was going to find out. I'd considered bringing Flynn with me today but had opted against it. According to Lenny, I had a lot of loyal employees who would have my back, no matter what. Of course, that's what I'd thought about Vanessa too. Mostly, I just wanted answers.

I got off the elevator and noticed Lenny standing in the lobby with Nellie. Nellie had two cups of coffee in her hand and I managed a shaky smile, since I knew one was for me.

"Hi, Ms. Lee." She gave me a nervous smile as she handed me the coffee. "I got your favorite."

"Thank you," I replied, accepting the coffee from her.

"They're having a meeting," she whispered.

"I'm late," Lenny said, shrugging.

"Go on ahead," I said to him. "I'll be there in a minute."

"You sure?"

"It's fine. Go."

I looked at Nellie. "Could you do me a favor, please?"

"Of course."

"Would you start packing up my office for me? Mostly personal things."

Her eyes rounded. "Are you…?"

"Please just do that for me. Okay?"

"Yes, ma'am." She turned and hurried in the other direction.

A meeting. One I hadn't been invited to.

Bitch.

I took a sip of coffee and let the flavor permeate my tastebuds.

Everyone in that room had most likely seen me having sex by now, which was humiliating in and of itself, but that Vanessa had orchestrated it just burned. I was beyond hurt at this point because hurt happened when you cared about someone. Like Lars. His rejection hurt because it was the end of a relationship that I'd messed up. But Vanessa? The shit she'd done had come from a place of hate, and I wouldn't cry over someone who obviously hated me.

I walked down the hall and didn't hesitate to push open the conference room door.

The sight in front of me was so much worse than what I'd envisioned, and the air left my lungs for a moment.

"Well, hello, darling." Hugh's smug smile made me want to puke. "So good of you to come congratulate me. I've just been made the newest president of Sheri Lee."

"You fucking bitch." The words came out before I could stop them as I faced Vanessa. "I want to see you in the hallway. *Now.*"

She arched a brow. "I don't take orders from you. In fact, you're not even supposed to be here. You're nothing more than a consultant, and this is an *executive* staff meeting."

"So you want to do this here?"

"Do what?"

"Why would you do this?" I asked quietly, my eyes never leaving hers. "After all I've done for you—"

"What you've done for me?!" She got to her feet, slamming her hands down on the table as she leaned forward, a snarl on her face. "Throwing me crumbs every time you made a million dollars? Millions of dollars you don't even deserve! You've never worked hard a day in your life. Everything just fucking comes to you. Modeling jobs, awards, endorsements —and all because you're fucking fat? It's disgusting. *You're* disgusting."

Though my stomach was churning with embarrassment, I'd die before I let her see it. "And you think you can run this company like I can?" I almost laughed at her, but I was too pissed.

"I've *been* running it!" she snapped.

"You've been doing what I tell you to do. You haven't had a creative idea of your own since—oh, I don't know…never."

"Fuck you." Vanessa's face was a mask of fury and I couldn't believe I'd never seen this side of her before.

"Come on, love, this isn't the time or the place." Hugh put a gentle hand on hers and it suddenly clicked.

"Oh. My. God. You're fucking him?" I threw my

head back and laughed derisively. "That's what this is all about? Talk about disgusting."

"Get out!" Vanessa shrieked. "Get out of my conference room right fucking now! Security!" She was screeching, and I just watched her, waiting to see if anyone would dare to try and walk me out of here. Technically, she couldn't fire me for six months, no matter what. Marian had seen to it. So although I had no desire to be here another second, I'd suck it up just to piss her off.

"I will fucking kill you!" Vanessa yelled, coming toward me.

"Babe, stop." Hugh grabbed her hand. "This is what she wants. If you lay a hand on her, we lose everything. Remember that."

Vanessa was breathing hard, her face red. "I've taken everything from you, you fat bitch. Your husband, more than half of your money, your company, and even that retarded boyfriend of yours —I have *everything* and you have nothing. How does it feel, Sheridan? Huh? How the fuck does it feel to be the one with nothing?"

I shook my head in disbelief. How had I missed this level of hatred and jealousy? If she'd wanted Hugh, I would have happily let her have him years ago, but the sad thing was that deep down I knew she didn't really want him—she just wanted to hurt me.

"At least I have my dignity, which is more than I can say for you."

"Dignity?" Vanessa's voice got even more shrill. "When that fucking video goes viral, you won't be able to look anyone in the eye ever again. And that's next. I'm nowhere near through with you, Sheridan."

My blood ran cold but there was no help for it now.

"Fuck you, Vanessa. See you in court, Hugh."

I turned and stalked out of the room.

I took an Uber home because I was carrying the box of personal items Nellie cleared out of my office. I was crying again, dabbing my eyes with a tissue as the driver watched me worriedly in the mirror. Even though I hadn't let her see it, Vanessa had truly taken everything from me. Releasing that video would be the end for me professionally. People would eventually forget but I'd probably never get another modeling job or be able to show my face in public again without being the fat chick who'd done unspeakable things on camera at sixteen.

I was so angry and frustrated I didn't even see

him standing there until I practically ran into his solid chest.

"Sheridan. What is wrong?" Lars gently reached out to lift my chin.

"I...nothing." I swallowed. "What are you doing here?"

"Can we talk?"

"N-no. I...can't right now." Tears were spilling over faster than I could stop them and Lars caught me around the waist.

"What is it? What happened?"

I looked up into his clear blue eyes and wished desperately that I could throw myself in his arms and tell him everything. But he'd betrayed me too. Not like Vanessa and Hugh, but he'd left me when I needed him most. And for me, that was unforgiveable.

"You lost the right to ask what's wrong," I said, stepping out of his embrace even though I wanted him to hold me more than I wanted to breathe.

"I am sorry. I... please don't cry." He looked miserable. "Please. Can't we just talk?"

I shook my head, almost losing my footing as I wrenched open the door to my building.

"Lady, your box!" The Uber driver was coming toward me and I was crying so hard I couldn't see.

"I'll take it." I heard Lars talking to him and then he was holding the door open for me.

"Miss Lee?" Barney was eyeing Lars suspiciously.

"Just give Barney the box," I whispered through my tears. "Please. If you care about me at all, just leave me alone. I don't have another fight in me today."

"Sheridan…" Lars's voice was a plea, but he didn't follow me inside.

He was still standing there watching me as the elevator doors closed. And I slid down the wall to the floor, sobbing uncontrollably.

CHAPTER TWENTY-EIGHT

Lars

Mavericks Group Text

Drew: Anyone else thinking about the fact that we're playing Nashville tonight and Keegan will be on the ice for the first time since he became enemy number one?

Nash: It may have crossed my mind.

Lars: I am looking forward to it.

Wes: Can we handle this shit with no major misconducts?

Boone: Doubtful. But it'll be worth it, Cap.

"Want some?" Nash asked, holding out a pack of gum.

I shook my head and went back to staring out the window of the bus that was taking us to the arena in Nashville. I hated gum, and I hated Nashville.

Right now, I kind of hated everything because I was so down and out over losing Sheridan. But even when I was in a good mood, I hated both gum and Nashville.

This city was too much for me. I preferred playing as far north as possible. Canada was my favorite. I loved mountains and trees and cold air. When I retired, I hoped to own a place in either Canada or Sweden.

I'd be living there alone, obviously. My one and only attempt at a real relationship had blown up in my face. I wasn't sure the dust would ever fully settle.

I'd hoped to apologize to Sheridan and start over. I'd let my inner caveman take over and overreacted to finding out she was married, but separated, from Hugh. The thought of her married to another man had made me too furious to see straight. And Hugh, no less? What the hell? He was the worst kind of human.

She'd been upset about something when I'd seen her outside her building yesterday, and it was eating me up inside that I didn't know what was wrong.

When I'd seen her agonized expression, my reason for being there hadn't mattered so much anymore.

I'd just wanted to be there for her. And that was big for me, because I'd never truly wanted to be there for any woman before.

"Hey," Nash said as we pulled into the arena parking lot. "You want me to order some food?"

"Yes. But not pasta this time. The last time you ordered pasta, it tasted like ass."

He gave me a look. "You're pretty picky for a guy who's being waited on, just sayin'."

"It was disgusting. Do you like to eat ass?"

He smirked at me. "Actually…"

"Fuck you."

"How many years are you going to be in a bad mood over Sheridan, just so I know?"

"A long time. Before I met her, you were the person I spent most of my free time with. You think I want to go back to that?"

Nash scoffed. "Dude, you are just a straight-up comedian lately. I never forced you to spend time with me."

"I don't mean I hate spending time with you. I just prefer Sheridan."

"So try harder to get her back instead of just pouting like a fucking baby."

I glared at him. "Do you think if I knew how to do that, I would do it?"

"It's *don't* you think if I knew how to do that, I would."

"I don't fucking care; you know what I mean."

"Give it a rest, you two," Beau said from the aisle across from ours as the driver parked the bus and people started standing up. "You sound like two grumpy old farts arguing about nothing in a nursing home."

"Fuck you," I muttered.

"This is going to be a super pleasant trip for all of us, isn't it?" Nash said. "Like being on the road with a grizzly bear who just had his honey stash stolen."

"What am I supposed to do?" I asked Nash.

"You mean to get her back?"

I narrowed my eyes at him, considering violence. "Yes. Enough with your bear bullshit. You said I need to try harder, so what do I do?"

Wes laughed and turned around from the seat in front of us. "Step one—don't take advice on women from Nash. He once broke up with a woman over some Nutty Bars."

"No, she broke up with me over it," Nash argued.

"How does that even happen?" Beau asked as we started filing off the bus.

"I left a box of Nutty Bars in the back seat of her

new car. Complete accident. They melted all over everything. I offered to have the car professionally cleaned, but she said I was too much of a child and she dumped me."

"That is not the whole story," I reminded him.

Nash rolled his eyes. "It's most of it."

"Bullshit." Wes scoffed. "She asked you if you took the Nutty Bars out of her car before they melted all over the place, and you said you did."

"I planned to," Nash said, shrugging.

"But you were playing a video game," I reminded him. "And you didn't want to stop playing."

"That may be true," Nash said, shrugging again.

Wes stopped walking and looked down at his phone screen. "Oh, shit."

"What?" Beau asked.

Wes looked over at me, and then back down at his phone screen.

"What?" I asked, stopping and walking over to him.

"A video Sheridan is in has gone viral. Hadley texted me to give me a heads-up."

"A video?" I scrunched up my forehead in confusion. "She is a model. She is in many videos."

"Yeah, this is…different."

"Shit," Nash muttered.

"It's a sex video, Lars," Wes said. "Apparently, it

was taken when she was a lot younger, and her douchebag husband is in it, too. It's been viewed more than a million times already."

I closed my eyes for a couple seconds, exhaling hard. What in the actual fuck? That had to be what was wrong with Sheridan when I'd seen her yesterday. And of course Hugh, who was out to ruin her in every way possible, had orchestrated it all.

A sex video, though? That was completely out of line. I was going to get him for this, one way or another. Sheridan didn't want me to have her back anymore, but that didn't matter.

I did have her back. And I always would, whether she ever spoke to me again or not.

As soon as we hit the ice, it was obvious Keegan was up to the same old shit, just in a new uniform. His sneer made my blood boil before the puck had even dropped. I was planning to wait for my moment and throttle the fuck out of him. He moved up my time line, though.

"Hey Lars, never knew you were a chubby chaser," he said as he skated past me during our first shift on the ice together.

My head snapped in his direction and he didn't

make it much farther. I dropped my gloves and knocked him to the ice, punching him as hard and fast as my hands would allow.

I was done. Done with all the hurt and anger Keegan and Hugh put into the world on a daily basis. They were both jealous assholes that couldn't stand seeing other people happy.

I felt myself being pulled backward, and I turned to see Nash, Sawyer, and Wes all working to pull me off of Keegan.

"You're gonna get yourself benched," Nash growled under his breath.

"He's not worth it," Sawyer added.

I didn't care if he was worth it. I glared at Keegan from the penalty box as he wiped the blood dripping from his lip. He could make fun of me for having autism and being weird, but I wouldn't stand for him insulting Sheridan.

As soon as the next period started, I waited for another shot at him. I wasn't thinking straight and I knew it. But some things were more important than hockey. And Sheridan was a hell of a lot more important than hockey right now.

Nashville's coach seemed intent on keeping us apart, making sure Keegan and I weren't on the ice at the same time. It couldn't last forever, though, and in the middle of the second period, I finally had my chance. We hadn't been out there ten seconds before Nashville got control of the puck and brought it into our end. Keegan was set up in front of Drew, trying to limit his view of the action. Drew gave him enough of a nudge to get a little separation as Wes dove to block a shot. The puck bounced to Nash, who took it back up the ice, but before Keegan followed the play, he swept Drew's legs out from under him, sending him sprawling.

Even if I hadn't been itching to grind my fist into his nose, one of my jobs as a defenseman was to protect the goalie and that right there was some bullshit. Especially since the refs had been watching the puck and hadn't seen it.

I didn't hesitate to hip check Keegan hard enough to knock him against the boards. He didn't have a chance to react because I punched him hard enough to send him flat on his back on the ice. I went down with him, my knee in his groin, holding him in place. The next punch knocked his mouthpiece out and drew blood, and then I lost it. I could only see red as I continued to pummel him.

"Fucking stop," Nash said to me in a stern voice as he and Sawyer pulled me off of Keegan for a second time. "This isn't helping anything."

"You're done, Jansson," the ref said. "Five and game."

I stared back at him, stunned. I'd never gotten a game misconduct before, and I'd been involved in worse fights than the two I'd just had. It didn't matter, though. This was about Sheridan and I wasn't done making Keegan—and anyone else who wanted a go at me—pay. Though I should have cared about disappointing my coach, all I cared about was not having another shot at Keegan again. Fighting was the only outlet I had for the way I was feeling about things with Sheridan.

I loved her, and I missed her with every fiber of my being.

Was it even possible to get her back? I wanted to believe it was, because without her, I was a different man. I wanted to be the man she'd shown me I could be.

As I headed back to the locker room, it occurred to me that maybe…well, more like *probably*, fighting Keegan wasn't going to solve anything. I needed to channel my energy in a different direction. I needed to fight for Sheridan.

CHAPTER TWENTY-NINE

Sheridan

I'D NEVER BEEN SO ALONE, SO scared, or so utterly devastated. As I'd known it would, that fucking video of me and Hugh had gone viral. In the forty-eight hours since he or Vanessa had put it out there, it had over ten million views on social media. My phone had been ringing nonstop, but the only people I'd spoken to so far had been my mother and Marian. Marian had mentioned suing both Hugh and Vanessa for child pornography or something, since I'd been underage when it had been filmed, but I didn't even care at this point. Nothing they did to him would change the fact that ten million people had seen it. Had seen *me*. Doing *that*.

I'd been holed up in my apartment for two days, and the doormen had strict orders to look out for paparazzi and that no one, not even people they already knew, was allowed up. I was hanging on by a thread at this point and I didn't know what to do or how to go forward. Marian was my lifeline right now, telling me she'd find a way to make the horror story of my life end. The divorce, the video, all of it. I'd told her I didn't care how, as long as Hugh was no longer in my life and no longer my agent. I'd go hungry before I gave him another dime once the papers were signed and finalized.

My phone buzzed and though I hadn't been speaking to anyone, Hadley had texted me multiple times and this was her again. She hadn't done anything wrong and I appreciated her checking in on me so I reluctantly opened her messages.

Hadley: Are you okay? Call if you need me.

That had been several hours ago.

Hadley: I'm sure you're hating life right now but I'm here for you. I don't care about the stupid video. It changes nothing for us.

That was an hour ago.

Hadley: I'm starting to worry. Please just let me know you're okay.

Sheridan: I'm as okay as I can be, hunkered down at home. Thanks for checking on me.

Hadley: Is there anything I can do? Annie and Nina are worried too.

Sheridan: There's nothing anyone can do, but my lawyer is working on forcing him to sign the papers. Beyond that, this is my life. I'm probably going to leave town for a while until things settle down.

Hadley: You don't have to run. We've got your back.

Sheridan: I appreciate you. I really do, but it's better for everyone to keep their distance. This is going to be a shit show of epic proportions and you don't need this raining down on your family.

Hadley: I'm not worried about it.

Sheridan: Right now, I just have to weather the storm. I'll call you in a week or two and let you know where I wind up. Thanks again.

I put the phone down and sighed heavily. I hadn't eaten since yesterday and was a little light headed but everything tasted like lead right now. I was considering running a bath when Barney buzzed the intercom.

"What is it, Barney?" I asked.

"There's an Annie Cain here to see you and she said she won't leave until I tell you she's here. That she's a friend."

"I…" I heard her in the background, arguing with Barney, saying he'd have to call the police and have her bodily removed and I almost laughed at the idea of anyone manhandling tiny, fragile Annie. "It's okay," I told him. "Send her up."

A minute later there was a knock on the door and I answered it.

"Hi." Annie took one look at me and immediately put down the bags she was carrying and hugged me tightly. "It's going to be okay," she whispered. "You'll see."

"God, I hope so." I led her into the apartment. "You shouldn't have come. The paparazzi are everywhere, and they'll follow you home."

"Sawyer will hurt them," she said, giving me an impish grin. "You know how protective he is."

"I do." I sank onto the couch, unsure what there was to say.

"I figured you weren't taking care of yourself so I've brought comfort food." She started unpacking the bags. "Chicken soup from the deli on fourth, baked ziti and cannoli from Giovanna's, and Lars said this is your favorite drink at Starbucks."

At the mention of Lars's name, tears filled my eyes. I was so fucking tired of crying, but it seemed to be par for the course these days. Especially when it came to Lars.

"Thank you," I murmured, taking the travel coffee mug from her. "I haven't been able to eat anything—it makes me want to puke."

"I know. But it's going to be okay."

"Everyone keeps saying that. My mother. My attorney. Hadley. *You*. But have you seen the fucking video?"

Annie met my gaze. "Yes. Sawyer and I watched it last night."

I groaned.

"We watched it so we would know how to defend you." She reached for my hand. "So we can help. We can't help if we're in the dark."

"There's no defending anything," I said angrily. "I was a willing participant!"

I wasn't mad at her but my whole life was falling apart and it was tiresome to hear everyone talking about it like this was nothing but a wardrobe malfunction that would blow over in a week or so. This video was online now and never going away. People for the rest of eternity would be able to watch it.

The thought made me want to puke. I hastily put the coffee cup down.

"Sheridan." Annie's voice was stronger than I'd ever heard it. "Anyone who watches that video, who really watches it, can see how scared and unsure you were. How *young* you were. How that pig was goading you and manipulating you…it's not sexy or even porn—it's a crime."

"Regardless. That video is forever and my life as I knew it is over."

"No. We're all here for you. Even Lars."

"The Lars ship has sailed."

"No. It hasn't. He loves you."

"I kept a huge secret from him. He said some… awful things to me."

"Awful things? Or just heat-of-the-moment, angry things?"

I gave a little shrug. "Does it matter?"

"Yes. It matters a lot."

"Not to me. I needed him more than I've ever needed anyone, and he left me."

"Oh, honey. He was hurt, but he knows he made a mistake."

I looked away, absently reaching for the coffee. It smelled good and my stomach was growling despite how upset I was. I took a sip and it soothed me a little.

"I can't talk about Lars," I whispered. "It hurts more than all the other stuff put together."

"Okay." She smiled. "Then how about eating a little?"

"I'll try."

She stayed for another hour, forcing me to eat, trying to make me laugh, and then running a bath for me so all I had to do was strip and get in once she was gone. She was a good friend, and I realized how much I was going to miss her and Hadley and Nina. Without Lars in my life, I would lose them too and that was yet another blow on top of so many others.

I put away the food and tossed the coffee cup before padding into the bathroom. I sank into the tub and it actually helped me relax a little. I was so tired of being stressed. Something had to give because I wasn't strong enough to do this much longer. Sitting there in the steamy water drained some of the tension from my back and I forced myself to breathe slowly and methodically. The last thing I needed on top of everything else was a back spasm.

Between the hot water, the soft music playing in the background, and half a glass of wine, I was considering eating when I got out.

I got dressed, grabbed my keys, phone, and the container of soup, and headed up to my studio. At least up there I could lose myself in art. I put the soup in the microwave and poured a glass of wine as I waited for it to warm. It had been sweet of Annie to bring it over and I'd have to remember to thank her if I ever got past this latest disaster.

Maybe it was time to go back to Europe. They were a lot more relaxed about nudity and porn, and maybe this would blow over faster there. I had a couple of acquaintances there that could help me start over, and if it worked out, I could move Mom there too.

I'd just turned on some music and pulled the soup from the microwave when my phone buzzed and I saw Hugh's name on the screen. He'd texted me and I stared at the phone for a second before forcing myself to open the app to see what he had to say. Marian had told me to save everything, in case we could use it in court, but my stomach always threatened to revolt when he contacted me.

Hugh: How does it feel to know I've taken everything from you, you fucking cow? Your virginity, your best friend, your company, that Neanderthal you were dating, and now your dignity. How does it feel to know you were nothing before I found you and you'll be nothing now that I've dumped your sorry ass? And we're not done with you yet—I have more videos. Maybe I'll even sell them. What do you think about that? Sweet dreams, baby doll.

The rage that filled me was so hot it felt like a tangible object that would burst from my skin in an explosion of anger. I threw my phone against the wall so hard it shattered into a dozen pieces and a scream came from my lungs that didn't sound like any noise I'd ever made. I threw the bowl of soup next and watched the sticky liquid splatter across a set of drawings.

I ripped the paper from one of the easels one sheet at a time, ripping and shredding them into tiny, unrecognizable pieces. Pens and pencils and paintbrushes went flying in every direction as I turned my studio upside down. I sliced through an abstract painting I'd been working on and threw it into a pile in the corner.

"I hate you, you fucking prick!"

I knocked over chairs and easels, my rage directed not just at Hugh, but also myself. How could I have been so stupid? He'd told me he would make me a star, and I'd believed every word. If I just hadn't listened when he'd said we needed to get married. I sobbed for the teenage girl who had signed over so much more than she'd realized on that fateful day, and then I opened the closest bottle of paint I could reach and threw it on the drawing I'd done of Lars. Bright purple liquid trailed down the paper, obscuring his face and dripping onto the floor. It was fitting—I'd destroyed my relationship with him, too.

I pounded my fist against the wall, tears pouring down my face as my back muscles began to tighten in protest.

There was nothing left inside me. I was as blank as the brand-new canvasses lined up along one wall of my studio. But this wouldn't be the end of me. I wouldn't let it. I needed some time to feel the hurt and start healing, but eventually, I would rise. Hugh and Vanessa thought they'd stripped me of my dignity, but I was stronger than they thought.

I frowned, getting up and walking over to turn down the music. Someone was knocking on the door.

Repeatedly.

Urgently.

And whoever it was, they were calling my name.

If the neighbors had heard me losing my mind, they might have called the police, and even in the middle of my pseudo nervous breakdown, I knew that was the last thing I needed.

Breathing heavily, I padded toward the door woodenly, my back still signaling I'd pushed it too hard.

I threw open the door, expecting to see a neighbor or Barney. Instead, Lars was standing there.

And before he could say a word, I fell to my knees, my sobs returning with full force.

CHAPTER THIRTY

Lars

I DROPPED to my knees beside Sheridan, wrapping her up in my arms. Her body went limp as she sobbed into my chest.

Other people murmured comforting words when someone they loved was hurting, but that just wasn't who I was. One way or another, Sheridan was going to be okay, but I didn't want to minimize her pain by saying so.

"Why are you here?" she asked, pulling back and wiping the tears from her cheeks. "And how did you get in?"

"Don't let anyone fire Barney," I said, my throat

tightening as I met her gaze and saw the anguish there.

A small smile danced on Sheridan's lips.

"Barney, huh? He's always concerned about me."

My heart raced with anticipation as I reminded myself what the doorman had said to me just ten minutes ago when I'd arrived at the building. *Tell her what you just told me, Lars. Don't change a single word.*

And I didn't.

"I'm here because I love you, Sheridan. I love every part of you. Every moment I've had with you. I didn't know what love felt like before you. And love —" I stopped, turning my face aside as I gathered myself, because I didn't want her to see the tears gathering in my eyes.

"Don't stop," she whispered.

I sighed softly, the brick wall I was focused on blurring into a swirl of maroon until I blinked and allowed my tears to fall. Balling my hands into fists, I forced myself not to wipe the tears away, and I looked back at Sheridan.

"Love is supposed to be hard for me," I continued, my voice choked with emotion. "Crying is supposed to be hard for me, too, because…I have autism. But with you…" I hung my head. "Nothing is hard for me with you, Sheridan."

"You have autism?" She cupped my cheek in her palm, raising my face so she could look into my eyes.

I nodded. "I did the testing. It was very difficult to hear."

"I can't imagine. How are you feeling about it now?"

"It makes sense. I always knew I was different. I know it doesn't change who I am, but it's going to take time for me to want to talk about it."

"I just wish I had known so I could have been there for you," she said softly.

"That night we fought, I was planning to tell you."

Her lips turned down in a frown and she dropped her hand. "I was planning to tell you about Hugh, too. And it hurt like hell that you accused me of lying about it."

"I was wrong."

"I just want someone in my life, just *one fucking person*, who doesn't hurt me," she said softly.

My chest tightened as I felt my future hanging in the balance. I'd come here to bare my soul to Sheridan in the hope that she'd give me another shot. But she wanted someone who had never hurt her, and that could never be me.

"I'm sorry," I said. "I was hurt, too, even if it does not make sense to you why."

"Can we stand up?" she asked. "My back doesn't like being on the floor like this."

"Of course."

I got to my feet and helped her get up, and she walked back into the spacious room.

It was more than just a room—it was an entire floor, with light pouring in through the many windows. Art hung on the walls and there was a turquoise sofa along one wall, the coffee table in front of it holding several Starbucks cups, notebooks, and pens.

Whatever this place was, it was a mess. Paintbrushes, bits of paper and pencils were scattered on the floor and a painting on a canvas lay destroyed in a corner of the room.

My gaze landed on a pencil drawing of my face, purple paint splattered all over it and dripping into a small pool in front of the easel.

"I drew that after our first date," Sheridan said, sitting down on the sofa.

"You are very talented."

"Not really. Creating art is just an outlet for me. It's something I don't share with anyone."

I turned to look at her. "Does Barney know?"

She shrugged. "He knows I rent this floor, and that I come here sometimes, but not why."

"The paint is wet," I observed, looking at the

drawing of my face again. "So you are still angry with me."

Sheridan smiled. "I'm angry at the world right now, Lars."

"I'm sorry about what Vanessa did. I am in love with you, but if you don't want a relationship with me, I will try to be a friend to you."

She looked at her hands, which were folded on her lap. "I didn't mean to hurt you. I wasn't trying to keep my…marriage to Hugh a secret. It's just that I was so ashamed. I still am ashamed and I probably will be until the day I die. I wanted to make it go away by divorcing him."

I sighed heavily and walked over to the wall, leaning my hip against it and looking out the window at the city skyline.

"I was ashamed when Keegan said those things about me," I said.

"Lars, autism is nothing to be ashamed of."

"My psychiatrist said shame is something many people feel, and that it is something we can't control."

"You're seeing a psychiatrist?" Sheridan asked.

"He's the one who did the autism testing, and I am going to keep seeing him, because…I am an imperfect man."

"Yes, but not because you have autism."

I walked over to the couch and stood across from her. "I am sorry, Sheridan. I was wrong and if I could go back in time and do things differently, I would. But I am in love with you, and that…" My throat tightened with emotion. "That is not something I want to let go of without a fight."

"You still want me, even now?" She sounded genuinely surprised. "I'm a worldwide laughing-stock, you know. Millions of people have seen every fat roll on my body, not to mention my vagina. I handed my company over to the two people who have fucked me over harder than I ever thought possible. And if everything goes like I want it to and Hugh signs off on this divorce, I won't have anywhere near the money I had before. I'm basically ruined."

I didn't hesitate before responding. "The answer is yes, I still want you. More than ever."

"I still want you, too."

Walking over to the couch, I kneeled in front of her. "You do?"

She cupped my face in her hands. "Of course I do. I love you. But being with me won't be easy, Lars. I'm going to be under more scrutiny than ever."

"None of that matters. I want to be with you through thin and thick."

She smiled. "Thick and thin. And why is it so damn cute when you mess up your English?"

I put my arms around her and kissed her tenderly. It wasn't a kiss of desire, but of affection. She loved me, too. I had a lot of work to do—both on myself and with Sheridan—but she was giving me another chance.

Soon, though, she was pulling me closer, her mouth hungrily demanding more. She took two fistfuls of my shirt and pulled me on top of her, lying back against the couch cushions.

"You missed me," I teased.

She cupped my crotch and I groaned in response. "By the feel of this, you missed me too."

"More than I can say."

"Show me, then."

Though I usually took charge when it came to sex, I was more than happy to obey her command. I kissed her neck and chest, an animalistic rumble sounding in my chest as she wrapped her fingers around my neck and buried her hands in my hair. Her nails grazed my scalp and a surge of arousal coursed through me, hard and fast.

She was wearing sweatpants, which were easy to get off, but I had to stand up to get my own jeans off. Every second I wasn't touching her felt like an hour.

I quickly stripped as she pulled her shirt off over the top of her head.

"I missed looking at you," I said tenderly. "You're so beautiful, Sheridan, just as you are."

Her gaze roved up and down my body, her nipples pebbling behind the thin fabric of her sheer white bra.

"I missed you so much," she said, her voice hoarse with emotion. "You make me feel more beautiful and worthy than anyone ever has. I love you."

I said a prayer of thanks that she was on the pill because I hadn't brought condoms. I hadn't even been sure I'd make it past the front door.

"I don't have condoms," I said. "But if you don't want—"

She cut me off, saying, "I do. Now."

Sheridan raised her hips and started to shimmy out of her panties. I reached for her hips and made short work of it, tossing them to the floor and climbing back onto the couch.

When I leaned down to kiss her, her eyes were glazed with a need that made me feel like a king. I didn't care if any other woman in the world ever looked at me again, as long as Sheridan looked at me just like this.

Part of me wanted to tease her, to make her wait

until she was desperate for me, but the truth was, I was desperate for her *now*.

She wrapped her legs around me, using them to pull me closer. When I pushed inside her, we both groaned with pleasure. It was the first time I'd been inside a woman without a condom, and it felt fucking amazing.

"Hard," she said in my ear. "Fuck me hard, Lars. Make me come hard."

"Fuck," I muttered. "You talking dirty is my weakness."

"Same," she said, moaning as I thrust all the way in.

"Yeah?" I put my hand in her hair and tugged with just enough pressure to get her attention, but not hurt her. "You like it when I fuck your wet pussy with my big cock?"

"Oh, God." She moaned again, her nails sinking into my back and sending a tingle down my spine.

"Don't take this pussy away from me again," I said, balancing on my forearm so I could look her in the eyes as I fucked her. "I plan to suck, fuck, and eat this pussy as hard as you can stand for a very long time."

She squeezed her legs tightly around me, panting as I pushed back one of her thighs to fuck her deeper.

"Like that," I said in a low tone. "You like it when I fuck you deep and hard, don't you, baby?"

"Yes," she said, her tone breathy. "Oh, God…yes."

Her pussy tightened around my cock as she started to come, her legs locked around my hips. I reveled in her scream of satisfaction, using all my self-control to hold on until I felt her ride out each wave of her orgasm. With one final thrust, I stiffened and came with a powerful groan.

I kissed her gently and then sat back on the couch, knowing I was too heavy to lie on top of her. We were both breathing hard as we came down from the high when Sheridan started laughing.

"Something is funny?" I asked.

"I just can't believe I'm naked in broad daylight in a room that's nothing but windows, and I'm not even self-conscious."

"You should never be self-conscious with me."

"It's hard not to be when you're a woman whose body has been criticized her entire life."

I quirked a brow and smiled at her. "Maybe it's time to stop listening to the world. I think you're the most beautiful woman I've ever seen."

She smiled. "Thank you."

I ran my fingers along the smooth skin of her calf, taking in the most spectacular view I'd ever seen. Sheridan's eyes were bright, her cheeks were flushed, and she looked happy. I had everything in the world I really wanted in this moment.

"I would like to have the picture of me," I said.

She burst out laughing. "That one? With purple paint all over it? No, let me make you a new one."

"I want that one."

"Okay, but what are you going to do with it?"

I grinned. "Hang it in my apartment. It will remind me of this every time I look at it."

"Of the time we fucked in my studio," she said softly. "It'll be a great memory."

"It will, because it will remind me of the *times* we fucked in your studio." I moved closer to her. "First, on this couch. And then, again on this couch, but with you on top. And then when I bent you over the side of this couch."

She gave me a sexy smile. "And when we smeared paint all over each other's bodies and then fucked on the floor?"

"Fuck yes. That, too."

CHAPTER THIRTY-ONE

Sheridan

Three weeks later

I'D NEVER LIKED DOING interviews because reporters inevitably asked me questions I wasn't comfortable with and it always made me hate them a little. This was different, though. Hadley was a good friend, and though we'd decided that nothing was off the table, I knew she wouldn't embarrass me. Interviewing me for her online magazine's podcast had been her idea, but I'd agreed for a lot of reasons. First, because I no longer had anything to hide. Second, because I was finally—*legally*—divorced, and it was a glorious thing. And last, I wanted to set the record straight. I was sure more people had seen the video than would hear my interview with Hadley, but at this point, it didn't matter as much.

I still had bouts of shame and frustration, but with Lars at my side and a good chunk of the Mavericks organization having my back, I didn't feel alone anymore.

"Are you ready?" Hadley asked me as we sat in her new home studio.

I took a breath. "Yes."

"You sure? You look queasy."

I shook my head. "No. I'm good. Really."

She smiled at me. "Remember, this is recorded and we can edit out anything you don't want in there. We can also pause anytime you want."

"Thank you."

She did her usual intro to the show and a little background on me. "Sheridan, thank you so much for coming on the show."

"Thank you for having me."

"Your life has been in the news a lot in the last year and a half or so. How are you feeling these days after your accident?"

"I'm much, much better. I've been in hard-core physical therapy and it's made a big difference. I do a lot of stretching and yoga, which has also helped, and I've lost about twenty pounds, which made a difference too."

"You're the most well-known plus-size supermodel in the world. Do you still worry about your weight?"

"Always. It may seem counterintuitive because obviously my career is partly based on my size, but the truth is I'm cognizant of every extra pound because I know for every fan I have, there's someone else out there who has something nasty to say. I've been doing this for nearly fifteen years now, but the meanness and bullying never get easier."

"Do you plan to go back to modeling?"

"I do. In fact, I have something planned in the spring that I can't talk about yet, but there will be a press release the first of the year."

"That sounds intriguing. Can you give us a hint?"

I chuckled. "Well, I loved combining the modeling world with the business world, so even though I sold Sheri Lee, I have a bigger, more innovative idea that I'll tell you about in January. Promise. First, I want to get through the holidays."

"What are you doing for the holidays now that you're officially divorced?"

"I'm spending them with my mom and my boyfriend, Lars."

"Now, you're talking about Lars Jansson, right? From the Mavericks?"

I gave her a playful grin. "I am."

"And how's that going?"

"Great! We're going to start house hunting soon, but he really doesn't like it when I talk about him, so I won't." I gazed over to where he and Wes were hanging out. He'd said he wanted to be close by, just in case I got nervous, and though it wasn't necessary, it was still sweet. Lars winked at me and I smiled back.

"Sheridan, I wanted to ask you about the now infamous video. You said you wanted to give your side of the story, so I'm going to let you do that."

"Well…" I'd thought long and hard about what I wanted to say, but decided honesty was the best policy. "I've always been heavy. So when my ex-husband, Hugh, started coming around, he was four years older than me, and handsome back then, so I was flattered. There weren't a lot of plus-size modeling gigs back then, which was nearly fourteen years ago now, when I was fifteen. So I kept getting rejected, agencies telling me I had a beautiful face but I needed to lose weight. Hugh would berate me, put me on diets, tease me, do all kinds of hurtful things. But then he'd tell me he loved me, and I believed him."

"I'm sorry," Hadley said quietly. "You were so young."

"Yes. I was sixteen when he recorded that first

video. He brought his friends around and…" I took a breath, glancing over at Lars, who was watching me intently.

"It's okay," he mouthed. "I love you."

I gave him a tremulous smile before turning back to Hadley. "He convinced me that porn was the only way I would ever be a star, so I had to practice. He was the only guy I'd ever been with and I guess I was a little brainwashed, you know? I was sure I was too fat to ever amount to anything, so I did the things he asked me to do. With his friends. Sometimes with strangers. Never intercourse, but everything else, and that's how he got me. He'd say that intercourse was just for him, since he was the first and would be the only. I feel so ashamed that I let him talk me into doing those things, even now that I know what a manipulative, predatory bastard he is, but I let my insecurity about my weight guide my self-worth."

"You have nothing to be ashamed of," Hadley said. "You were young, and he was a sexual predator."

"He was. And that's my message to all the women listening—young or old—be true to yourself. Don't base your worth on a man or society's version of attractiveness. Be who you are. Because even at my weight, with all my insecurities, big modeling agencies did come calling. I'm known all over the world for being a beautiful, full-figured woman, and I'm not the only one."

"Have you ever considered mentoring other young women like yourself?"

"I have and I will again once I get my new business off the ground. The modeling world is treacherous, it really is, and if I can save even one young model the agony I've gone through, it'll be worth it."

"Do you have a message to young models, and aspiring models, who are listening?"

"Whether you're plus size or double zero, or anywhere in between, make sure you don't sign anything until your own lawyer looks at it. If you're involved with your manager or agent—and I can't say don't do it because there are good people out there too—make sure you still have a little separation. Just in case. Prenups, stuff like that. You don't want to go through the divorce battle I just got through."

"Can you talk about that?"

I chuckled. "I really don't ever want to say my ex's name again, but it took me more than two years to get him to sign the papers. I'd been with him since I was fifteen, married since I was eighteen, and I trusted him implicitly. Be careful out there, ladies, because there *are* predators."

"As the mom of a little girl, your words hit me

right between the eyes," Hadley said. "She's only four but I can't imagine watching my teenage daughter go through what you went through."

"And that's the thing—they make you so dependent on them, on their praise, their love, their touch—you lie to protect them. I know if I ever have a little girl, I'm going to watch her like a hawk when it comes to those kinds of things."

"Ooooh…" Hadley's voice turned playful. "Does that mean there's a little Lars or Sheridan to look forward to?"

I laughed, looking over at Lars again. "We haven't gotten that far. We'd like kids someday, but we haven't discussed timing or anything. First, we're going to find a house and I'm going to start my new business. We'll see about everything else later."

We talked about a few less serious topics and then, finally, it was over.

"You were very good," Lars said, coming over to me and leaning down to lightly kiss me.

"Thanks. I was nervous."

"You did great," Hadley said. "And I'll let you listen to the finished product before I upload it."

"Thank you. This means so much to me." I reached out and hugged her.

"Anytime."

"I wish we could have talked about all the shit

Hugh did," I said ruefully, "but it's honestly better that we didn't. I wanted to explain that damn video, so people would understand how awful it was for me, and now it's done. I don't ever intend to talk about it again. I've hired a crisis management publicist to help bury the whole thing, and for the first time in my life, I don't wake up in the morning afraid of what he's going to do to me next."

"And you never will." Lars wrapped his arms around me and kissed the side of my face. "Not as long as I'm breathing."

I smiled up at him. "Have I told you how much I love you lately?"

He smiled back. "Yes. Often. But you can tell me again. Is nice to hear the words."

"You guys want to open a bottle of wine or run upstairs real quick first?" Wes asked, arching a brow in our direction.

"We can do this?" Lars asked, his face a mask of nothingness. "Go upstairs?"

Everyone was silent for a beat and then Wes laughed. "You almost got me, buddy."

Lars just smirked.

I slid my fingers through his. "Did I tell you I heard from Nellie today?"

He frowned. "Your old assistant?"

"Yes. She's been giving me all the gossip and she quit today."

"Yes? What happened?"

"Apparently, Vanessa and Hugh melted down during a staff meeting and the rest of the executive staff walked out. Lenny and Marnie had already quit, and everyone else did it today. So she has literally no one to help her run the company. And the best part is, even if she hires people, there's no one there to train anyone."

"This is good news." He squeezed my hand. "The new company will be amazing. Even better than Sheri Lee."

"I had a thought for a name. Hey, Hadley? Wes? I was thinking of naming my new company Annie's Closet."

"Oh, I love that," Hadley said. "I think she will too."

"It is very sweet," Lars agreed.

"Just make sure she's on board," Wes said. "You know how private Sawyer can be."

"Don't worry. I will."

We sat in their family room in front of the fireplace and Wes poured us all a glass of wine.

"I can't believe Christmas is in three days," Hadley said, looking over at the tree. "You think we overdid it on gifts for the kids?"

"No?" He grimaced as he said it.

They laughed.

"To first Christmases," he said, picking up his glass as he looked at his wife. "Our first Christmas as husband and wife."

"And as parents," she agreed, holding up her glass.

"Our first Christmas together," I said to Lars, lifting my own.

"The first of many," he said, nodding.

"Cheers." We clinked our glasses together.

EPILOGUE

Lars

Mavericks Group Text

Boone: Hey, I know it's Valentine's Day, but it's opening day for my buddy Cal's new bar. He was supposed to open in two weeks, but renovations got finished early. He's a good dude who's putting his life savings into this place. I'd appreciate it if any of you could stop by. It's called Calypso and it's on Cherokee St.

Drew: Sounds like fun. Nina and I will come by after dinner.

Konstantin: I'll be there.

Wes: Hadley and I are staying at a hotel tonight, but if we're up for a break from our sexathon, we'll drop by.

Lars: Sheridan and I will come, but it may be late.

Nash: Yeah, I'm in, and I'll tell you guys tonight about the news I got this morning. It's fucking epic.

"MR. LARS, PUT SALAD ON TABLE," Rosalina said in a scolding tone.

"I do not want it on the table."

She shook her head and opened the lid on the marinara sauce she'd made from scratch. "Salad eat first, Mr. Lars."

"I know, but that doesn't mean it has to go on the table. I only want the champagne on the table."

"You make apartment pretty. I make apartment clean, and I cook food." She glared in my direction. "Next time, you do all yourself."

Tonight was a special occasion—the first Valentine's Day for Sheridan and me. Rosalina had been on board with helping me make a special dinner for her, but she wasn't one to do anything without a little bickering. I was just glad to have something to keep my mind off of how nervous I was. I wanted everything to be perfect tonight.

I'd had practice today and Sheridan had gone to work at her new downtown office space. She'd come a long way with Annie's Closet since December, and since Annie was feeling a lot better these days, she was working there part-time as a consultant.

Lingerie for all. That was the Annie's Closet motto. There would be beautiful items for women in every size, but also those who had been left behind by most clothing manufacturers. Breast cancer survivors. Colostomy bag users. Trans women. I was enormously proud of Sheridan for promoting inclusivity, and based on the research she'd done so far, the market was hungry for it.

"Food is ready, Mr. Lars," Rosalina said. "I go now."

"Thanks for all your help. Are you doing anything for Valentine's Day?"

She picked up the box of chocolates I'd given her when she arrived and put on her coat.

"I stay with granddaughter. Son and daughter-in-law go out to dinner."

"That'll be fun. Do you have to cook dinner for her?"

Rosalina smiled. "Yes, but I like cook dinner. Good luck tonight, Mr. Lars."

"Thanks. I'm going on the road tomorrow, but I'll see you when I get back."

After she left, I checked my watch and saw that Sheridan was due at my place in ten minutes. I exhaled hard, double-checking the twinkle lights I'd strung across the chandelier over the dining table, the long-stemmed red roses waiting on the kitchen counter, and the bottle of champagne chilling on ice.

Everything was ready. I was ready. But still, I was nervous. Sheridan had told me Hugh always said Valentine's Day was just a commercial holiday, and he'd never gotten her anything to celebrate. She deserved to be treated like a queen, and I hoped she'd feel that way when she walked into my apartment.

Loki was perched in the windowsill, and as soon as I went over to pet him, the doorbell rang.

"You ready?" I asked my cat, who stared back at me nonchalantly.

"Hey," Sheridan said, grinning when I opened the door.

"Happy Valentine's Day," I said, stepping aside to let her in before giving her a kiss.

"Happy Valentine's Day. It smells amazing in here."

"Rosalina made pasta and salad."

"That sounds wonderful. I worked through lunch."

"You look beautiful." My gaze roamed down her outfit—a formfitting dark gray dress, black stockings, and black booties. "Wow."

"Thank you."

I held out a little black box wrapped with a red ribbon. "I hope this will match your outfit."

She smiled warmly as she slid out of her coat. I traded her the coat for the gift box.

"I have something for you, too," she said, reaching into the pocket of her coat.

We walked over to the couch together and I looked at her expectantly, waiting for her to open her gift. It was the first time I'd bought anyone a present for Valentine's Day, and my heart pounded nervously as I waited to see what she'd think.

"Oh, I love them!" she cried. "Lars, they're beautiful."

I'd gotten her star-shaped diamond earrings. Round diamonds were too boring for Sheridan; in my eyes she was bright and beautiful, just like stars.

She immediately took off the earrings she was wearing and put on the new ones. I smiled, relieved and thrilled in equal measure. I was still working with David on identifying and working on things that were hard for me as a person on the autism spectrum. Reading people's feelings was something I struggled with. It helped that Sheridan was a straightforward person, and we prioritized communication in our relationship. But still, I wanted tonight to be perfect.

I opened my gift from her—custom-made cuff links shaped like hammers, for Thor.

"These are wonderful," I said. "Thank you. I will wear them after every game."

I kissed her again, inhaling the sweet scent of her perfume. It made me want to skip dinner altogether.

"I'm too hungry to think about sex right now," she said, reading my mind.

I smiled. "I am hungry, too. Let's eat."

"Lars!" Sheridan cried as we walked toward the kitchen. "You did all this?"

"Rosalina cleaned, but I put up the lights and set the table."

She kissed me again. "This is amazing, thank you. It was a crazy day at work today, and it feels so good to come home to this." She gave me the dazzling smile I loved so much. "Well, to *your* home."

"Your home is my home these days," I said. "I think Loki and I should just move in with you."

"Maybe? If we can't find a house we like soon, you should. I know it sucks having so much of your stuff here when you're at my place so much."

"It's not a big deal. But I do love your apartment, and I think Loki would, too."

She told me about her day at work as we ate. Our dynamic was the same as it was on our first date— she did more talking than I did. I liked that, though.

I'd seen a picture of a cherry tree recently, and it had reminded me of us—I was the strong, solid trunk, supporting the branches that were Sheridan as they flowered and spread their beauty into the world.

"Did you see my text about going to that new bar tonight?" I asked her.

"Yes, and I told everyone at the office about it. It's only five people as of now, I know, but I told them to tell people, too."

"Want to go sooner or later?"

"Sooner," she said. "And then we can stay here tonight since your place is closer."

"Okay."

"Let's get the dishwasher loaded now so we don't come home to a mess."

I shook my head. "Rosalina can clean up tomorrow."

Sheridan arched her brows. "We aren't leaving crusty, tomato sauce–covered plates for your house-keeper to scrub tomorrow. Let's load the dishwasher."

"I hope you don't mess up your dress."

"It'll be fine."

My stomach churned nervously. I was eager to get to the bar, where I was going to surprise Sheridan with one last thing on our first Valentine's Day together. I didn't want to spend time cleaning up the kitchen, but she was right; it was best to do it now.

"You scrape the food off dishes and put away the leftovers. I'll prerinse everything and load the dishwasher," she said, looking out of place doing housework in her glamorous makeup and dress.

These were my favorite times together. I loved doing domestic things with Sheridan, especially on those rare weekend days when we were both wearing sweats and didn't have to run off anywhere.

"We got coffee from that new place next to the office today," she said as we both worked.

"Yeah? How was it?"

"Marginal. It wasn't hot, and they only filled Annie's coffee three-quarters full. I think I'll just buy a really nice coffee maker for the office."

She dropped a spoon on the floor and I said, "I've got it."

As I bent down to pick it up, I felt the bulge of the small box in my pants pocket and I got an idea.

It wasn't fancy. I hadn't planned it this way. But something about this moment felt perfect. I took the box from my pocket and opened it.

"Depending on the day, the Starbucks line is worth it, though," she was saying. "It's—"

"Sheridan?"

She looked down at me, at the little black box

with a sparkling diamond ring in one hand and a dirty spoon in the other. I set the spoon back down on the floor.

"I love you more than measure," I said, my pulse pounding. "You're my best friend. I want to load the dishwasher with you for the rest of our lives. Will you marry me?"

She grabbed a dish towel and dried her hands, eyes welling with tears as a huge smile overtook her face, and she said, "Yes!"

Relief and joy flooded through me as I stood up and she jumped into my arms. I held her tightly and we kissed. She pulled back and wiped her cheeks, saying, "I'm going to get makeup all over you."

"I don't care."

"Oh my God! I've never been so surprised in my life!"

I took her left hand and slipped the ring onto it. "I was going to do it tonight, with everyone there, but it felt right for it to just be me and you."

"It was perfect," she said softly, looking down at the pear-shaped solitaire on her finger. "I still can't believe it!"

I kissed her again. "If you hadn't bid on that date with me, I never would have found you."

"Oh, you never know. We may have run into each other somewhere else. Would you have noticed me?"

"Absolutely."

She laughed and a fresh round of tears spilled onto her cheeks. "I just can't believe how happy I am. I've never been this happy."

"Me either." I smiled and reached for the spoon I'd set down, loading it into the dishwasher's silverware rack. "Now let's finish this so we can go celebrate."

————

"ENGAGED?" Annie cried an hour later when she and Sawyer walked into Calypso shortly after Sheridan and I had arrived. "Oh, Sheridan! I'm so happy for you guys!"

Hadley hugged me, and then Sheridan, and then me again.

"You are a wise man, Lars Jansson," she said in my ear. "You picked a great one."

"Thank you."

"Sheridan, welcome to the family," Wes said. "Although it feels like you're already part of it."

Boone bought a round of drinks for everyone and we toasted to the engagement. Usually, Sheridan was off with Hadley and Annie when we were at team gatherings, but tonight, she'd stayed by my side. Tonight was about us.

I couldn't stop looking at her and smiling. She was going to be my wife. Six months ago, I'd thought the bachelor life was the greatest. Little had I known.

"Congratulations, man," Nash said when he arrived and I told him the news. "You guys are great together. I can't think of anyone better for you."

"Will you be my best man?"

He grinned. "Nothing would make me happier. But…I may have a scheduling conflict."

"We haven't scheduled it yet."

"I'd love it if the wedding was before or after my thing."

"What thing?"

"Well…" He cleared his throat and looked around the large table our group was occupying. "Can I have everyone's attention, please? Hey! Guys! Can I get like, a fraction of everyone's attention?"

I cupped my hands around my mouth and yelled, "Mavericks!"

Everyone went quiet and looked my way.

"Thanks, dude," Nash said. "So I have an announcement to make."

"You better not be retiring," Boone said.

"Nah, nothing like that. I'm going to be doing a photo shoot in the Bahamas because I was chosen as one of the Sexiest Athletes Alive."

"No way!" Drew said.

"Yeah." Nash grinned.

"Did no one submit my name?" Wes asked.

"I just beat all you ugly mofos, fair and square," Nash said.

"Congratulations," I said, clapping him on the shoulder. "This calls for another round of drinks."

"No, it's nothing like you and Sheridan getting engaged. But I said I'd tell everyone about it tonight, so I wanted to."

"Are you posing nude?" Wes asked.

Nash shrugged and said, "If they want me to."

"We can get you a baby sock to cover your wanger," Boone cracked.

"Whatever." Nash just laughed, and they continued busting his balls, but I'd lost interest.

Instead, I glanced over at my fiancée and marveled at just how beautiful she was.

And the best part?

She was mine.

Forever and always.

The next book in the St. Louis Mavericks series is Hard Pass. It releases May 17, 2022.

ABOUT THE AUTHOR

Brenda Rothert lives in Central Illinois with her husband, children and dogs. She loves to hear from readers through her website or her Facebook Group, Rothert's Readers.

ALSO BY BRENDA ROTHERT

CHICAGO BLAZE SERIES

Book 1 - Anton

Book 2 - Luca

Book 3 - Victor

Book 4 - Knox

Book 5 - Alexei

Book 6 - Easy

Book 7 - Jonah

Book 8 - Kit

Book 9 - Olivier

SIN CITY SAINTS SERIES

Book 1 - Maverick

Book 2 - Pike

ST. LOUS MAVERICKS SERIES

Book 1 - Hard Fall

Book 2 - Hard Limit

FIRE ON ICE SERIES

Book 1 - Bound

Book 2 - Captive

Book 3 - Edge

Book 4 - Drive

Book 5 - Release

On the Line Series

Book 1 - Killian

Book 2 - Bennett

Lockhart Brothers Series

Book 1 - Deep Down

Book 2 - In Deep

Book 3 - Drawn Deeper

Book 4 - Hidden Depth

Filthy Series

Book 1 - Dirty Work

Book 2 - Dirty Secret

Book 3 - Dirty Defiance

Standalones

Come Closer

Buried

Sweet Sixteen

His

Alpha Mail

Healing Touch

Barely Breathing

ABOUT THE AUTHOR

USA Today Bestselling author Kat Mizera was born in Miami Beach with a healthy dose of wanderlust. She's lived from coast to coast, and everywhere in between, but home is wherever her family is.

A devoted mom and wife to her wonderful and supportive husband (Kevin) and two amazing boys (Nick and Max), Kat loves to travel the globe with her adventurous, hockey loving family. Greece is at the top of that list. She hopes to one day retire there, spending her days writing books on the beach.

Kat is former freelance sports writer who now writes steamy hockey romance about her favorite fictional teams, the Las Vegas Sidewinders and the Alaska Blizzard. The library of novels she's penned also include sexy contemporary stories about baseball stars, alpha sex club owners, special forces heroes, rock stars and royalty. Regardless of genre, her books about bad boys with hearts of gold will steal your breath, rock your world and melt your heart.

WHERE TO FOLLOW KAT:

WEBSITE
FACEBOOK
TWITTER
INSTAGRAM
BOOKBUB
KAT'S PRIVATE FACEBOOK GROUP

ALSO BY KAT MIZERA

Las Vegas Sidewinders:
Dominic
Cody's Christmas Surprise
Drake
Karl
Anatoli
Zakk
Toli & Tessa
Brock
Vladimir
Royce
Nate
Sidewinders: Ever After
Jared
Dmitri's Christmas Angel
Ian

Sidewinders: Generations:
> Zaan
> Tore
> Anton

Alaska Blizzard:
> Defending Dani
> Holding Hailey
> Winning Whitney
> Losing Laurel
> Saving Sara
> Chasing Charli
> A Very Blizzard Christmas
> Tending Tara
> Calling Cassie
> Playing Peyton

St. Louis Mavericks (with Brenda Rothert)
> Hard Fall
> Hard Limit

Lauderdale Knights:
> Slap Shot
> Big Shot

Rock Hard:
> *Play*

Pause
Rewind
Fast Forward

The Royal Trilogy:
Nowhere Left to Fall
Nowhere Left to Run
Nowhere Left to Hide

Royal Protectors:
Sandor
Cocky Protector (book 1.5, part of the Cocky Heroes Club series)
Xander
Axel
Dax (*A Royal Protectors/Sidewinders crossover novel*)

Inferno:
Salvation's Inferno
Temptation's Inferno
Redemption's Inferno
Tropical Inferno (formerly "Tropical Ice")

Romancing Europe:
Adonis in Athens
Smitten in Santorini
Lucky in Lugano

Other Books:

Special Forces: Operation Alpha: Protecting Bobbi (Susan Stoker's Special Forces World)

Special Forces: Operation Alpha: Protecting Delilah (Susan Stoker's Special Forces World)

View Kat's entire collection of books at www.KatMizera.com